The middle-aged woman waiting in reception raised Kate's hackles immediately, but not, she hoped, too visibly. 'Mrs Duncton?'

'Oh,' she said, making no effort to get up, though Kate knew from experience that the chairs were not designed to encourage sitting, 'I expected someone – you know . . .'

Kate did know. Punters wanted avuncular men, not young women dressed with more regard for the weather than for sobriety. Punters wanted Sergeant George Dixon of Dock Green, not Sergeant Kate Power of Kings Heath.

*Also by Judith Cutler*

Power on Her Own
Staying Power
Power Games

# Will Power

Judith Cutler

NEW ENGLISH LIBRARY
Hodder & Stoughton

Copyright © 2002 by Judith Cutler

First published in Great Britain in 2001
by Hodder and Stoughton
A division of Hodder Headline

The right of Judith Cutler to be identified as the
Author of the Work has been asserted by her in accordance
with the Copyright, Designs and Patents Act 1988.

A New English Library paperback

2 4 6 8 10 9 7 5 3 1

A CIP catalogue record for this title
is available from the British Library.

ISBN 0 340 76825 8

Printed and bound in Great Britain by
Mackays of Chatham plc, Chatham, Kent

Hodder and Stoughton
A division of Hodder Headline
338 Euston Road
London NW1 3BH

For Peter and Liz, the truest of friends

# ACKNOWLEDGEMENTS

Who would have thought that the simple signing of my own will would lead to a crime novel? Thank you, David Henson, for your support and encouragement throughout the project, and for your and Pam's kind hospitality.

Tom Davis, the forensic handwriting expert based at the University of Birmingham, also provided invaluable information, as did Raymond Flynn on fraud and Mick Bickerton on jewellery: Thank you all. A special thanks to Sigrid Ruschmeier, who loves words as much as I do.

# Chapter One

DI Lizzie King pushed herself away from her desk, running a hand through her mop of red hair. 'Now you're here, Power, I suppose we'll just have to make the most of it,' she said, by way of welcome to the Fraud Squad.

Kate Power nodded with matching enthusiasm. She'd worked in Fraud before, with varying degrees of pleasure. Her relationship with Lizzie wasn't among the high points. But while she was awaiting the results of her inspectors' exams, Personnel had moved her – still as a detective sergeant – from her squad in Birmingham's city centre CID. There might, of course, have been other reasons. The promotion to uniformed sergeant of one of Fraud's most experienced detective constables, for instance. And others she didn't want to discuss with Lizzie.

'Do you want me to pick up Bill's case-load?' Kate asked, wondering when she'd be invited to sit down.

Lizzie's face said that no one could replace Bill. 'Oh, why not? It'll take Ben hours to fill you in, and weeks to train you. But until something else comes up, you might as well.'

'Right. I'll read through everything in the in-tray and then talk to Ben. Thanks, Gaffer,' she added, with a smile even she didn't think would be convincing, and made for the door.

'Any idea how long you'll be here?'

Kate turned back. 'Your guess is as good as mine, Gaffer.'

After a morning's unremitting poring over paperwork on which she had only the most slender of grasps, Kate allowed herself to stretch and look out of the window. No Ben this morning – he was in court. And – perhaps taking their cue from Lizzie – none of her other colleagues had gone out of their way to invite her to join them in the canteen for lunch. That was their prerogative. Kate had had to earn respect and comradeship before; she could do it again, though she'd have preferred not to have the odds against her stacked quite so high. She could simply wander down to the canteen and take pot luck with the company. As it was, the bright sun called her. She owed herself a new summer outfit to celebrate the end of the exams, and this might be just the day to go hunting for it. And for lunch there was a Prêt à Manger close to Rackhams, which was where she could start her hunt.

So it was by genuine coincidence that as she crossed the Cathedral Close she ran into Graham Harvey. Genuine but delightful. Almost as delightful as the joyous disbelief in his face lightening his usually sombre features. Pity the joy had to be suppressed and transformed into a workaday nod.

'All right, Kate?'

After all these months, she still couldn't get her head round the Brummie greeting as anything other than an enquiry after her health. 'Fine. And you?'

'Fine. What are you doing?'

It would have been nice if he hadn't had to look furtively round as he asked. But that was the price you had to pay, she supposed, if you were illicit lovers. No matter how hard they tried to keep the relationship secret, rumours started. Hence, probably, Lizzie's hostility. Lizzie was a fully paid-up member of the DCI Harvey Fan Club. Had been for years, according to gossip, which added that they'd once been lovers. Whether this was true or not, Graham was still married to the woman he always referred to simply as 'my wife', though a little espionage by Aunt Cassie in her residential home had disclosed that she not only had a first name, but that it was Flavia.

'Going to buy a sandwich,' she said. Her smile invited him to join her.

He looked at his watch, shaking his head. 'I've got a meeting. Look, what time are you finishing tonight?'

'Sixish, unless anything comes up.'

'If I dropped in at – let's say seven? – you'd be home by then? I'll phone if I can't make it.'

'Not at work,' she said, too quickly.

His eyebrows shot up. She said, evasively, 'Lizzie's hot on personal phone calls.'

3

'I could make it police work.' He pulled himself up and put on his official voice. 'DCI Harvey, here — can I speak to DS Power?' And he grinned, looking less like the schoolmaster for which he could usually be taken than a mischievous schoolboy.

It was hard to respond sensibly, but she did. 'She'd want to know why, chapter and verse. Just leave a message on my answerphone. No message, and I'll get the beer into the fridge.'

'I'll be putting on weight.' No smile. This might not be a joke.

She couldn't quip back that she knew ways of exercising calories off. Not yet. Graham was still too anxious a lover. So they exchanged smiles, no more, and went their ways.

Beer was supposed to be evidence to Graham's wife that he'd had a drink with the lads on the way home. Most evenings he did and his squad was — Kate was sure — the happier for it. But the occasional evening — an hour of the occasional evening — was theirs.

What if Lizzie wanted her to work late? Abandoning the shopping, she scuttled back to work. An extra half-hour's effort now might just save their evening.

'Kate.' Maybe Lizzie was impressed to see her back at her desk within the half-hour, a baguette in one hand, a highlighter in the other. Certainly her voice was friendlier, Kate suspected, than it would have been if Kate had done her shopping and now had a designer carrier bag beside her desk. 'No sign of Ben?' she continued.

Plenty of signs of Ben. His sandwiches on his desk, a can of Diet Coke, the *Mail* open at the crossword.

'Loo, I think.'

'Tell him I want to see him.'

'Gaffer.'

Lizzie'd got brusquer, hadn't she? Even brusquer. It wasn't just the red hair, fiery tempter cliché: she'd always had that hair, that temperament. There must be some squad rumours. But Kate would hate them to involve menopause or PMS. And – yes – she'd hate to ask. Maybe when she and Ben got on gossiping terms. She'd never worked closely with him, though she and Bill had evolved a very good partnership.

She was highlighting the next obscure page when Ben returned, collapsing into his chair and grabbing his biro. Not the demeanour of a happy man.

'Problems in court this morning?'

'Fucking adjournment. As if I hadn't enough on my bloody plate without having to sit on my arse all morning.' He bit into his sandwich.

'Reckon you might be getting even more on your plate. The gaffer wants to see you.'

'What? Now?' He slammed the sandwich back into the box.

'I'd eat first. No point in getting yourself an ulcer.'

'Any idea what she wanted?'

'She had an air about her that made my in-tray quake.

'Which reminds me, Ben, when you've got a moment, I could do with picking your brain about some of this.'

He looked at her coldly: 'I thought sergeants were supposed to have an extra dose of brains. Specially those on the accelerated promotion scheme.'

She raised an eyebrow. 'You'd know about the sergeants' brains, Ben. After all, you passed at the same time as Bill, didn't you?'

'Fat lot of good it's done me.' Yes, still a constable approaching forty, and her a high-flyer not yet thirty. A bit of tact was called for.

'Same as the inspectors' has done me. Come on, Ben, you know you can have all the letters of the alphabet after your name and still be no good because you don't have the experience. And because you can't mind-read. Some of the stuff Bill thought important doesn't mean a thing to me.'

'Good cop, Bill.' He shrugged. 'Want to bring them over here?'

'Not till you've finished your sarnies. And the crossword.'

'That might take a little longer.' There was no doubt the deep lines from nose to chin softened a little, but you couldn't say he'd managed a smile. 'I suppose I'd better see the gaffer before I look at the stuff for you.'

'You better bloody had,' Lizzie snarled from the door.


Ben might be getting a bollocking but there was no doubt he wasn't taking it quietly. You could hear the raised voices all along the corridor. Tammy, a constable who looked as if she'd just finished her GCSEs but who had in fact an accountancy degree, popped her head round Kate's door.

'Any idea what's going on?'

'A free and frank discussion by the sounds of it.' Kate grinned. If it took a row to bring her colleagues along to see her, well, pity about the row but nice about the mellowing of relations.

'She's been like this ever since Bill went,' Tammy continued, drifting further into the room.

Kate got up and shook the kettle. Tammy nodded, perching on the edge of Ben's desk.

'Must be bad,' Kate said, dropping a tea bag into a clean mug, 'losing someone as experienced as him, and getting me to replace him. And then only after having to wait about — what, six weeks?'

Tammy snorted. 'You think it's his work she's missing! I'd say it was something else.' She mimed.

Kate wouldn't bite. Not in her situation. She hoped she wouldn't have anyway. Before she could say anything, Ben stormed back into the room. 'Her majesty wants you,' he said. 'Now.'

'You might as well drink my tea,' Kate said, putting the mug in front of him. There were some meetings with bosses to which you could take a drink, and others you couldn't. She had a nasty feeling that this was the latter.

\*

'At least even you won't have to break into a sweat over this file,' Lizzie said, without preamble. 'Not a figure in sight. Just words. Plenty of them.'

Kate bent to pick it up off Lizzie's desk.

'Let me have your thoughts on it tomorrow.'

'Ma'am.'

It looked as though she was in for a late evening. No. It would have to be an extremely early morning, wouldn't it? She turned to leave.

'And for God's sake, Power, stop picking on Ben. He's got enough to worry about without having to help you.'

Kate had a nasty feeling Lizzie was going to repeat all the stuff Ben had come out with about exams and brains. Hell, Lizzie was a graduate herself, so there was no excuse for her inverted intellectual snobbery. The only problem was that she'd got her promotions the hard way, not via the accelerated promotion scheme Kate was on – which Kate wasn't at all sure she wanted to be on any longer. But now wasn't the time to confide her doubts to Lizzie. Personnel knew about them, and so did her previous gaffer, Rod Neville. He, however, was now running the Murder Investigation Teams, and well out of her orbit. The only person with whom she could chew over her doubts now was Graham Harvey, and their time together was too precious to waste on career plan discussions.

'Will that be all, Gaffer?'

Lizzie, already opening the next file, flapped a dismissive hand.

The words came out before Kate could stop them. 'Are you all right, Gaffer?' she asked, in the tone of voice she'd use to a friend, not a boss.

'The Superintendent's off sick, they've cut back two DCIs, I'm doing the work of all three on a DI's pay, and you ask if I'm all right? Get real, Power.'

There was something else, though, wasn't there? Surely there must be. However stressed, however resentful, good bosses like Lizzie didn't turn into raging monsters. She didn't think she bought Tammy's theory, either. Kate had seen nothing during her partnership with Bill to suggest that he might be having or indeed concealing an affair. Indeed, he'd always seemed rather fond of his wife, and proud of her achievements. But she didn't have time to speculate now. She had to get her head down to some good hard work, and make sure she was home in time for Graham.

Ben was on his own when she came back, elbows on desk, his forehead supported by splayed fingers. The tea she'd passed him was untouched. She shut the door quietly and pulled a chair across. 'Problems?'

He looked almost relieved to have his thoughts interrupted. 'Sounds a cliché, doesn't it? But I'm worried about Lizzie.'

'Losing it, isn't she,' she agreed. 'But you don't have to take what isn't due to you.'

'She's a mate,' he said. 'And I give as good as I get. But I don't like to see her like this. She's always had a rough tongue, no doubt about that. It couldn't – it couldn't be a woman's thing, could it? You know, the change or something?'

'She can't be much over forty. But I suppose it's possible. Or is it a work thing? She seems to be doing the work of three.'

'And you and me both. And we don't go ballistic like that every time someone gives us a new case. I see she's lumbered you with it, by the way.' He nodded at the folder she'd dropped on her desk. 'Actually, she should have given it to you in the first place. It's a nice little one-off-er. You should be able to start and finish it on your own.' He grinned. 'And it leaves me to finish Bill's fag ends. Just as easy to do that as to tell you what to do.'

She glanced at the door. 'I've a nasty suspicion that you'll have to do that anyway. I reckon the gaffer will be checking up on my progress.'

'You're probably right. When do you want to start? Over a snifter tonight?'

*Snifter*? Ah, Black Country for drink.

She sighed. 'Have to take a rain check on that, Ben. I've got to get home – plumber. How about tomorrow?'

'Fine. Only one thing, Kate: would you mind not calling me Ben?' he added in a rush. 'It was Lizzie's idea of a joke – you know, Bill and Ben, the Flowerpot Men. We're both keen on our gardens, see, and swapped cuttings and such like. And it stuck. Would do, while Bill was here. But I'm really Derek.'

'And you probably have a surname too. I ought to know in case people ask for you. Though I was here all those weeks and everyone always called you Ben – and nothing else.'

'Baker. Derek Baker.'

She reached to shake his hand. 'Hi, Derek.' This time both smiles seemed genuine. 'But how public do you want to be about this? Isn't Ben a bit of a shibboleth. If I call you anything else I'll be marked down as an outsider?'

'As far as I'm concerned, Kate, it marks you as an insider.'

'Sufficient of an insider to bum cuttings and advice about my infant garden? I had it completely reorganised. My great-aunt – you know how she gave me her house – wouldn't recognise it. Nice paths. Seating area.'

He whistled. 'That must have cost a bit. No problem with the plants, though. I'll be splitting quite a lot of stuff this autumn.' He looked at his watch. 'Tell you what, let's check through that in-tray now, so you'll please her majesty, and you can tell me what you need tomorrow over half of mild. Oh, and we might talk a bit of shop too.'


Would the red light be flashing? God, how absurd to have your pulse-rate ruled by a tiny light.

Kate fumbled her keys into the locks, killed the alarm and headed for the answerphone. A message.

'I'm sorry. I really am. But my wife's ill. She phoned work – pulled me out of that meeting. Talk to you as soon as I can.'

No greeting. No farewell. No endearment to hold on to.

And, of course, no Graham.

Kate wandered blindly back to pick up the post and close the vestibule door. As an afterthought, she went back and bolted the front door. No need to leave it for Graham, who seemed to derive an extra pleasure from letting himself into her house. Presumably his wife's checks on his private life didn't extend to his key ring.

*Come on: this is what you get when you have an affair with a married man.* Except it hadn't been like that with her and Robin. She poured herself a glass of wine and wandered into the garden. The plants were so tiny the place looked more like a pin-cushion than a garden, but everything would grow. Even the seeds she'd scattered between the new shrubs to give some green, some colour in the garden's first season. At the far end, instead of the ancient shed and the hoard of buttons it had concealed, were a bench and table. She tipped her head back to absorb the evening sun. She and Robin had been police partners months before they became sexual ones. Partners, not DCI and sergeant, so there was never any hint of promotion politics. And Robin had left his wife before they so much as kissed. So they'd never had to be furtive. They'd never had it easy, and the circumstances surrounding Robin's funeral had been especially hard to bear. But at least, ninety-nine per cent of the time, they could be open and frank about their love.

So was that what she and Graham shared? Love?

The phone!

She ran back to the house.

Lorraine from the Domestic Violence Unit. Did she fancy a game of tennis? She and Midge had found a third keen player, and needed a fourth.

Sit around hoping against hope that Graham might phone, or an evening with the girls? Come on, what sort of woman was she?

'So long as there's a balti afterwards,' she said.

It was a good hard game, and an excellent meal with rather more lager than she should have had.

But there were no more messages on the answerphone, and no matter how much she despised herself for doing it, she cried herself to sleep.

# Chapter Two

Kate was just boiling the kettle for the first office coffee of the day when Derek appeared. She flourished a second mug.

'Why not?' he asked, dumping his raincoat and flopping on to his chair. 'By the way, the gaffer says there's some punter being a pain down in Reception and will you deal with her?'

'Punter? Here?'

Lloyd House was the West Midlands Police head-quarters building, not, like Steelhouse Lane nick, a natural target for Joe Public.

'That's what she says. Don't ask my why and how.'

'Or even who?' Not to mention the rest of the six honest serving men.

He shook his head, taking the coffee and staring into the mug. 'No idea. She said there was no hurry – the gaffer, that is. Said you could let her cool her heels a bit.'

'I love Lizzie's idea of public relations,' Kate said, replacing the file she'd been working on in the in-tray and picking up her notebook. 'If she means it, of course. She's just as likely to bollock me for keeping whoever it is waiting.' She swigged the too-hot coffee. 'Why the rain-coat, Derek? They're forecasting sun all day; twenty three degrees, no more than thirty minutes out in the sun without your SPF fifteen and pop your hay-fever pills.';

'I'd rather trust my instincts,' Derek said, opening the *Mail.*


The middle-aged woman waiting in Reception raised Kate's hackles immediately, but not, she hoped, too visibly. 'Mrs Duncton?'

'Oh,' she said, making no effort to get up, though Kate knew from experience that the chairs were not designed to encourage sitting, 'I expected someone — you know . . .'

Kate did know. Punters wanted avuncular men, not young women dressed with more regard for the weather than for sobriety. Punters wanted Sergeant George Dixon of Dock Green, not Sergeant Kate Power of Kings Heath.

Smiling politely and bending to shake hands, she intro-duced herself, adding, 'Inspector King has asked me to speak to you. Would you like to come upstairs? Let's get you a visitor's pass. Oh, I need your first name, too.'

'Maeve.' She didn't ask Kate to use it.

She couldn't work out if the woman was nervous or plain clumsy: whatever she did with the clip fastening, the label slipped off either her suit jacket or the co-ordinating blouse. Mrs Duncton had dressed well to meet Sergeant

Dixon. Leather bag, leather sandals. Discreet gold jewellery and some make-up.

The label fell to the floor again. At last Kate did the sensible thing and, picking it up, leaned forward herself to clip it on. 'There,' she smiled.

'Are you sure it won't tear my blouse?' The woman peered at it, turning her mouth down at the corners and pulling her neck into four double-chins.

'I'm sure it won't.' Kate crossed her fingers behind her back. With the other hand she summoned the lift. When one eventually arrived – how long could you keep small-talk going with a complete stranger – the doors opened to release her former boss, Superintendent Rod Neville, who nodded at her impersonally and strode off, the handsome personification of authority and busy-ness. It was clear whom Mrs Duncton would have preferred to talk to.

But punters didn't get detective superintendents; they shouldn't really have got a detective sergeant. Still, she'd got one now, and was entitled to some courtesy. A smile, at least, as Kate held back the lift door to usher her into a corridor and thence to a meeting room far too large for her immediate purpose. She sat Mrs Duncton at the corner of the conference table, and drew up a chair for herself. Then she pulled herself up short: Come on, Kate: what about a bit of PR from you? She offered tea or coffee: Mrs Duncton wanted neither.

'It's about my mother's will,' she said. 'It's a forgery.'

Taken aback by the sudden announcement, Kate asked foolishly, 'In what sense?'

'What do you mean, "in what sense?" Someone's forged it. And not just someone. I know who and I know why.'

Kate looked at her. 'So whom are you accusing, Mrs Duncton? And why do you allege he or she did it?' She kept her voice as neutral as possible.

'Max Cornfield. He was her handyman for years. And he did it to get his hands on her money.'

'And your mother's name was – ?'

'Sylvia Barr.'

'And she lived – ?'

Mrs Duncton gave an address in a very smart road in the smart suburb of Edgbaston.

'When did she pass away?'

'In June. And then we found this will. And it's a forgery. Here.' Mrs Duncton reached inside her shopping bag for a pink card envelope folder. She extracted a single sheet of paper, which she laid with something of a flourish on the table.

The paper was a photocopy of a hand-written document, purporting to be the last will and testament of Sylvia Hermione Barr. It was signed in a different hand by Mrs Barr, and by two witnesses, neither of whom, for some reason, lived in the UK. One lived in Berlin, the other in Portugal. The will left everything Mrs Barr possessed to Max Cornfield.

'Why do you think this is a forgery?'

'It's not her writing. It's Max's, I'd stake my life on it. I mean, look what she's left him. Everything.'

Kate read again, more slowly. 'And nothing, it seems, to anyone else. Apart from yourself, Mrs Duncton, did she have any family?'

'My brother. Michael.'

'Michael Barr.'

Mrs Duncton shifted slightly in her chair. 'Michael Barton, actually.'

'Son of a different marriage?' Kate asked.

The shift was more obvious. 'Not exactly.'

Kate said nothing. The pause deepened. Should she prompt her? Or wait? Sometimes a pause said more than words, and this might just be one of those pauses. She maintained her alert, listening posture, her head cocked slightly to one side, and waited.

'You'll be wanting his address,' Mrs Duncton said. She gave one in Tamworth.

Kate wrote it down, repeating it.

'And I don't think I gave you mine.'

'No, you didn't.' She dictated one in Four Oaks, a nice part of Sutton Coldfield.

'Neither of you lives in Birmingham itself,' Kate noted.

Mrs Duncton jerked back her head. 'That's what it's like these days. People leave home. Live in different places. You're not from round here, are you? London, is it? Somewhere in the south, anyway.'

Kate smiled. 'I lived down there for a couple of years.'

'Funny how you pick up accents, isn't it?'

So should she go along with this digression? Why not? Give her some more conversational rope . . . 'I never stayed in one place very long,' Kate said. 'Goodness knows what I shall sound like at the end of my life.'

'My mother tried to make sure we didn't have an accent. Birmingham. Well, it was in the papers the other day, wasn't it, that people respect Scots but think that if you come from Birmingham you're stupid. Not that you get a Birmingham accent if you come from Edgbaston. And we were privately educated, of course. Michael went off to boarding school somewhere, and I went to Edgbaston High School. Just five minutes down the road. I used to walk there.'

'What did you do when you'd left school, Mrs Duncton?' Had she left home then? And how often had she returned?

'Oh, training college, that was what they called it in those days.'

'So you're a teacher. Goodness, I don't envy you!'

Another of those fidgets. 'Actually, I didn't like it. Not all that much. No, I got my secretarial qualifications, and then I married and we had our family. I wasn't one of these modern mothers, I stayed at home and raised them myself.'

Kate jotted. There was a lot of history being concealed here, wasn't there? 'What about your brother? Michael, wasn't it?'

'Oh, he went off to university, of course.'

Was there an edge of resentment there? That the boy had been better treated, and thirty-odd years later it still rankled?

'And what did he do then?'

'He became a very successful man. A doctor. He's retired now, of course.'

'So does Dr Barr—'

'Dr Barton. I told you.'

'Of course. I'm sorry. When did he change his name?'

No fidget at all this time. But another jerk of the head. 'That's his business.'

Was it indeed? Kate jotted again. 'Now, tell me about this Mr Cornfield. Was he your mother's . . .' She hoped the hesitation was both delicate and insinuating.

'He called himself a handyman. Imagine, leaving everything to a handyman!'

Kate smiled: 'I can imagine leaving a fortune to a good plumber!'

The joke fell flat.

'No, he forged it. He must have forged it. She was proud of her family, proud of us. She wouldn't leave it to a stranger. The will's a forgery, I tell you.' Her colour had come right up, a pulse going in her neck.

'So how long had Mr Cornfield worked for her?'

'What do you mean, how long?'

Oh, yes, there was something there, wasn't there? 'A few months? A few years?'

'Yes, quite some time. Quite some time. But he was only a handyman.'

So what was the real problem? That Cornfield was merely a working man? Or had Cornfield and Mrs Barr been lovers? One way or another, he'd ousted the family in her affections. Clearly she'd have to talk to Cornfield.

She looked at his address in the will. The Coach House, at the same address as the deceased. Well, that was a good start.

'Have you taken any advice, Mrs Duncton?'

'Advice?'

'Legal advice. Talked to a solicitor, your mother's solicitor—'

'She didn't have one. She hated the whole tribe, she said.'

'What about you?'

'I took it to a graphologist,' Mrs Duncton said. 'To get an expert opinion. Here it is.' She produced another file, blue this time.

Kate opened it, and ran her eyes quickly down the first page of the report. Graphologist's report this might be, but any use in a police investigation it was not. It wouldn't even have been much use as part of a candidate selection procedure, not that she could see. It was full of florid assertions, unburdened by any concrete examples. That didn't mean it was harmless. Could the writer really be secretive, mean and vicious-tongued? For all she knew the adjectives could have fitted Mrs Barr perfectly. But here was a nugget. 'The writer is male.'

Kate tapped the folder. 'May I keep this?'

'Of course. And the will.'

'You have the original? Our experts would need to see it.'

Mrs Duncton bit her lip. 'It's been lodged for probate already.'

'No problem. There's not much the police can't get hold of if they need to see it.' She smiled. 'Tell me, was there much property involved?'

Mrs Duncton flushed again. 'Oh yes, quite a bit. I mean, her house is on a prime site. And all the contents: she never threw anything away – probably sitting on a gold-mine. And that bastard thinks he'll get the lot.' She gathered up her bags and stood up. 'And I'll tell you something else, Sergeant. A man who's capable of forging a helpless old lady's will is quite capable of killing her.'

Not a bad exit line, and Kate was quite sure Mrs Duncton had meant it as such. She thought, on the whole, she'd let it be just that. She too got to her feet, and courteously opened the door for her. She could somehow see Mrs Duncton regaling Mr Duncton with her account of her morning, repeating her last words again and again for emphasis. She'd told the police her suspicions, hadn't she? All of them. Yes. All of them. They'd have to act now, wouldn't they?

And Kate rather supposed they would. Divesting Mrs Duncton of the visitor's badge, she shook hands and politely saw her off. She'd get ten out of ten for manners, if not for her rank.

What remained to be seen, of course, was the mark she'd get for the case itself. Because she'd got a nasty suspicion that however little she'd taken to Mrs Duncton, she'd got an unavoidable investigation on her hands.

*

'There's something fishy going on, Gaffer,' she told Lizzie. Could she trust Lizzie's mood enough to ask her for a cup of what smelt like very good coffee?

'Fishy enough for us to get involved? You're sure?'

'My hope is that there's a perfectly simple explanation and it'll take ten minutes' conversation to sort everything out. But even to my eye there's no doubt that whoever signed the will didn't write it. Someone ought to talk to him.'

'You,' Lizzie said. 'You've nothing special on, after all.'

'There was the job you got me to look at last night,' Kate pointed out. 'But I don't think that'll come to much.'

Lizzie looked ostentatiously at her watch. 'Talk me through it at lunch-time. We'll nip out for half a pint. Half-twelve, in the foyer. OK?'

It was hardly a question.

'OK, Gaffer.'

One thing they'd have to discuss, of course, was whom she should work with. Derek Baker? No, he had enough on his plate for two, garnished by a fine dollop of stress. One thing was certain, it would be better to let Lizzie make any dispositions rather than provoke any tempests with her own suggestions.

*Come on, Kate: what's happened to your assertiveness?*

She meandered into the loo. Graham hadn't phoned. That was what had happened to her assertiveness. Crazy! Stupid! If you had to give marks out of ten for technical expertise in bed, if you had to give a grade for lover-like behaviour in the matter of flowers and gestures, he wasn't even a very good lover. No man could be worth this.

*Except he is. Love doesn't come much more painful than this.*

And there was an e-mail from him waiting for her when she switched on her computer. Since he was using official police channels, he used official police language. Would anyone be deceived?

Kate:

*There are one or two matters I'd like to go over with you before the Simmons trial next week. Could you suggest a couple of convenient times?*

Graham Harvey

The worst thing was that he might simply be suggesting precisely that. But at least they'd be in the same room; at least words could be exchanged. She'd better mention his request to Lizzie at lunch-time. And make sure she wasn't grinning like a monkey with rictus at the time.

# Chapter Three

Kate had already left her office to meet up with Lizzie when Derek yelled down the corridor to call her back.

'Gaffer's on the blower for you, Kate!'

Shrugging, she turned back, wondering whether she should break into a canter, but settling for a brisk stride.

'Something's come up, Power,' Lizzie announced. 'I should be free by five. I'd like an action plan for both the case I gave you and whatever crap that woman came up with this morning. OK?'

*Sure, sit round outside your office like a lemon for half an hour, then endure half an hour of criticism and get home too late for Graham to drop in.*

'Fine, Gaffer. Just one thing, they want me back at Steelhouse Lane for a confab about a case that's coming up in the County Court next week.'

'You're based here, Power – haven't they noticed?'

'I'm sure they have. Which is why I'm asking you if I can sort out a couple of free-ish slots and confirm them with you before I get back to them.'

'For them read Graham Harvey, I suppose?'

*Have you stopped beating your wife yet*, and other unanswerable questions. 'Graham Harvey's arranging the meeting, ma'am. You know what it's like, pulling people together now they're scattered out to sector nicks.'

'We'll talk action plans first. Then you can talk to Graham. OK?'

'Ma'am.' She spoke to a dead phone. She looked up: Derek, chin on hand, was watching her.

'It's not just you, you know,' he said. 'I'm worried about her, Kate. Five years I've known her, and she's always been – what do they call it? – feisty. But nothing like this. I mean, she's a good career cop and she's pissing round like some bloody opera singer – prima whatsit. Hormones, I suppose.'

Kate shoved her hands in her pockets, shaking her head. 'If she were a bloke, what would we put it down to? Overwork, family problems, illness.'

He pulled at his lower lip. 'But she's a woman. And it's well known that women her age—'

'Like I said the other day, she's a bit on the young side to be menopausal, I'd have thought.'

'My sister-in-law was only thirty-five when she had hers. Come on, Kate, if it's a woman thing, you should talk to her.'

She flung her hands in the air but not in a gesture of surrender. 'No way. In case the rumour hasn't already reached your ears, I'm not her favourite person at the best of times. I shall do my action plans and my paperwork and keep my head well below the parapet.'

He didn't look convinced. He looked at his watch. 'I forgot my sarnies this morning. Coming down the canteen?'

'Sure,' she said. No, she mustn't even contemplate the possibility that Graham might have been free for a sandwich in the sun.

She was entitled to e-mail Graham back, wasn't she? To explain that she had to prepare something for a meeting late in the afternoon, but would get back to him about the Simmons case and a couple of other things as soon as she could. How was his wife, incidentally? She was sorry to hear she was ill. Then she deleted the last two sentences. Just in case anyone else should read them and want to know how she knew. Just in case.

She sent the message and closed down the system. Paper files, now, she told herself sternly. But what she wanted, oh, what she wanted more than anything else, was to hear his voice. Simply his voice. It didn't matter what he was saying. He wasn't a man for luscious endearments, never would be, she suspected; if he expressed tenderness, he did so by offering her a cup of tea in his office. And their conversation could be as prosaic and business-filled as you like, but it was still talk with him. And if they were on their own, there'd be eye contact, there'd be that electricity . . .

She forced herself to concentrate. Ironically, the first case concerned lovers too. She read through the notes again, although she was already almost word perfect on them. A young man had bought his girlfriend a pair of ruby earrings from an antique shop. When they got engaged, he wanted to have a ring to match them, so he took them along to a shop in the Jewellery Quarter which not only sold but also made jewellery. There he learned that the 'rubies' were in fact garnets, worth perhaps a tenth of what he'd paid. The shop he'd originally bought them from was profusely apologetic, and refunded his money, but he wanted action taken against it.

*Action*, she wrote: *talk to: Jewellery Quarter firm manufacturing jewellery and possibly Trading Standards. Time allocation: an hour.*

As far as the will allegations went, she was afraid that if you lifted up what seemed to be a rotting log, you might find all sorts of unsavoury insect life underneath it.

*Talk to: Michael Barton, Max Cornfield, forensic graphologist, witnesses to will. Time allocation, two days.* She looked at the witness signatures again. One had a Portuguese address; the other lived in Berlin. *Maybe longer, if the witnesses are not based in the UK.*

Two-ten. What if Graham were free now?

Her hand was already on the phone. But she drew it away swiftly. 'Any chance you could spare me ten minutes on this in-tray, Derek? Then maybe I could wrap up one or two of them for her nibs.'

He looked up, sighing.

'OK,' she said. 'I'll be off to the Jewellery Quarter, then.'

'Nice day for a walk down there,' he nodded.

'Walk?' She still forgot that, however sprawling its

conurbation, the centre of Birmingham was remarkably compact.

'Shouldn't take you more than ten minutes – fifteen in this heat.' He grinned, sardonically. 'Take your brolly, though.'

The trouble was, the old misery might be right. Though the sun was still hot, and bright enough for sun-glasses, the sky above Birmingham was taking on a milky brownness. No, that was just pollution, surely: all those particles of dust and chemical that blended into an atmospheric soup, the sort of haze you saw over every big city. She didn't want it to rain tonight. She wanted a sunny evening, to sit out in her new garden. She might even have a barbecue for one – though a barbecue for two was infinitely preferable. *Oh, Kate, in your dreams. Graham will always go home to eat. Think of the stress you caused him that time you tipped his lunch sandwiches into the bin so he could go and eat with you. No, solo eating's the price you'll have to pay as long as you and Graham are together.*

She paused: this must be St Paul's churchyard. She'd heard people talk about the church itself, a neat, elegant Georgian building. It was supposed to have very good acoustics as she recalled, good enough for concerts. And across there should be – yes, that must be it – a pub which did great food, and over there a couple of clubs. She pressed on. And stopped, thunderstruck. She had never seen so many shops – some big, but mostly small – all selling jewellery. Real jewellery, not the china and resin stuff that filled so many high-street shop windows these days. There was gold in them there shops. Gold and diamonds. And a museum. Not far from the museum was the shop she wanted, the one that had alerted the young man to the problems of his fiancée's earrings. Yes, there it was, next to the Metro station, lying slightly back from the kerb from which its bow-window was protected (from ram-raiding?) by a big square brick-built planter, burgeoning with petunias and, ironically enough, busy lizzies. It shared its outer front door with a gem-cutter; there was a buzzer system to let customers into the shop itself. She had to remind herself she was there on business, or she could have spent the whole afternoon drooling over the items on display. What intrigued her was what lay behind one of the counters; a workshop, complete with gas burners. It wasn't just for show, either. Young men were working there, to the quiet accompaniment of a local radio station.

Thank goodness the assistant was an intelligent-looking woman in her forties, not some vacuous kid. She had diamonds to die for on her ring fingers.

Kate introduced herself and explained the problem.

'You have to do it sometimes,' the woman said simply. 'You get to know the stones – the colour, the cut. But I always refer them to Mick – he's the boss – or Stephen, just in case.'

At the mention of his name, one of the young men got up from his bench and came round into the shop. He nodded. 'Happens the other way round, too,' he said, smiling. 'Sometimes we get to give good news. I had this customer with an opal so big I thought it was a doublet—'

'A doublet?'

'An opal covered with a thin skin of glass to make it bigger and stronger,' he explained. 'But it turned out it was one lovely big stone. Whoever sold it to her would have torn his hair out he'd let her have it so cheap. They're antique dealers, you see. Not gemmologists.'

'So you don't see this as some nasty big scam designed to rip off Joe Public.'

'If there are scams, we get to hear about them soon enough. It's all done by trust in the trade, Sergeant. Has to be. We have to trust our gem suppliers; sometimes we have to send a customer's stone away to be matched. We've got to know it'll come back. That one. Not another quite like it. We have to trust the gold suppliers, because the assay office will pounce on anything sub-standard.'

She nodded. 'But if you do come on any scams, you will tell me?' She put her card on the counter.

'Sure; it's in everyone's interest, isn't it?'

She grinned. 'What I'm interested in is that chain, there. Tell you what, I'll come back when I'm not on duty!'

There were friendly smiles and good-natured laughter. But the smile left her face as soon as she stepped into the street.

Any diamonds she wore would be diamonds she bought herself, wouldn't they?

*

As she'd predicted, Lizzie's five o'clock was actually five-thirty, and the criticism was ready to crackle. However, Lizzie was disarmed, temporarily at least, by the news that the garnets and ruby case was still-born.

'That's something, I suppose,' she said. 'But what about this morning's punter? You don't want to get us involved in some family feud, Power.'

Kate nodded. 'Quite. But it may turn out to be bigger than that. In fact, Gaffer, my nose tells me it's going to.'

Lizzie treated her to a long, level stare. At last her face softened. 'That's what makes a good cop, Kate. A nose. You use that and you'll be all right.' She sat back and stretched, grimacing as something clicked audibly in her back.

'You all right, Gaffer?' Kate risked.

'Sounded bad, didn't it? I could use an hour in a sauna, I admit. But—' she gestured helplessly at her desk. 'And I wanted to talk to Ben before I left.'

Kate took another risk. 'Why not talk to him in the pub? A day like this, we'd all be the better for a long cold beer.'

Lizzie managed a half-smile. 'You're telling me it's time to go home. Maybe. Tell Ben I'll see him tomorrow.'

Taking that as dismissal, Kate got to her feet. The angle of Lizzie's eyebrow told her to sit down again.

'This business of a partner for you. I've been talking to Personnel. And one or two others. The feeling seems to be that you might as well get on with things on your own. You're not going to be dealing with violent criminals here, after all. You've got a good deal of police experience and we're understaffed. QED. Oh, you'll be reporting back to me, and anything really needing two cops – like an arrest – we'll find you someone. OK?' This time there was a definite dismissal.

Kate nodded, getting to her feet. It wasn't as if she hadn't worked on her own before. When she was under-cover in that home, she was well and truly isolated. But she'd come to enjoy being part of a team. Well, if there was no team to be part of, that was that.

Ben shrugged when she told him the news. And packed up like a schoolboy late for half-term when she told him his session with Lizzie could wait. So much for that half of mild. Well, he had a family to go home to.


If there'd been any single-use barbecues left in Sainsbury's, she'd have bought herself one, and some steak to cook on it. But the locusts had landed before her. There were only a few salads hanging around, tatty as Cinders waiting for a fairy godmother. Next year, she'd grow lettuces and radishes and some young onions. In fact, she was so taken with the idea, she nipped round to the seed stand. There was a chance that some might germinate even at this late date. There!

Back to the salad area. Tomatoes and basil: that would do. And some pâté. And some nice bread. No strawberries; the locusts were evidently partial to them, too. And she'd bet her pension there wouldn't be much in the way of quality ice-cream, either. But there was a good offer on white wine.

Displacement activity, of course. Because she didn't want to go home to find no message from Graham. That would be even worse than a message saying he still couldn't see her. She chose a long queue, and dawdled back up Worksop Road. To find a familiar car just about to pull away.

'I waited and waited,' Graham said, still panting slightly. 'I reasoned that if your car was outside you wouldn't be long away.'

She passed him a glass of wine. 'I'm glad you waited. Oh, I'm so glad.' Deliberately, she slopped some of her wine on to his stomach, licking it up. 'Or should I say, I'm so glad you came.'

'I might come again,' he said.

And did.

But he was showered and dressed and out of the house twenty minutes later. And, as she'd known she'd have to, she ate alone in her garden.

# Chapter Four

'The key is to be absolutely meticulous,' Derek said, first thing next morning, passing her a coffee. 'Not just paper-work. Everything. Because if you aren't, if Lizzie suspects you of being the tiniest bit sloppy, she'll slice you up into tiny pieces and have you on toast.'

'So what's new?'

'And for all she says you'll be working on your own, you'll find she wants chapter and verse every day, and she'll be running the show. In her own highly individual not to say eccentric way. You'll just be her gofer. You'd be better off partnered with one of the kids.'

'I'm sure I would. But in this job I want doesn't get. Any more than it got me jelly at Aunt Cassie's when I was a kid.'

'How is the old bat? As bad as my ma-in-law? God, we all have our crosses to bear!'

Kate pulled a face. 'Getting stroppier. She used to say she didn't want to interfere in my life, didn't want me to visit her, even, if I had anything else to do. But things are

37

changing. She says *she* worries about *me* if I don't pop in every other day.'

'And do you?'

Kate spread her hands. 'In this job?'

Derek shook his head. 'Don't get me wrong. I'm not criticising. Every other day's quite often, if she's being cared for by someone else. It's not as if she was stuck in a house on her own all day with nothing but the telly for company.'

'I feel guilty, all the same. After all, she's been very generous to me. Very generous indeed. And all I can manage – no, all I make time to do – is pop in twice a week. Sometimes once.' Nor did she always make the effort to stay and talk as long as Cassie would have liked. But conversation was becoming more and more difficult, the more institutionalised Aunt Cassie became. 'Any road,' she added, 'better get on with the job. Soon as I've finished this I'll be on my way to sunny Edgbaston.'

'"Any road"! Anyone would think you lived round here! You'll be getting a Brummie accent next.'

'According to the punter who stirred this lot up, people think you're thick if you talk Brummie. So at least I'd be in good company.' She drained her mug, and picked up her bag. 'Right; into battle!'

'Take a brolly!' he yelled after her.

She dodged back into the office: 'You said it would rain yesterday. And look at it, it's gorgeous out there. I think I might even walk.'

'Unless you want to go by bus, you'll have to. We're down to two cars today, and Lizzie's bagged one. And I'm having the other.' His face invited her to challenge him. When she didn't, it softened a mite. 'I suppose I could always give you a lift.'

'Only if you're going that way. It's only a step, after all.'

'True. Still, like I say, take your brolly. Too bright too early if you ask me.'


As houses went, Mrs Barr's wasn't particularly attractive. It was obviously later than some of the elegant Georgian and Regency houses in the area, its windows smaller, its overall proportions less right. And it lacked the sheer cheek of some of the neighbouring Victorian piles. But it was on such a prime site that it would no doubt fetch a mint on the open market, particularly if someone slapped some paint on it and fixed the rough-cast.

The term Coach House had been somewhat generously applied. To Kate's eyes it had far more the look of a twenties garage. In the side were a couple of windows, inviting Kate to peer through; which she duly did. Into a tidy bed-sitting room. Hmm. Had anyone got round to notifying the council of a change of use? Did anyone pay council tax on what was clearly a dwelling? Perhaps she didn't care. What she wanted was the place's front door, surely not the big wooden ones appropriate to the original use? She dodged round to the back, but a fence ran between it and the house. So was the only access through the house itself?

Before she rang the front bell, she'd go and rap on the window of the big doors. No. No response.

Back to the front door, which lay within a deep porch. She'd have wanted a security light to greet her comings and goings if she'd been the owner. The bell – an old-fashioned one helpfully labelled 'Press' – echoed loudly enough for her to hear it through what she suspected was a very solid front door. But no one responded.

Turning away, she looked straight into the eyes of an elderly golden retriever, tugging half-heartedly at its leash. Its owner, an immensely tall woman who might be any age between seventy and ninety, peered over what looked like bifocals from the end of the drive.

'May I help you?' Her county vowels might have carried a further fifty yards. She hadn't raised her voice, simply projected.

Kate stepped away from the door, and smiled. 'Good morning. I was hoping to find Mr Cornfield at home.'

The old lady shook her head. 'Today is Thursday. That is Mr Cornfield's day for travelling.'

Of course! What an obvious mistake to make! Kate bit back a sarcastic quip and approached her, letting the dog sniff as much of her hand as it could be bothered to. 'Where does Mr Cornfield travel to, Mrs – er?'

'Hamilton.' The eyebrows, bravely pencilled in on an age-spotted face, rose elegantly. Or had once.

'My name's Power. Kate Power.' To flash the ID, or not to flash? On the whole, Kate thought not, just at this point.

'And you are what, Miss Power?'

Kate produced a bright, positive smile. And her ID. Mrs

Hamilton would let her get away with nothing. 'I'm a police officer, Mrs Hamilton.'

'And your interest in Mr Cornfield?'

'A simple need to talk to him.'

The eyebrows conveyed disapproval of her cheek, but approval of her reticence. 'I should imagine — and do not for one moment imagine that I would wish to pry, Miss Power — that you may wish to talk about his legacy. Which is, after all, in the public domain, or very soon will be. It will be published, will it not, in *The Times*? Not that one would read it, these days. But one must stay informed.'

'What do you know of his legacy, Mrs Hamilton?'

'Enough to prefer not to converse in the public street about it. Miss Power, Mrs Barr was my neighbour for forty years or more. If you would like me to reminisce, I will be happy to do so. But in the privacy of my own home. Edward would appreciate a bowl of water.' The dog's ears pricked. 'And I myself usually drink coffee at this hour of the morning. Would you care to join me?'

Though next door, Mrs Hamilton's house was authentically Georgian in proportions, making Kate utter little gasps of pleasure as she passed through the square hall into a rear drawing room as faded but still elegant as its owner. The silk of the curtains and upholstery might be sadly worn, but was silk none the less. The chairs looked too fragile to support adult weight, but were surprisingly comfortable. While she waited for Mrs Hamilton, Kate made a stern resolution: she would never be able to afford a place like this – she suspected her entire ground floor would fit into this room and the hall with room to spare – but the furniture she bought to replace that damaged in the fire would be the best she could afford.

Mrs Hamilton's china, on an oval mahogany tray with brass handles at each end, looked quite like the stuff Kate had in her kitchen, courtesy Habitat. But it was so fine as to be translucent, its lines even more delicate. No, Mrs Hamilton was not a Habitat customer. The coffee was in a matching jug. Kate feared for its life as Mrs Hamilton struggled to force her arthritic joints to grasp the slender handle.

Her concern was noted, but did not seem to cause offence. 'Perhaps you would be good enough to add your own milk and sugar. Now, a biscuit, Miss Power? It is "Miss", is it? Or are you an awful "Ms"?'

'I'm actually a detective sergeant, Mrs Hamilton. Many people prefer simply to call me Kate.' If only Aunt Cassie could have been like this, in control of her own home. Even if it meant Kate had had to find her own place to live. 'You were saying that you had known Mrs Barr for many years.'

Mrs Hamilton smiled, shaking her head. 'I said, Sergeant, that we had been neighbours for many years. The two statements are not synonymous.' She paused long enough to gesture towards the biscuits fanned out elegantly on a plate.

Kate couldn't resist. Biting as delicately as she could, she

42

had an idea that she'd be unable to resist if they were offered a second time.

'Mrs Barr always respected her neighbours' privacy, and expected them to respect hers. Latterly, she went much further than that. She became reclusive. I understand that her health was very poor in recent years. Perhaps the explanation lies in that.'

Kate nodded. If only all witnesses were like this.

'She came to depend – no, utterly would not be too strong a word – on Mr Cornfield. He had always been a presence in the garden. I fancy he made up in enthusiasm and hard work what he lacked in expertise. Unfortunately Mrs Barr insisted on a hedge of those confounded Leylandii. Quite out of keeping with the original conception of the garden, but at least Mr Cornfield kept them at a reasonable height.' She gestured. The hedge was perhaps seven feet high. 'Mr Cornfield did his best to maintain the house, too. Though without access to proper funds, his ability to make more than cosmetic improvements was limited. Another biscuit, Miss Power? Sergeant!' She produced a smile of surprising sweetness. 'Kate. I made them myself. *Langue de chat.*'

Kate made no effort to resist. 'Mr Cornfield seems to have been a good friend to Mrs Barr?'

'Friend? Yes, I suppose in a strange way they were friends. Not that they didn't argue, latterly, at least. It must have been so hard for them both. She was bed-bound these last three years and depended, as I said, utterly on Mr Cornfield.'

Kate hesitated: how did Mrs Hamilton know? And how to ask?

'My source of information, my dear, is the district nurse, or whatever they call them these days. I was foolish enough to scrape my shin, and it needed dressing. Apparently the same district nurse had tried to treat Mrs Barr, but had been turned away.'

'By Mrs Barr or by Mr Cornfield?'

The wrinkled lids lowered slightly. 'I understood that it was Mrs Barr herself, but that would be hearsay, would it not? I suggest you contact the medical practice that sent the nurse. I can provide you with the number. It's in the hall, on the wall by my phone.'

'You don't have an extension in here? Or anywhere else?' Suddenly Kate found herself in carer mode. But it had to be said. 'What if you were to fall? Or if you were taken ill? My great-aunt had an alarm I made her wear all the time.' She took another risk. 'I could get you details, if you liked. But I do beg you, get the phone people to install more extensions.'

The response was a frosty smile. She'd gone too far. Coughing slightly, she pretended to refer to her notebook. 'You said that Mr Cornfield travelled on Thursdays, Mrs Hamilton. I suppose you wouldn't know where?'

The old lady shook her head. 'I used to see him set off at the same time every Thursday, returning at the same time. Where he went I have no idea.'

'His day off, perhaps?'

'I'm not sure that Mr Cornfield ever enjoyed the luxury

of a day off. Kate, I suspect that when Mrs Barr's will is finally published, the vultures will descend. But I will testify that I never knew Mr Cornfield leave the house for more than a few days, and I will also testify I never saw anyone except the friends Mr Cornfield introduced me to come near it.'

'Mr Cornfield introduced his friends to you?'

'Of course. If we met in circumstances like those in which I met you. Very distinguished gentlemen, some of them. But as for family, if Mrs Barr had nearest, believe me, Kate, they were certainly not her dearest.'

# Chapter Five

Nice day it might be for a trip to rural Tamworth, but if Kate was using public transport or subsidising West Midlands Police by using her own car, she'd better make sure that Michael Barton was at home. She certainly wouldn't class the morning so far as wasted, but Lizzie might. If she drew a blank with Barton, she could write up the interview with Mrs Hamilton and try to find a tame forensic graphologist: just the sort of person that Lizzie might be expected to know. Kate herself wasn't sure of the set-up here in Birmingham. Back in the Met, there was the Document Section in the Forensic Science Lab. She'd never had to refer material there herself, so she didn't have a useful contact who might have a mate in Brum. Presumably there was the equivalent up here, with its official channels, but in forensic science as in everything else, someone who'd whiz things through the system because you'd shared a pint or two was always worth cultivating. And, given Lizzie's penchant for speed, she'd know just the guy. About to tick herself off for the male term, Kate laughed sourly. Lizzie was not a woman for sisters. With Lizzie, it would be a guy.

And it was.

'You didn't hear?' Lizzie sat back from her desk and ran disbelieving hands through her hair. 'Oh, you folk in the Met, you're so bloody parochial. It was a national scandal. Oh, ten years ago now.'

Kate bit back an observation that ten years ago she was still an undergraduate. It was information she needed, not a few cheap points, each one of which would further fuel Lizzie's hostility. 'What happened?'

'Oh, the people there started whinging away about pressure and overwork and bad working conditions. And then one person left for the private sector, then another, and then, hey presto, the whole lot went private.

Kate opened her eyes wide. 'So you're saying there are no official experts?'

'There's a branch they split off from the Met down in Swindon or somewhere.'

'Nothing here in Brum?'

'Only your independent ones. Who charge a fee. So if you want anything doing, make sure you really want it doing. Mind you, the forensic science people charge a fee too, of course, so I usually argue – for convenience sake – that we use one here. Provided it's essential.' Lizzie favoured her with a hard stare.

'I think it's essential in this case. So who would you recommend I talked to?'

Lizzie reached in the cabinet behind her and slung a file on to her desk. 'Come on, Kate, use a bit of initiative.'

'Initiative's one thing, boss, but I'd rather go for someone tried and trusted. By you, preferably.'

'You mean I won't be able to query the expenditure if I tell you who to try? OK.' Lizzie managed a grin. She burrowed through the papers, coming up with a sheet of paper flimsy enough to have been through a typewriter. Another grin. 'Remember those days – hunt and peck and Tippex by the gallon?'

'My first squad, they delivered it in tankers. Thank God for the delete button!'

Lizzie was running a finger down the paper, finally stabbing it with her left forefinger and scribbling on a pad. 'Try this bloke. Or – he was getting on a bit, as I recall – you could try him. Say hello from me in either case.' She checked her watch. 'Doing anything for lunch?'

Another accolade. OK, it would have been nice to stroll in the sun again, nicer still to have risked a phone call to Graham. But she had to work with this woman, and though she expected a complaint about quality or flavour or texture with each mouthful, she'd better smile and say, 'Nothing. Canteen or pub?'

As predicted, the chicken was both tough and flavourless, the salad was probably dirty, and how Kate could eat that granary bread, Lizzie had no idea. If Kate had hoped – belatedly, but she had indeed hoped – to probe for possible causes of Lizzie's angst, there wasn't much opportunity. They talked about the lack of transport, the lack of clerical support, the hiving off to hicks from the sticks of cases needing Fraud expertise: Kate had the feeling that she would have expected a similar conversation with a middle-aged man. It was as if Lizzie lacked the small change of gossip. Kate herself touched on Derek's preference for his given name, but she wasn't sanguine that Lizzie would take the hint. She also dragged in references to her own health which she hoped might free Lizzie to speak of any scares she might be having, but she felt a distinct waning of respect, so she switched briskly back to her car, and the possibility of changing it. Cue for horror stories of Lizzie's garage.

'Why don't you change? Go somewhere else?' Kate asked.

'Oh, you get used to a place, don't you? And I suppose it's convenient.'

'Having to take it back each time you have it serviced can't be very convenient.'

'That's what you get, these days. Just bits of kids, not even proper apprentices.'

Kate had found herself a garage in a side street in Selly Oak. The mechanics there were so good she'd be embarrassed to take custom from them if she bought a new car under guarantee. But even as she opened her mouth to tell Lizzie, she closed it again. She didn't want Lizzie in full throat descending on lads she'd come to regard as mates.

'So what are you planning for this afternoon?' Lizzie asked, grimacing over coffee, which was, however, fully deserving of a grimace.

'Talk to one of your experts, I hope. And talk to the deceased's son. There's something funny there. I thought, if it was OK by you, Gaffer, tomorrow I'd go straight to talk to our friend Cornfield. Before he goes on any more travels.'

Kate got through to the second of Lizzie's forensic scientists, Dr Walcott, and arranged to meet him at his office, which turned out to be a lab in a technology park sandwiched between the A38(M) and a canal. Nicely within walking distance. The site was unexpectedly pleasant, a modern purpose-built development of interesting brick low-rise buildings, not out of place with the blue-brick of the canal-side itself.

Dr Walcott couldn't have been far from retirement, which he told her Lizzie's other choice had embraced five years before. He sported enormous, Dickensian side-whiskers, perhaps to compensate for having no more than Bobby Charlton wisps across his cranium. He also sucked on a pipe, a Sherlock Holmes affair, which Kate never saw alight. Apart from these minor eccentricities, he was charming and affable, producing Perrier from the lab fridge and seating her in his computer chair. Their conversation covered the weather, traffic and the current state of public spending before settling down on the matter in hand, or, more precisely, in the folder Kate handed him. At this point he shook his head sadly.

'Lizzie King told you to bring this to me?' This?' He tapped the photocopy. 'What for?'

Kate flushed. 'I need preliminary advice on whether this could be forged. I mean, even I can see that the writing in the body of the will isn't the same as the signature . . .'

'My dear, *anyone* can see that.' He gave the sort of patient smile that curled Kate up inside more effectively than any Lizzie bollocking. 'My area of expertise – such as it is – is in the chemical make-up of paper and ink. I can tell you just when a piece of paper was made, and almost certainly where. I can give you similar information about the ink. Mine is a scientific background, in other words. If you wanted to prove that someone could not have written something because that type of paper wasn't available at the time he is supposed to have written it, then I'm your man. But for that – why . . .'

'You'd need the document itself, not a photocopy. I'm sorry. I've wasted your time.' She hung her head. Then she perked up again. 'But I bet if I asked you to suggest a reputable graphologist, you could.'

'Do I notice,' Walcott asked, 'a stress on the word *reputable*?'

'One whose word would stand up in court. I'm not interested,' she said, 'in that stuff they have in women's magazines. You know the sort of thing: *you are good at ball-room dancing because the loops on your g's look like a foot.*'

He snorted. 'There are plenty of people like that around.'

She took a risk. 'Someone alleged that whoever wrote this was secretive, mean, vicious-tongued – and male.'

'There are people who will say they can differentiate

male and female writing,' he conceded. 'I'd have thought they had a sixty to sixty-five per cent chance of being right. Not that that's good enough for a court. Men, they say, have messier, more angular writing, because boys are encouraged to be individual. Whereas girls are supposed to present themselves nicely, so their writing, as part of their presentation, is more likely to be tidy and rounded.'

Kate covered her notebook ostentatiously, pulling a face.

'As for the secretive, mean and vicious-tongued part, well, can you see anything that would suggest such characteristics? No, not suggest: *prove!*'

Kate peered, wrinkling her nose. 'How would you suppose mean people write? No gaps between the words so they don't waste paper? Tiny margins?'

'You may be into *post hoc propter hoc* arguments here.'

If Kate had had more than GCSE Latin she might have been able to give an opinion. She went for surer ground. 'So these tight o's – the writer really has tied a knot at the top – don't mean someone's tight-fisted? Or secretive?'

Walcott shrugged. 'Who am I to question those who say so? All I can say is that there is no reliable scientific or academic evidence to show that someone with those very pointed t-strokes – see how they're thick to the left, fine to the right – is sharp-tongued. Or a good swordsman. Or anything else. Oh, call me an old cynic, Sergeant Power, but I'd rather talk about what I can prove. And I have colleagues in the ranks of independent handwriting analysts who can provide evidence of their assertions.'

'You couldn't give me a couple of names, could you?'

'They too will almost certainly want the original. Which is not in your keeping?'

'The will is up for probate at the moment. It's retrievable.'

'Don't tell me. It's the old, old story. Some bloodsucker's persuaded an old biddy to change her will in his favour! And oh no, there's no need to call in a solicitor because he can do it perfectly well.' He shook his head, drawing stertorously on the empty pipe. 'One of these people should be able to help: she's particularly good.' He flipped a couple of business cards her way. 'Off you go, Sergeant, and nail the bastard!'


Clearly the first thing to do was to get hold of the original will, so Kate faxed an application through to the probate court. The independent handwriting analyst whom Walcott had recommended was very busy, but promised to try to see Kate as soon as the document came through. What next? A trip to Tamworth? No, no reply from Dr Barton's number. She left a message asking him to call her. Not especially keen on confessing to Lizzie about her mistake, she tried to frame the notes as if they had been a premeditated attempt to discuss Mrs Duncton's expert's allegations. She wasn't sure how convincing she'd made the account, but it would have to do. Meanwhile, there was that in-tray to tackle: surely she could do something to lighten Derek's load.

She was so engrossed by her attempts to select facts which seemed salient and present them in some sort of coherent order she hardly registered the phone. At last she picked it up, with the most perfunctory greeting.

'Kate. Are you all right?'

'Graham!' Her voice expressed in almost equal measure delight and disbelief that he would risk calling her at work.

'The Simmons case, Kate. I've been trying to get you all day. We really do have to talk. I've OK'd it with Lizzie. She says first thing tomorrow's fine.'

Bloody Lizzie! 'I'm supposed to be talking to— No problem, I'll put it off. What time and where?'

'I suppose – I suppose you couldn't give me a lift in? Only my car's—'

'Of course I'll give you a lift.' *Oh, Graham, I'd love to.* 'Where shall I pick you up?'

'End of my road? Say, ten past eight?'

So how long would it take her to get from Kings Heath across to his leafier suburb? If she had to set out at six, she'd be there.

'Ten past eight it is.'

'Thanks.' He cut the connection.

On impulse, looking round guiltily, she reached for her organiser and fished out from the back flap a note Graham had once sent her. Nothing personal, heavens no, and nothing remotely romantic. But she'd kept it because he'd written it himself, not on his computer, but in his own handwriting. She peered at the t's, at the o's: she hoped to God Dr Walcott was right. If he wasn't, she was having a love affair with a secretive, vicious-tongued man.

# Chapter Six

'Shorts? Coming visiting in shorts?' Aunt Cassie demanded. 'Goodness me! When I played tennis we used to go to the club properly dressed and change there. We wouldn't have gone through the public streets wearing shorts. And what do you call that vest thing?'

Time to sidestep. Kate was wearing an admittedly skimpy top and shorts because it was a hot evening, that was all. It was a shame the self-tanning lotion had gone streaky in places, but her legs still looked good. 'Come on, Aunt Cassie, you told me you used to wear daring dresses for tennis. You were going to look out your photos.'

'Well, I haven't had time. You've no idea what it's like at this place. Come here, go there. Oh, you'll tell me it's all for my own good, but they've got this idea we should be out in the garden in this weather. And they gave us a barbecue last night.'

Kate laughed. 'That's wonderful, Aunt Cassie.'

'It may be if you like meat that's black on the outside and bloody in the middle. Actually, the sausages weren't bad. Or the salmon.'

Salmon! Some barbecue. But Aunt Cassie was paying enough for this residential home: she was entitled to salmon, yes, and caviar too.

'I should think this hot, dry weather's good for your arthritis,' Kate suggested.

'I've known it worse,' Cassie conceded. 'So when are you going to show me this new garden of yours, then? You promised, but I expect you've forgotten all about it.'

Forgotten! Fat chance of forgetting. Cassie raised it each time she came.

'I've got the car outside waiting for you,' Kate said.

'But it's time for *Coronation Street*. You wouldn't want me to miss that.'

Kate shook her head. 'I'd forgotten about that. What about tomorrow night?'

'They say they'll have something special for us. Some kids from the Conservatoire are going to play in the grounds for us. A little concert. I can't let them down, now, can I?'

'We'll try and make it this weekend, then.' Kate smiled. 'Now, shall I fix you a gin?'

'If you like. Then you might as well push off. But you can see me down to the TV room before you go. It's nice to have a bit of company while you're watching,' she added plaintively.

'I'm sure it is. Now, shall I carry the drink for you?'

Cassie shook her head vehemently. 'I'll have that now. Or they'll all want a glass, won't they?'

✻

Kate wasn't sure which part of her anatomy Graham Harvey's wife noticed first, as they came upon each other at the door leading to the car park. Flavia Harvey was rather more modestly dressed, in long skirt and loose blouse. Both women wore sunglasses and sun-hats, Kate's a stylish Greek straw to the other's cotton floppy, so there might conceivably have been a reason for Mrs Harvey's apparent failure to recognise Kate. But Kate — there must be some of Aunt Cassie's cussed DNA in her genes — decided to both recognise and greet the other woman. No. Kate was the other woman. Mrs Harvey was Graham's lawful wedded wife.

Kate whisked off the dark glasses. 'Hello!' She smiled. 'How are you? And how's Mrs Nelmes?'

It was easier to ask after Mrs Harvey's mother: at least Kate knew what to call her. She was loath to address anyone she knew by their title plus surname, but she was fairly sure that 'Flavia' would be objectionably intimate.

'She finds the heat distressing.' There was a hesitation. 'And your great-aunt?'

'Pretty crotchety.'

'It's a sad thing, growing old.'

Kate risked a caustic grin. 'But it sure as hell beats dying young.' Like Robin. And to her horror, tears came to her eyes. Damn! After all this time! She turned quickly away.

To her amazement, Mrs Harvey put out a hand, not quite touching her arm. 'I heard. I'm sorry.' She went quickly inside, leaving Kate no time to say anything.

*

Who was it told people to go and dig in their garden? Some French philosopher. Rousseau or Voltaire. Just at the moment, it didn't matter which. The d-i-y store Kate passed on the way home still had pots of herbs, and, grabbing a selection and what she was sure was really a strawberry grower and some potting compost, she breezed up to the checkout as if the operator hadn't been drumming her fingers and sighing ostentatiously for the last five minutes. That was what she'd do for the rest of the evening. Dig in her garden.

Something might grow. She dug and raked till she had a fine tilth: lettuce seeds here, radish – why not – here. Rocket? Well, it cost enough in sophisticated salad packs, so why not grow her own? Mindful that the local cats had queued on the fence, with, she would swear, feline lavatory rolls under their arms, while the garden was being planted, she watered the little plot and criss-crossed canes over it. As for the pot, at least the little tufts of basil, thyme, marjoram and coriander would bring some instant green and might cultivate – she winced at her own pun – her still elementary cooking skills.

'Are you all right?' Graham asked as soon as he'd fastened his seat-belt. 'My wife said you looked upset last night.'

She nodded: if she concentrated long enough on finding a gap in the traffic steaming past, eventually she would find some acceptable explanation. Mentioning Robin's name might not be the most tactful thing. But then,

Mrs Harvey might have put her upset in context.

'Cassie seems to be going downhill,' she said at last, pulling in between a bus and a people carrier. 'She'd have been better off in her own home, I'm sure.'

'It was her choice. And – with due respect – your house wouldn't be ideal for someone with mobility problems. You both know you couldn't have looked after her, not with your job. She didn't like having that nice black family next door, so how she'd have coped with those new Asians the other side I don't know.'

'No, not one for cosmopolitanism, Cassie.'

'And she always looks remarkably well to me,' he concluded positively. Graham made a point of visiting not just his mother-in-law but Cassie as well. Usually at a time when he knew Kate wouldn't be there.

'Even so . . .'

'Mrs Nelmes plays up something shocking,' he added. 'To hear her carry on, she's at death's door, and totally neglected. And every time we raise our concerns, the staff laugh at us. They took her and some more old biddies out for a run in the country the other day. They even had a drink at a pub! Mother-in-law, a life-long tee-totaller, nipping sherry! But my wife and I have never heard about it, not from her. You ask Cassie what she's been up to.'

'She did moan about having to go to a barbecue. And she's compelled to listen to an alfresco concert. Kate grinned.

'There you are,' Graham said. 'If I were you, I'd take a

left here. It's a longer way round but the traffic jam at the far end is usually marginally shorter.'

Would anyone have judged from their conversation that they were lovers? What if instead of turning left, she turned right, back to Kings Heath and her bedroom? The way he was sitting, her hand brushed his knee every time she changed gear. What if the brush became a stroke?

The answer was easy enough. He wouldn't cope with either. Not in broad daylight, not at eight-fifteen in the morning. The relationship had to be on his terms. Maybe she could encourage him to change those terms, but it would all have to be done terribly slowly. And in the full knowledge that however hard she tried, they might never change at all.

One kiss. That was all they had. And she'd had to contrive that, leaving her notebook under a file on his desk and, after dutifully leaving his room with the others, having to dash back for it. She'd been careful to sit where they couldn't have eye contact without meaning to, had made a point of arguing her corner when it was clear he disagreed. And had drifted out talking about tennis to DI Sue Rowley, the best boss she'd ever had, with no exception. She'd even popped into the squad office to pick up any stray post and pass the time of day with the folk in there. It was then, only then, that she dared smack a hand to her forehead and 'remember' the notebook.

At least now she knew he'd wanted her as much as she'd

wanted him. Even if that knowledge would have to keep her going all weekend.


Derek smiled as he picked up his raincoat. 'You've been a real mate, Kate. Shifting that lot. I never thought you'd do it, not without help.'

'I'd rather you didn't take my word for it. I mean, whole cases could stand or fall and—'

'OK. I'll run an eye over everything before I discuss it with the gaffer.'

'Discuss what with the gaffer?' Lizzie demanded, materialising apparently at will, like a smile-free Cheshire cat.

'These cases,' Derek said, putting down his raincoat.

Lizzie sniffed. 'I thought you were supposed to be talking to that Cornfield scrote, Power.'

As if she herself hadn't double-booked Kate.

'I tried phoning first, this time. Or I would have done, if I could have found a number for him. The dead woman's phone is still live. But there was no reply—'

'So you just gave up.'

Kate flared. 'Rather than waste any more time, I thought I'd work on this backlog. I suspect the DPP won't be impressed by those but might buy these.' She patted the files. 'Ma'am,' she added. Christ, on a gorgeous afternoon like this, wouldn't she rather have had a gentle stroll out to Edgbaston and a gentle stroll back, with nothing achieved between the two? She'd spent five solid hours in an overheated office picking up the threads of other people's work, and this was what she got.

Lizzie looked at her coldly, but said nothing. 'So when are you proposing to see him?'

'Monday morning, if that's acceptable to you.' She tried to keep her voice pleasant and low.

'Graham Harvey can dispense with your services, can he?'

'This morning's meeting with him, Inspector Rowley and DC Roper tied up everything before the case goes to the County Court. I was involved in other cases which may necessitate further such meetings, ma'am. Subject to your permission.' She bit back another 'ma'am'; it would sound insolent. Which is what she would have liked to be. Flaming, blazing insolent.

'I take it he'll approach me in the usual way.'

'I'm sure he will, ma'am.'

Lizzie nodded and left. Derek caught Kate's eye, touching his lips. Kate nodded. She couldn't have said anything anyway. She turned back to her desk, giving one more superfluous adjustment to the tidy piles. Derek gathered his case and raincoat and walked noisily to the door. Nodding, he stepped back.

'She's gone. Come on, you need a drink.'

'I'm fine.'

'You might be. Lizzie's not. And that is what we're going to talk about. What we're going to do about Lizzie.'

# Chapter Seven

Kate and Derek were walking past Lizzie's half-open door, Kate trying not to tiptoe like a particularly guilty Pink Panther.

'Is that you, Kate?'

They exchanged a look.

'Gaffer?'

Lizzie pulled open the door. 'Look – Kate. I'm ... I was out of order there; well out. D'you fancy a jar? Oh, and you, Ben,' she added, managing a grin in his direction.

'Good idea,' they said together.

'Have you got an umbrella?' Kate added. 'Derek's got this idea that it'll rain any moment.'

That was the first laugh: embarrassed, stilted, but still a laugh. While Lizzie locked up, Derek risked a thumbs-up. Kate winked back. They both heaved silent sighs, however: fun evening this was not going to be.

The city centre bars and the pavements outside them were heaving.

'Maybe somewhere further out?' Derek suggested.

'Forget Brindley Place: that'll be solid,' Lizzie said.

'Let's head towards that place in St Paul's Square, and if we find anything with so much as a window-sill to park our glasses on, we stop there.'

'Sounds good,' agreed Kate, loathing the whole thing. Loud, laddish laughter seemed somehow even more unlovely in the street than in a bar. It was is if the hilarity had to be inflicted on the world, not just fellow drinkers, and if you were simply making your quiet way home, your very sobriety made you less of a person.

In the event, they found a pub in the business area where they could not only drink, but drink inside.

'My shout,' Lizzie announced, heading for the bar before either could argue or, indeed, say what they wanted. She turned, drawing a question mark in the air, and seemed unimpressed by the thought of two orange and lemonades.

But she bought one for herself, and crisps for them all. This was not going to be a one-drink evening, was it? And of course, as far as Kate was concerned, there was no reason why it should have been. There was nothing else on the agenda, after all. No need to visit Aunt Cassie, no point waiting in for a call from Graham. She could make a night of it, do a club: except that clubbing seemed so much more the province of the young, not the coming-up-to-thirties. And it was best done in gangs, and not as a loner. God, she'd better sort her social life soon, hadn't she?

Derek's was obviously more organised. He was already glancing at his watch. What if he sneaked off and left her tête-à-tête with Lizzie? Forgiving and forgetting this afternoon were not the same at all as enjoying a quiet drink with a friend.

The talk circled round the weather. It was agreed that Derek – still Ben, as far as Lizzie was concerned – was likely to need his rainwear this weekend, on the principle that it always rained at weekends. The gardens needed a drop, anyway.

'Mine certainly does,' Kate said. 'All those poor little things struggling to put out roots, and what does the weather do? It starves them. I'm watering them every night.'

'Haven't you got a water-butt?' Lizzie asked, almost accusingly, as if water would somehow transfer itself by osmosis from the butt to the earth.

'Emptied that. And I've had the first crop from my worms.'

'*Worms!* Did you say *worms?*' Lizzie demanded.

'Absolutely. I've got a little wormery. I thought it was time I had a pet, if only to get my revenge on my neighbours, for all their cats. So I bought my worms. They're conversationally challenged, but at least what they do for the garden is useful, unlike the several tons of cat-crap I've been shovelling recently.'

'You don't like cats, then,' Lizzie said.

Oh, God! She was probably a patron of the Cats' Protection League!

'Don't get me wrong. I like cats. I love cats. In *their* homes and in *their* gardens. We always had a cat at home. There was one that never went outside, and another that insisted on using potted plants as litter-trays. And I loved each and every one. We had a little cats' cemetery at the far end of the garden.' If only she could stop talking.

'I'm a dog man myself,' Derek said. 'Basset hounds.'

Of course! That explained the deep frown lines! He'd come to look like his pets!

'Do you have animals, Lizzie?'

She drained her glass and leant forward. 'Do you know,' she began, 'I've always had a yen for a pot-bellied pig . . .'

So it wasn't so bad. They'd had only one more drink each, and simply gone their separate ways. Kate toyed with the idea of a barbecue, and was just setting off to get some meat when Zenia, her next-door neighbour, rang the doorbell. Joseph was just lighting theirs, and since Kate would get the smells, it was only fair she got the food too.


It turned out to be a party, organised just like that. And well organised: to get to the garden guests had to go through the kitchen, where they acquired a glass of Joseph's special punch and a plate and fork. Once in the garden Kate found bowls of salad and rice and peas to accompany wonderful things from the barbecue. This was better than a Friday evening mope. As it got darker, the place was lit by fairy lights and anti-bug candles. There was even dancing indoors.

'You men – you go and move the furniture,' Zenia had said.

'Why not out here?' someone asked.

'Because I have to live with my neighbours,' she said. 'OK?'

'Oh, come on—'

'Look at these houses, cheek by jowl: one person parties today, the rest party tomorrow or the next day. Think of the noise, sweetheart. No, indoors with you all.'

Expecting – well, perhaps the kids' CDs – Kate got the Cole Porter songbook. And Zenia's tall, handsome cousin Rafe to dance with, singing along with Ella Fitzgerald.

'You OK, kid?' he asked after a while, looking genuinely concerned.

'I'm sorry. This always makes me want to cry. "I Love Paris" – all those dark minor chords.'

A slight pause. She'd forgotten that not everyone was an occasional church organist.

Rafe asked, 'And is your love there? In Paris?'

'He's dead,' she said briefly. 'Car crash.' What on earth was she thinking about? He was alive and down the road!

'My girl – she went off,' he said. 'Seems to me we could cheer each other up a bit. Let's find something less mournful.'

'You're on.'

'No shouting, no slamming of doors, no revving, no burning rubber,' said Zenia, as she kissed everyone good-night. 'You're grown-ups, remember, not kids. And people round here are asleep in their beds. Now what do you think you're doing, Kate?'

'What does it look as if I'm doing?' Kate gathered another clutch of glasses and carried them through into the kitchen.

'You're my guest!'

'And you're my friend. Many hands and all that.'

It didn't take them long to get the place back into shape. Zenia pointed to the kettle. 'You deserve a coffee. Or,' she added, winking hugely, 'what I'd prefer, this time of night. One of Joseph's amazing mugs of cocoa. Which he will get us while you tell me how you're going on. And that Aunt Cassie of yours . . .'

They were halfway down their cocoa when Zenia said, 'Rafe would like to see you again. But I said I wasn't sure if you were ready . . . Hello, what have I said? Hey, you've got yourself a man already!'

Kate shook her head. It would be such a relief to chew everything over with someone, especially someone not remotely connected with the police. Well, it could only be with someone not remotely connected with the police. But she'd had a lot of that punch, and couldn't risk, even with Zenia, being indiscreet.

'So if my Rafe asked you out, you might go?' Zenia's face lit up. 'He's a great guy, Kate. He's – what – thirty-five next birthday. Solicitor. Own place out in Solihull. Plays tennis like Arthur Ashe. And cook – can that man cook! Shall I tell him, go ahead, ask you?'

Kate bit her lip.

Zenia looked her hard in the eye. 'Come on, Kate, why not?'

'It's just that . . .' She tailed off, shaking her head, at last looking away in embarrassment.

'Kate, are you telling me you've got problems because he's black?'

She shook her head again. 'Can we talk about it in the morning Zenia? He's really nice, really sexy. It's not him and his blackness that worries me. It's me.' She heaved herself to her feet.

Zenia got up too, and hugged her. 'You *have* got things on your mind, haven't you? Well, I'd guess one of them is that guy I've seen at your place a couple of times. About forty – looks, for all he's good-looking, a bit like my old headmaster. Like –' she hunched her shoulders – 'like he's tired. Or stressed. No, I've said nothing to anyone, not even to Joseph. I'll tell you for why: that man's got "married" written all over him.'

# Chapter Eight

Kate set out so early enough to see Max Cornfield on Monday morning that she got thoroughly snarled up in the rush-hour traffic. To add insult to injury, she found she couldn't park outside Mrs Barr's — Mr Cornfield's? — house for another hour; not just legally but morally: to shove any obstruction into this tangle would surely be to cause tail-backs long enough to paralyse the whole city, maybe, she thought ghoulishly, the whole of the West Midlands. Shrugging, she pulled on to the drive in front of the converted garage. No access, of course, except via the main house.

This time when the doorbell pealed the response was immediate. The door — held on a security chain — opened a few centimetres to reveal a grey-haired man.

Kate produced a smile and her ID. 'Good morning. Are you Mr Cornfield? Might I have a few words with you? I'm Detective Sergeant Kate Power, West Midlands Police.'

The man peered at the ID, then nodded. 'To open the door fully I have to close it first,' he said.

So where did he come from? For all the name Cornfield

sounded quintessentially English, Englishman Cornfield was not. His accent was middle-European, maybe German, maybe from further east.

The door opened, and Mr Cornfield gestured her courteously inside. The hall was much darker, much narrower, than his neighbour's. Kate recognised the tiles as Minton precursors of those in her vestibule, but they were badly worn and in some places missing.

'How may I help you, Sergeant?'

'It's a matter of some delicacy, Mr Cornfield: perhaps we could sit down somewhere?'

'You are not arresting me and dragging me off to the Tower of London? After you, please.' He pointed down the hallway.

'We don't do things like that,' she smiled. 'This way?'

'Into the kitchen, please. It gets the morning sun.'

It did. But it was still gloomy. The sash windows were too high and too small: servants were no doubt not intended to enjoy the advantages of bright light.

Cornfield pulled out a chair for her. 'Coffee, Sergeant? You can see I'm about to have some myself.'

'And smell!' she said, with an appreciative sniff. 'Hmm! Yes, please.'

'Good.' He reached for another cup and saucer, stretching rather stiffly. He was about sixty-five, she thought, maybe older, with his face surprisingly unlined and hair only now receding. The grey woollen cardigan he wore over a white shirt and grey flannels was pilled and darned on the elbows, but was clean.

The kitchen itself was in a time warp, stuck in the nineteen-fifties, maybe early sixties. From the colour of the walls to the kitchen units, such as they were, everything spoke of a time before she was born. The paint was very shabby, but it looked very clean, as did the porcelain sink.

'May I offer you a biscuit? I didn't make them myself, I'm afraid,' he said, opening a tin and laying some on a plate. *Langues de chat*! 'My neighbour did. Mrs Hamilton. She mentioned that you had been to see her, but seemed uncharacteristically vague as to the reason.'

'She makes wonderful biscuits,' Kate said, taking one, 'but that doesn't entitle her to know what business I may have with you, does it?'

He poured their coffee, offering milk and sugar but apparently pleased when Kate took neither. 'So what is your business with me?' He sat down at right angles to her.

'It's about Mrs Barr's will. I'd like to talk to you about that. This is very good,' she said.

He nodded. 'Mrs Barr insisted on so many economies, Sergeant. But coffee was one I would not let her make. Camp Essence, indeed!'

'Did she need to make economies?'

He shook his head. 'She was a very rich old woman, but she lived in constant fear of debt.'

'Very rich?'

He shrugged. 'Look at the position of this house, Sergeant. It may be shabby and in need of more maintenance than I was able to give it, but I cannot imagine it fetching much less than half a million if it went on the market. And she had other property too.'

'"If it went on the market" – is there any doubt that it will?'

He smiled sadly. 'It is my home, Sergeant. I have lived here for more years than I care to remember. Absurd as it may be, I am strangely loath to leave it.'

'Mrs Barr left it to you?'

'Mrs Barr left everything to me,' he said simply.

'But she had a family?'

'They quarrelled with her years ago and never came near her. Never. She never saw hide or hair of them, Sergeant. They sent her Christmas cards all right, because at least they could presumably remember when Christmas was. As for her birthday, forget it. Family? They were not her family!' His accent was becoming more and more pronounced.

'Had you become her family?'

'I was all she had,' he said simply. His voice was so sad he might almost have added that she was all he had. He straightened. 'I suppose, Sergeant, that the family wish to dispute the will. I have told my solicitor to expect that. What I cannot understand is that they should have involved the police. You.'

Kate would have liked to believe him. 'They allege that there are certain . . . irregularities about it, Mr Cornfield. Do you know of any?'

'I knew it, I knew it!' He beat a fist into his palm. 'I begged her to have a solicitor. "Fifty pounds," I told her, "that's all it would cast!" But she was stubborn. All her life she was stubborn, Sergeant, and towards the end . . . She became, shall we say, very . . . very difficult.'

Kate nodded. Mrs Hamilton had implied as much, hadn't she? 'But she wouldn't have a lawyer?'

'Under no circumstances. Indeed, Sergeant, when I persisted — believe me, I persisted — she became so distressed I was afraid she would have a stroke or heart attack and drop down without any sort of will at all. So eventually I simply let her dictate it to me. She signed it. There you are.' He spread his hands expansively: they encompassed years of fruitless battles and now, with a tiny spreading of the fingers, his new domain. 'I suppose, as a police officer, you'll wish to inspect the premises,' he added suddenly.

'As a human being, I'm always interested in other people's houses. I'd have loved a conducted tour of Mrs Hamilton's.'

'Ah, this doesn't have the elegance of Mrs Hamilton's. Architecturally, I would say it has very little to commend it. Take this kitchen, for instance: if you turn round you will see a door to the dining room. Whoever conceived of a room with virtually no natural light should have been condemned to eat in there forever.' He pulled himself stiffly to his feet. 'However, since it hasn't been used for its true purpose for at least forty years, I suppose we can truncate his sentence.'

He pushed open the door and reached for the light switch. Kate followed, gasping. The room should have been dominated by a dark oak dining suite worthy of Balmoral – a sideboard that must have been eight feet tall, a table that could without additional leaves have seated ten, high-backed chairs and matching carvers. But it wasn't. It was dominated by newspapers. Piles of papers rose five feet up each wall. More piles swamped the sideboard and the table. The chairs groaned under further piles. Someone – Cornfield, no doubt – had ensured that there was a canyon about a foot wide between the great cliffs of newsprint. She picked her way carefully along it.

'Take care – they're very dusty.'

'Nineteen sixty-six!' She pointed to the date on the top of a *Times*.

'They go back further than that. To nineteen fifty-six, in fact. I tried to get rid of them, handful by slow handful. But Mrs Barr noticed, and I had to stop. She always intended to re-read them for her research.'

'Research into what?' She started to pick her way back.

He lifted his shoulders in a huge shrug. 'Who can tell?'

'Are you saying her mind was unsound, Mr Cornfield?'

'Is your mind sound? Is mine? Oh, Mrs Barr was unusual, maybe eccentric, but she knew her own mind. No doubts, no hesitations.' His hand sliced the air. 'Decision made – there. There are some more newspapers elsewhere, as it happens. She always planned to do that research, you see. Or for me to do it – it would have come to the same thing. Shall we move on?'

'It's a wonderful old place,' Kate said, as she stepped back into the hall.

'Wonderful! Believe me, it needs thousands spending on it. Thousands.' He smiled suddenly. 'I understand that the National Trust or English Heritage or some such is now preserving properties as they were when they came into their hands, not as they were at their peak. Now, Sergeant, do you think I should ask them to take over this place? Item, dining room! Item, butler's pantry.'

'Butler's pantry!' She gazed at not newspapers but rank upon rank of cardboard boxes.

'The wooden sink, for washing precious glasses. The store cupboards. Maybe it was a housekeeper's store, but butler's pantry was what she always called it. All those boxes are full, by the way. China, glass: I should take a couple along to the *Antiques Road Show* – see what they make of them. Now, the living room.'

This wasn't as funereal as the dining room but was far from cheerful. Although it had windows at either end they were too small for the overall size of the room, and certainly out of proportion to the high ceiling and deep cornices, which needed dusting at the very least. The emulsion on the ceiling and at the top of the walls was grey with age. Originally the wallpaper might have been expensive, but now it was faded. The carpet was threadbare, the leather of the three-piece suite bruised and split. But there was a baby grand in one corner, music open on the stand, and what looked to Kate's untutored eye some good paintings on the walls. The curtains – heavy brocade, once – had been unevenly bleached by the sun.

'Quite rotten,' Cornfield said, sadly. 'Thank goodness

we have the original shutters. I use them too, Sergeant, for both warmth and security. I tried never to be away overnight – and never was, once Mrs Barr took to her bed. The house was too vulnerable. Too vulnerable.' He held open the door. 'The other rooms down here—'

'*Rooms!*'

'Oh, yes – the drawing room and the study. They are in very poor shape. I hardly like anyone to see them before I rehabilitate them. And upstairs – well, you may wish to see where Mrs Barr lived her last years.'

Kate nodded, not because she had any ghoulish inclinations but because this house had gripped her imagination almost as Mrs Hamilton's had. Almost, but not quite. Whereas Mrs Hamilton's called out to be lived in, she found this almost repellent. She longed – perhaps as Mr Cornfield longed – to strip everything out and start again.

Upstairs she saw no reason to change her mind. The same air of decay hung about it, now augmented by a sad smell of unwashed old age, the smell of Aunt Cassie's residential home multiplied several-fold.

'I did my best,' he said. 'I urged her to keep active, to use the bathroom. She could have done. But not latterly.'

He was weeping. The old chap was weeping.

'The only thing to do with her room is to empty it completely. Every stick of furniture, every thread of fabric. And there are times when I believe I shall have to strip the wallpaper and sand down the floorboards. Oh, Sergeant, forgive me but if you go in there, you go in alone.'

She nodded.

Yes, the smell was bad. The bed had been stripped down to the utility wire spring sub-frame: no mattress or blanket left. No books on the bedside cabinet, more surprisingly no medicines. Just what looked like a doorbell, with a thin cable running down to the skirting-board. But illness and death lingered everywhere, despite the wide-open window. She walked across. Again, the window was too high for the proportions of the room, again the curtains rotting. She looked down at the garden. It was as huge as the house.

'Could we go down into the sun?' she asked, coming back into the corridor.

'Permit me to show you the bathroom first,' he said. 'Lavatory here, you see, and next door . . .'

An enamel bath, feet exposed. No means of heating, not that she could see. No comfort. None in the towels, almost too threadbare to be able to dry anyone.

'Which is your room?' Kate asked. If she were having a conducted tour it might as well include the parts behind the green baize door.

'My room? Sergeant, you do not understand. I never slept in the house, never. Only recently, when she was very ill, and I slept on a camp-bed out here, on the landing. Within earshot, you see.'

'What was that press-button by the bed? Wasn't that to summon you?'

'It's a big house and she was too ill to wait that long,' he said gently. 'My room is the one it always was, the garage. You can see in there with pleasure. Shall we go down?'

A conservatory ran right across the back of the house. Nothing uPVC about this one, however: cast iron, with Victorian curlicues. Old glass, too, nothing like as uniform and clear as modern. Inevitably, she supposed, where panes had broken, they'd been replaced badly, the putty ugly, or cardboard had been taped across the gaps. At one end was a Welsh dresser, inexplicably painted turquoise, stacked high with empty jam-jars. At the other were beautifully maintained garden tools. Between lay a jumble involving, as far as she could see, canvas deckchairs, broken washing-baskets, both wicker and plastic, a pram and a half-full wine rack.

'You see,' Cornfield said sadly, 'it's not just a matter of having a skip on the drive and slinging everything in. Some of that wine — and there are a couple more cases under there somewhere — may not simply be drinkable, it may be valuable. And if you should ask why a man with several millions in real estate should want even more money, it is because I, like Mrs Barr, hate waste. When I first knew her she was — newspapers apart — merely economical: she became obsessive only in later years.'

Kate turned to him. 'She must have been a difficult employer. Why did you stay with her?'

'Why does anyone stay with anyone? There are answers, but maybe only a psychiatrist could make any sense of them.' He opened the door to the garden, stepping out before her, then pausing to gesture. 'How far are we from the city centre, Sergeant? Two miles? And a garden like this!'

An estate agent would have referred to mature trees: these were woodland trees, the sort you found in parks, not in the average garden. Why, they were bigger than those Kate had had to have uprooted from her patch. And they were not out of keeping with the rest of the garden. They shielded it from the gaze of most of the surrounding houses, but not an office block some planner had unaccountably permitted.

'I did my best, Sergeant. But I'm no longer a young man, and latterly Mrs Barr needed me more than the herbaceous border did.' His face crumpled again.

'Were you originally her gardener, then?' Kate asked at last.

'Originally, Sergeant, I was a waif, a stray. A refugee. An economic migrant. A bogus asylum seeker. Miss Widdecombe would have given me a voucher or sent me back on the next boat. Mrs Barr took me in and gave me shelter and a job.'

'A refugee?'

'An old story. I'm now the proud holder of one of Her Britannic Majesty's official passports. Or at least, the EEC version.'

'The newspapers date from 1956, you say. So we're talking Hungary?' Was it really Mrs Barr who'd kept them, or Cornfield himself? He was surely the more likely to hoard information about such a traumatic year.

'We are.' He turned abruptly.

She followed him along the back of the house to a wooden door.

'You asked to see my room, Sergeant: here it is.'

Yes, the converted garage. And although it was as shabby as the rest of the place – the armchair looked as if it had been discarded from the main house as being too battered even for that – it was clean. The roof had been insulated and sheets of heavy-duty polythene covered it and the big garage doors. She took in a single bed, neat enough to have satisfied the most pernickety sergeant at police training college, a single wardrobe, and a coffee table with a wooden chess-set laid out ready for play. A bookshelf crammed with a heterogeneous collection of books, a wooden chair and a desk completed the furniture. The only modern items were spotlights over the bed and desk, a jug-kettle and – so out of place Kate walked across to take a closer look – a lap-top computer of a generation later than Kate's own.

'Virtual chess,' Cornfield volunteered. He tapped a key. A chessboard materialised. 'I play with friends all over the world.'

'All over the world?'

'A lot of us were displaced in 1956,' he said.

They returned via the garden to the conservatory.

'I'd ask you if I've replied to all your questions satisfactorily, Sergeant,' Cornfield said, 'but you don't seem to have asked very many.'

'You've given me a lot of answers, though. You came here during or after the Hungarian uprising as a refugee.

You'd have been about twenty? Mrs Barr took you in as a gardener, and for some reason, though she had plenty of room in the house, offered you accommodation in the garage.'

'She didn't have so much room then. Her husband was alive, and she had her son and daughters living here too.'

'Daughters?'

He nodded. 'Edna and Mavis. Edna would have been about eighteen, Mavis thirteen when I came. Then there was Michael. A very bright boy, but troubled. He was about sixteen then.'

Kate wrote in her notebook. 'What happened to Edna?'

Another of those continental shrugs. 'Who can tell? It wasn't a very happy family, Sergeant. The father . . . was a very strange man.'

Stranger than a woman who kept newspapers dating from the year dot?

'In what way strange?'

'Had he been anything other than a perfect English gentleman I would have called him a brutish lout. But I hesitate to speak ill of the dead, and he passed away – oh, back in 1963. It was a very cold winter, lots of snow, and he gave himself a heart attack pushing the car he would have done better to leave at home.'

'He didn't mind a handsome young gardener on the premises?'

'I might have been young, and I might have tended the garden, but I was never handsome, Sergeant.'

She wasn't sure she believed him. His bones, quite

striking now, would have given a good structure then. In any case, as Cassie would have observed, you don't look at the mantelpiece when you poke the fire.

'In any case, I don't suppose he noticed me. He spent more hours at the office making money than today's city workaholics are rumoured to do. Well, a place like this takes a lot of maintaining—'

'But it hasn't been maintained – hadn't even then, surely!'

He smiled sadly. 'Things may fall into desuetude quite gradually. One room falls out of use, then another. They used the drawing room as a dining room, for instance: Mr Barr believed that his furniture was too valuable to sell, let alone throw away, so he left it in situ and bought G-Plan.'

'Which is still there?'

'Under Mrs Barr's clothes. I had to move them from the bedroom when – when she became . . . bedridden.' He was ready to weep again. Turning to her he said, 'Sergeant, would you mind if we continued our conversation over more coffee?'

'I think you've answered enough questions for one day, Mr Cornfield. I've only a couple more.'

He nodded.

'I take it Cornfield is an anglicisation of another name?'

'Yes. I was born Maxim Kornfeld. Not a difficult transliteration.'

'But Kornfeld sounds more – more German?'

'Polish. After Auschwitz my family drifted to Hungary.'

'Auschwitz!'

He smiled. 'You know the newsreel shots of kids pressed up against the wire? I was one. Happy ending for me. Both parents and I – all saved.'

'And what happened to them when the tanks rolled into Budapest?'

'They chose to stay.'

It seemed impertinent to ask more. And irrelevant, surely.

He looked at her wearily. 'You said you had two questions.'

'Yes,' she said, wishing she didn't have to ask the second. 'Did you forge Mrs Barr's will?'

# Chapter Nine

'You don't want him to be guilty! What sort of fuckwitted answer is that?' Lizzie demanded, raising her eyes in exasperation and pushing away the last of her lunchtime sandwich.

'An honest one. On the face of it, he's the only sane man in a family for whom the term dysfunctional might have been coined. We've got a missing sister, a brother who seems to have changed his name and my tight-arsed Mrs Duncton, so far. The late Mr Barr appears to have been unpleasant in an unspecified way, and Mrs Barr seems to have made eccentricity an art form. Mr Cornfield's neighbour says that he nursed the old lady through her last years, which is confirmed by the district nurse the two old ladies shared. The district nurse, by the way, declared he was a blessed saint, the way he put up with her carryings on. Sure, Cornfield's sitting on a goldmine, but he's already spent more years than I'd care to imagine excavating it – and I'd have thought it would take him twelve months' tedious work to finish.' She explained about the house.

'What you really want me to do,' sighed Lizzie, 'is tell

you to file the case at the very bottom of your in-tray and get on with something else. Tell you to let it go.'

'Ultimately that wouldn't solve anything, would it?' Kate said, regretfully. 'No, Duncton's not the sort of woman to let go once she's got her teeth into something. Tell you what, Gaffer, I've already got the probate people to pop the original of the will into the post—'

'Are you or they off their heads?'

'Guaranteed delivery. I'll get a handwriting expert to cast her beady eyes over it before I ask you to tell me to let it go.'

Lizzie pulled a face. 'I thought you high-flyers were supposed to be able to string a decent sentence together. OK. It's what I'd have wanted you to say, incidentally. If not quite like that. There's something altogether too pat about what you've told me. He's too good to be true. The happy ending would definitely be too good to be true. No, Power, don't stop sniffing till we're sure there isn't a bone. What I'd like you to do this afternoon is to go and talk to the brother.'

'You're sure we shouldn't wait for this report to come through? We may simply have a weird family with one one decent person in it. Which is what I'd go for, after this morning at least.'

'OK. I suppose so. Yes, if Ben's around we could go through those cases you looked at. Wheel him in.'

'There is just one thing, Gaffer. Now Bill's left – now there's no reason for his nickname – I think he'd rather be called Derek.'

'Derek? You're telling me his name's Derek?'

'Yes.'

'I'd have thought any name preferable to Derek. Especially Ben.'


The rain Derek had been predicting for so long arrived during the evening rush hour, reducing traffic to a snail's pace. And snails were what Kate found in her garden that evening. Snails and slugs. In profusion, but definitely not gay. Well, at least she had slug pellets.

Slug-killing apart, her evening felt very empty. No exams to revise for. No tennis – it was the others' night for aromatherapy classes. Nothing on TV. If only she could have reached for the phone. She didn't want to say anything, just to hear Graham's voice. And couldn't.

So thank goodness for Aunt Cassie. At least ten minutes with her would give a focus to the evening. They could chew over yet again all the things that had prevented Cassie from coming out to see her garden: the heat, the garden party, the second barbecue, the pain in her hip. No, the truth was that Aunt Cassie hadn't wanted to go back to what had been her house, and any protestations that she made were simply token, Kate was sure.

Since she'd eaten, Kate risked a gin and tonic when she mixed Cassie hers.

'Tell you what we had yesterday, in the garden,' Cassie said, 'Pimms. And very nice it was too. You could get me some of that, if you like.'

'Wouldn't it be a bit of a pain – trying to store your cucumber and mint and so on?'

Cassie withered her with a look. 'You can get it in tins or bottles or something, ready mixed. You could bring me a couple of those.'

Kate nodded. 'No problem.' Except it was. Where on earth could you get ready mixed Pimms, for goodness' sake?

Meanwhile the gin was going down, if not as sweetly as a Pimms would have done, very briskly. So she was topping up Cassie's glass with her back to the door when she heard it open.

'Hello, Aunt Cassie.'

Graham! Oh, Graham!

He was walking across to Cassie's chair, would be taking the old woman's hand and kissing her cheek. If only she dared hope that one day he might take her hand, kiss her like that. But married men mustn't.

'Fancy a gin, Graham?' she asked as casually as she could. Aunt Cassie's hearing might not be what it used to be, but sure as God made little apples she'd pick up any intonation she wasn't meant to hear.

'You know, I just might.'

He strolled over to where she stood. She risked a quick sideways glance, to be rewarded by the warmest of smiles. He could have touched her without Aunt Cassie seeing, but he didn't.

'Would you pass Aunt Cassie hers, while I wash out this glass?'

'No need. I'm sure you haven't got foot and mouth.' He

spoke as lightly as if they'd been in the canteen. But his eyes crinkled intimately. 'I hear you people have been having high jinks,' he said, squatting at Cassie's feet. 'Thanks, Kate. Cheers.' He clinked glasses with Cassie.

'We pay enough,' Cassie observed. 'And like they said, we might as well take advantage of the weather.'

'Good job you did. It's throwing it down, now.'

'Thought it was cooler. At least young Kate's got decent clothes on tonight. You should have seen her the other day, here in her nothings.' Cassie sounded genuinely disapproving.

He looked up swiftly, eyebrows raised, but then said, 'But I bet you lot were all in your nothings too. Come on, Aunt Cassie, I bet you wowed them in your bikini.'

'Enough of your lip, young man,' she snorted. But there was no doubt that she liked his teasing.

Young? He'd be forty this year, wouldn't he? No doubt his wife would organise a big party, to which, of course, she would not be invited.

'Mrs Nelmes tells me she's getting new swimmies,' he pursued.

They all laughed: Mrs Nelmes, rather like her daughter, was not the sort of woman to strip off for summer; almost certainly never had been.

And then, as Kate had known he would, he looked at his watch. One of the hairs on his wrist curled over the strap, as it always did.

'Enough of this debauchery,' he said, pulling himself to his feet. 'And thanks for the drink.' He'd barely touched the gin, but he passed Kate the glass. Their eyes met. Quickly she sipped from where he'd been drinking.

He bent to kiss Cassie and straightened, in the same movement brushing his lips against Kate's. And was gone, leaving behind the echo of his cheery good nights and the draught from his wave.

Tuesday morning saw Kate with not only the original of the will in her hand, but an appointment booked for the middle of the afternoon with the forensic handwriting analyst whom Dr Walcott had recommended: Dr Kennedy. Over the phone Kennedy's voice sounded full of energy, so Kate wasn't surprised to meet a woman in her early forties, with good clear skin and blonde hair cut into a stylish bob. What she hadn't expected was to find her ensconced in the English department at Birmingham University, surrounded by books on Elizabethan theatre and with a thick file of what looked horribly like exam scripts on her desk.

'Eng. Lit?' Kate asked. 'Am I in the right place?'

'Eng. Lit is what I trained in. Textual criticism. Comparing literary texts to find out what the author wrote in the first place.'

Kate stared.

'What A levels did you do, Sergeant?'

'Oh, Kate, please. Sociology, Psychology and English. Oh, and General Studies.'

'OK: what English texts did you study?'

'I can hardly remember. Oh, Shakespeare, of course –
*Hamlet* –'

'So you'll know there are two main editions of the play?'

'Hang on!' She dug in her memory, '1602 and 1623?'

'Well done. But did you also know that there are
some fifteen hundred differences between these two
editions?'

'I knew there was that argument about flesh – whether
it was *sullied* or *solid* . . . So how do people know what it's
supposed to be?'

Kennedy smiled. 'That's where people like me come in.
At Oxford, then later at Yale, I learned how to decipher
and identify the handwriting of various authors – it's not
just Shakespeare whose work comes out in different
versions. And then I discovered those skills could be
employed in forensic work too. So here I am and here you
are.'

A cue for action, if ever there was one. So Kate dug in
her briefcase for the will, secure in its folder.

'There. What we're interested in, as I said on the phone,
is whether—'

'Hang on. If you tell me what to look for, I may find
that, but miss something else.' She pulled out the sheet of
paper. 'Hmm. Ballpoint. OK. Now, how soon did you say
you wanted this?'

'Yesterday. Seriously, as soon as you give me an
informal report, nothing fancy, nothing time-consuming,
I can decide whether there's a case to build or whether I
can get back to harassing motorists, or whatever we're

popularly supposed to do. If there's to be a case, then we'll need the big, detailed analysis.'

Kennedy looked again at the will, and then at the pile of scripts on her desk. 'Do I gather you can't do anything till I get back to you? Well, I suppose it might make a pleasant displacement activity.'

Kate left the Arts Building to find that the sun had come out. She checked her watch: the interview had been far shorter than she'd expected, so she might as well look round the campus before she headed back to the office. To her right was a tower block swathed in tarpaulin and bristling with scaffolding. Someone had found a plank of wood and painted on it, 'This way to the leaning Tower of Muirhead'. Then there was the library: that might be useful one day. Further off were more fifties or early sixties buildings she had no particular wish to explore. What about those grand Victorian edifices across the grass? You'd get a superb view from the top of the clock tower. What did they call it? Joe, that was it. After Joseph Chamberlain. Well, all very impressive, but not on her way back to the car park. Shrugging – one lot of civic pride was much like another, after all – she told herself it was time to retrace her steps, and picked her way across the granite setts. Why had no one ever told architects that fine though these might be for men with big feet wearing heavy shoes, for women with small feet in summer-weight sandals they were murder? Murder! At least that was one advantage of being back in Fraud; there were no bodies to worry about.

Another sign caught her eye: an official one, this time.

BARBER INSTITUTE. So that was where it was, this art gallery she'd read about when she'd checked out Birmingham before she moved up. No. She really had no time now. But the very next wet weekend, she promised herself, she'd be there.

Kate was back at the university rather earlier than that. The following afternoon to be precise. And not in the Barber Institute, but in Dr Kennedy's room.

She hadn't been in the office to take the call summoning her herself, however. She'd been down in the increasingly familiar meetings room talking to Dr Michael Barton.

The family resemblance between him and Maeve Duncton was very strong, though his hair was now quite white. Like her, he dressed well, if not in a suit: his jacket was as well cut as Graham's favourite. He carried himself well; upright, strong about the shoulders. Unlike his sister, he'd shown every sign of pleasure when Kate had met him in reception. He'd had no difficulty with the ID badge, either.

He'd started to talk as soon as they got to the lift. 'I gather Maeve came to see you the other day,' he said. 'Well, Mavis, really. She changed her name very early in her life, and who would blame her? Celtic-romantic beats old-fashioned English any day.'

'And you changed your name too,' Kate observed, holding the doors back for him to step out. 'Here: along to our right.'

'Oh yes. No big secret about that. I had this rich cousin who wanted to leave me a lot of money, only she brought in this dreadful Victorian proviso that I change my name. No problem. So now I live in this gorgeous Queen Anne house in Staffordshire.'

She unlocked the room, and showed him into the chair that his sister had occupied. Like her, he declined refreshment.

'Maeve's got this bee in her bonnet,' he said as soon as she was seated too. 'About the will. She's got the idea that it's forged, that Mother really wanted to leave everything to us. It's nonsense. Absolute nonsense. I want you to stop any enquiries you've set in train. Let the poor old bugger have her estate. He's earned it, believe me.'

'That's very generous,' Kate said.

'Well, have you seen the place? I've not been back for years, but it was a tip when I saw it. Absolute tip. Max did his best, but it would have taken a proper complement of staff to run the place properly – indoor and outdoor.'

'Why didn't you visit her recently?'

'I didn't visit at all. Full stop. We had a row. Mother never offered an opinion; she stated facts. And once she had stated one, it was set in tablets of stone. To be honest, if I had turned up it could have been fatal: she could have had a heart attack or a stroke at any minute, or if she hadn't I might have strangled her.'

Kate nodded: that tied in with what both Mrs Hamilton and Cornfield himself had said.

'So there you are, Sergeant. Let's not waste police time and public money chasing after something neither of us needs.'

She smiled. 'Have you discussed this with your sister?'

Did the charm slip?

'She knows my views. She's entitled to hers. But believe me, the whole thing's a chimera.'

'I take it you two don't exactly see eye to eye,' she said mildly.

'Siblings don't always,' he said.

'Quite. But it's a bit unusual to fall out with your mother and your sibling — and isn't there another sister somewhere?'

'None of this is pertinent to the case,' he said sharply. Then he managed an apologetic smile. 'I'm sorry. Look, Sergeant, let's just agree that if you want to play Happy Families then you should go for Mr Bun the Baker, not the Barr family.' Looking at his watch, he got to his feet. 'Now, since the case is closed, may I make a suggestion I wouldn't have dreamed of making under any other circumstances? May I invite you to make an old man's day happier by joining him for lunch, Sergeant?'

Heavens, that was quick! 'If I could see an old man,' she laughed, standing up too, 'I might. As it is, I've got to report to my inspector.'

He seemed quite unabashed. In the lift he produced a card from his wallet. 'If you change your mind, you know where to find me,' he said, handing it and his temporary ID over in the same elegant movement.

\*

'Curioser and curioser, as Alice said,' Lizzie observed. 'So are you going to talk to the sister and see if you can persuade her to drop the accusation? After all, you've got plenty to suggest the old dear wanted Cornfield to have her loot.'

'I'd love to,' Kate admitted. 'But for one thing. Derek's just fielded a phone call from our expert at the university—'

'I do wish you'd be more precise. Birmingham has three universities. I take it you mean Birmingham University?'

'Yes.' Jesus, did the woman have to be so bloody awkward even when she was being given hard news? 'Our Birmingham University expert, Gaffer, wants me to go round at two this afternoon. And I don't somehow think it's to discuss interpretations of *Hamlet*.'

# Chapter Ten

Dr Kennedy was deep into red-penning an essay when kate knocked and popped her head round the door.

'You would not believe,' she said, 'that a second-year student at a major university could manage to write the following sentence: "Neither Lear or Hamlet see any point in the prolongisation of their struggles. If he was to keep going, things would only get worse."'

'Depends whether it was under exam conditions, I suppose.'

'Hmm. But even exam conditions shouldn't excuse two apostrophe mistakes in the rest of the paragraph. A Level English, they're supposed to have. An A or B grade pass. What do they teach them at school these days? Still, you're not here to listen to me griping.' She got up stretching. Her neck emitted a couple of ominous cracks. 'You don't know a decent osteopath, do you? Now, I can't walk without a mug of coffee in my hand. Care to join me?' It was clear she wasn't about to divulge anything quickly.

Kate nodded. But she couldn't resist an urgent, 'Dr Kennedy—'

'Oh, come on. If you're Kate, I'm Sam. And I know I'm keeping you on tenterhooks, but that's where you should be. And will be until this bloody kettle boils. Ah! Now, if you come with me, all will be revealed.'

Locking her door behind her, she led the way to an identical room fitted up not with bookshelves and desk but as a small lab.

'Have a peer down those eye-pieces,' she said. 'And tell me what you see.'

Kate obeyed. But came up, shaking her head. 'I'm sorry – I'm just a cop. I do need to be told what to look for.'

Sam laughed. 'I thought you would. But take another look. What you've got in front of you is a piece of paper on which someone has written in ballpoint. Now, to the naked eye, when you write in ballpoint you see a fairly uniform line.'

'But this is striated.'

'Quite. Those little white lines are caused by defects on the housing of the ball from which the ballpoint gets its name. The ball has to be spherical or it won't rotate. But the socket or housing into which it's fitted often has little irregularities, little protrusions, which interrupt the free flow of ink.'

'I see.'

'Now, can you tell me anything else about the striations?'

Kate blinked and focused again. 'They go in the same direction. Or rather, they go in the direction' – she mimed writing – 'the ballpoint would go in when you were writing.'

'Well done. Now, I gather that you're right-handed. So most of your striations would go from left to right, because that's the way right-handers write.'

Kate straightened. 'But so do left-handers! Unless they're writing Hebrew or something.'

'Not quite. There's evidence that when we write we prefer, if we can, to pull the pen, not push it. So if you write an "o" I'd expect you to start at the top, come back in an anti-clockwise direction and join up at the top. OK? Try it.'

Kate obliged.

'Now, some left-handers don't do it that way. They start at the top – yes – but then continue in the same direction, so their circle is clockwise, not anti-clockwise.'

'You know,' Kate said slowly, rubbing her chin, 'I've never noticed that.' She wrinkled her nose in silent disbelief.

'OK, when did you last watch someone closely when they were writing? When they were writing you a cheque? You're more interested in what they write than in how.'

'OK. So where does this get us?'

'Whoever wrote the will was left-handed, in my opinion. Look at this "o" – and this. Check them all out if you wish.' Sam waited. 'OK? Now, there are other characteristics of this handwriting which suggest to me that whoever produced it had his education somewhere other than in the UK.'

'Why's that?'

'Come on, Kate, you must have had pen-friends when you were at school. Or been served meals by foreign waiters. You'll have noticed that for various reasons different regions produce different shapes—'

'OK. Like all those American loops—'

'Right. So I'd say whoever wrote the will was an Eastern European male. I don't know if that's what you wanted me to tell you?'

If Kate was disappointed she'd better not show it. 'One of the things,' she said.

'How about another one? That in my professional opinion' – she not only fell into the language of the courts, she reduced her pace – 'whoever wrote the letter also made one of the signatures. There – Leon Horowitz. Compare the "o's".'

My God! My God! Kate forced herself to ask, 'But what if this Leon Horowitz were also educated in Eastern Europe and were also left-handed?'

'Nice use of the subjunctive, Kate. I wish you could teach my students. Well, if he were, it would be more difficult to say. But I have a hunch . . . there's something about the quality of the line that interests me . . . No, you tell me if he is or not, and show me his normal signature, and I'll be able to offer a considered opinion.'

They were walking back along the corridor, Sam having locked the will into a safe and then punctiliously double locked the lab door, when Kate said, 'I would never have asked you to look for that, you know. Never in a million years.'

Sam slowed to a halt. 'You look what my students would call gobsmacked. Are you all right? No, you're not, are you? Come and have another coffee?'

'I ought . . . And you've got those essays to mark . . . But, hell, yes, I really could do with one. Yes, please.'

From the top drawer of her desk, Sam produced a packet of German biscuits, rich with ginger and cinnamon. 'My bloke lives in Berlin,' she said.

'Berlin! That's hardly down the road. How do you manage to keep going?'

'The phone, e-mail and monthly commuting. We manage. But I wish he were nearer. Or, I suppose, that I were nearer to him.' She sighed.

Kate nodded sympathetically. A partner that far away must be almost as bad as having a married lover. Worse, maybe. 'How do you manage for all the things people are supposed to do in couples?'

Sam grimaced. 'Oh, I should do them on my own, shouldn't I? I'm a grown-up woman. But – well, what I do is work most of the time. Concerts, plays – they're more fun, aren't they, with someone to chew them over with in the interval? Sometimes friends invite me, and I've got a gay friend I go with. But that's not good for his street cred.'

'Unless he needs a beard. My best mate's gay,' Kate added.

Sam passed her her coffee. 'Tell you what, we should

get together next time there's something either of us wants to see. Let me see — yes, here we are.' She burrowed in her in-tray and flipped across two brochures, one for the RSC, another for Birmingham Rep. 'You do like the theatre?' she asked anxiously.

'My partner was a bit of a philistine,' Kate said. That must be about the first time she'd ever criticised Robin, mustn't it? 'Preferred his football and his beer. So I'm out of touch.'

'Past tense?' Sam asked gently.

'Past tense. He was killed in an accident. That's why I came to Birmingham — to get away from everything.'

'Was that a good idea?'

'It seemed so at the time! Actually, yes, I think it was. I've made some good friends up here — even if none of them is inclined to go to the theatre. Or music.'

'Hang on, what have I here?' Sam burrowed again, this time coming up with a Symphony Hall leaflet.


All of which seemed very positive, Kate thought, as she went back to her car. Even if there were nothing that particularly grabbed her, she'd make a point of contacting Sam again — maybe even for a balti. There was that nice place in York Road, the place where Rod had taken her. Why not?

Meanwhile, back to her immediate problem. Max Cornfield and the will.

There was a theory that letting someone talk enough

would encourage whoever it was to betray him or herself. Since Mrs Barr's house lay not far off her route back into the city, what about another conversation with Mr Cornfield? Despite this afternoon's evidence, in her bones she was sure he was a decent man. Perhaps the knowledge that something was nagging the police would drive him to confess, simply to clear his conscience – always assuming, of course, that he had anything to confess.

Parking the car on the road this time, she hesitated. What if talking to him simply put him on his guard? This was the sort of situation where a partner was invaluable for chewing over pros and cons. The one person who would require her to talk through events was, of course, Lizzie, who would, of course, almost certainly blow up big time, if Kate presented Sam's evidence unvarnished, ordering Cornfield's immediate evisceration. If Kate made a wrong decision – or, in this case, indecision – Kate could be eviscerated too.

She put the car into gear, signalled and pulled away.

Since Rod Neville was parking and locking his car at the same time as she was parking and locking hers, he could hardly avoid speaking to her. But he never did so without embarrassment these days. Silly man. Love affairs ended, didn't they? Except there'd been more lust than love in their short encounter. Perhaps he felt he'd taken advantage of his rank; more likely, a stickler for convention – and what detective superintendent wouldn't be? – he'd been shocked, possibly even offended, by Kate's occasional forays into maverickdom.

Anyway, he was now not just speaking, but smiling at her in very much the old way. In fact, though she was prepared to fall into step with him as they went into the building, there was something about his smile that detained her alongside his car.

'How are things?' he asked.

Not a particularly impressive or original line, but he put his briefcase down and looked ready to listen to more than the conventional 'OK'.

But she wasn't prepared to say more than that, not yet.

'I mean, really. Are you over . . . all that . . . trauma?'

'Yes, thanks. House and garden doing well. No more buried hoards, no more fires. And a new tennis coach.'

'And a new posting here. With Fraud.'

'Typical of Personnel, isn't it? Pull out all the experienced guys and shove in a rookie.'

'You're hardly that. You're an experienced officer. Come on, didn't I hear you've finished your inspector's exams? In fact, I'd say that calls for a drink.'

She'd had a good night on the booze with all her mates. Yes, even Graham had looked in for half an hour.

He must have understood her silence. He lowered his eyes.

'I'd better get along,' she said. 'I've got to report something to Lizzie King.'

He picked up his briefcase, and started towards the

entrance. But then he stopped. 'It was about her I wanted to talk to you,' he said.

Really?

Despite herself, as if she really believed him, she looked around to check no one was within earshot.

'I thought so. There *is* something wrong, isn't there? Why don't you come along to my office and we'll talk about it?'

She took a deep breath. 'Do you want an honest reply? I don't think that would be a good idea. If Lizzie gets wind of the tiniest rumour I've been alone in your company, she'll . . .'

A couple of very senior officers strolled by. They all exchanged salutes.

'She'll what? Come on, Kate!'

'It's no good, Rod. I can't. I shouldn't have said that.' It was one thing gossiping to a fellow victim like Derek, quite another talking to someone who could have an effect on someone's career. Sure, she might have said something last week, when Lizzie seemed to be spinning out of control, but, though still tetchy, she seemed much better this week.

He dropped his voice, lowered his eyes, 'Kate, you've every reason to believe you can't trust me as a lover. God knows . . . I – I'd really like to talk about that. Hell . . . But surely you know you can trust me as a colleague?'

'You're not just a colleague. You're a senior CID colleague. And anything I say to you about a colleague will almost certainly be seen as grassing.'

'You didn't volunteer, I asked you. Damn it, Kate, if the woman's ill—'

Ill? Well, if that was the rumour, OK. 'So long as it's in absolute confidence.'

'Thanks. The only question, then, is where and when. And I'd like to suggest a quiet meal somewhere. It'll save us both cooking,' he added, with a mocking sideways glance.

'Let me think about that,' she said. It was unlikely that Graham would come tonight but not impossible. 'Could you phone me – eightish?'

'Eightish.' His smile was worryingly intimate.

Mistake, Kate, big mistake.

But not as bad as having been seen talking to him by, inevitably, Lizzie.

'Still got the hots for Rod Neville, then?' Lizzie yelled, as Kate walked past her half-open office door.

Did the woman control the security cameras, for God's sake?

'He wanted to know how my house was, after the fire. Now, Gaffer, I could do with advice and a cup of tea, but not necessarily in that order.'

Lizzie raised her eyebrows coldly. 'What's the verdict on the will?'

'What I simply can't understand,' Lizzie exploded before Kate had drawn breath on her final sentence, 'is that you didn't hightail over to his place and pick him up and grill him. For God's sake, Power, you're supposed to be the *crème de la crème*. Act like it for once.' She picked up a folder, pretending to leaf through it. Then – feigning surprise – she looked up again. What are you hanging round here for? I thought I told you to go and bring him in.'

'With respect, I'm not sure—'

'You don't have to be sure, Power. You have to do as you're told for once.'

'Ma'am.'

So it was back to the big house in Edgbaston. Obediently she applied an unwilling thumb to the bell marked 'Press'. There was no reply. Tomorrow, then.

It was only as she pulled away that she remembered: Thursday was Cornfield's day for travelling.

# Chapter Eleven

The phone rang promptly at eight. Not even daring to hope it might be Graham, Kate wasn't surprised to hear Rod's voice.

'OK, it's eight o'clock, and you said I might phone you then. So may I take you out for a meal?' He sounded absurdly boyish.

She couldn't resist laughing. 'OK. Why not?' Except there were a hundred reasons why not.

'I'll be with you in two minutes, then.'

'*Two minutes?*'

'OK. One minute. I'm parked right opposite your house.'

The bastard. And double bastard to flourish a bunch of flowers in her face as she opened the front door.

Her vestibule and hall were both too narrow for her to do anything other than stand back and let him through into the living room. But as soon as she could, she said, 'Rod, you shouldn't have bought me flowers. We're – we're not in a relationship any more.'

His face fell. But not for long. 'Accept them for when I

should have given them to you. Kate, shove them in water, for goodness' sake. It'd be a shame for them to die. Come on, wouldn't it?'

She pulled a face. 'No more, though. OK?' If she sounded grudging, she meant to. Assertive would have been better, but grudging was better than nothing.

He followed her into the kitchen, watching her snip the stems and add food to the water in a big cut-glass vase that Cassie had left behind. She couldn't resist pulling one stem here, pushing another there: flowers deserved more than merely to be plonked into a container. But she knew even as she repositioned the gypsophila that she was sending out the wrong messages. She'd just have to correct them later.

He looked at his watch. 'Kate: would you mind if we set off now? I've got a table booked.'

'A table! You were pretty bloody sure of me!' Oh, Rod would never lack for confidence: his looks, his brain, his physique, his position – they all added up to one alpha male.

'I'd have gone on my own if you hadn't agreed. I got a last-minute cancellation. The Siam – the Thai restaurant at the far end of the High Street.'

'I need to change.'

'Two minutes? It'll take us ages to find anywhere to park.'

'We could always walk? Ten minutes at most.'

'There's a storm coming up. Can't you feel it?'

*Feeling storms?* Well, that was a side of Rod she'd never

seen before, she reflected, peeling off her work clothes and pulling a dress over her head. She knew the colour suited her – red picked up the colour of her hair – and that the cut flattered her figure. Hairbrush, make-up, a quick check in the mirror told her that at least Rod had nothing to be ashamed of when they sallied forth together. On impulse, she dug in her drawer for perfume – what would be light enough for summer? No! Wrong message. She shut the drawer again.

'In the police, it's almost impossible to complain about a line manager,' Kate said, laying her spoon in her bowl after a gluttonous final scrape. Rod knew how to pick a restaurant. 'You must see that.'

Their conversation accorded ill with the quietly civilised décor and relaxed service.

'Impossible?'

'The whole ethic's based on loyalty, isn't it? Grassing's the ultimate crime. At my last London nick, someone mentioned his DCI's alcoholism – in absolute confidence of course – to his super and ended up with piles of lawn-cuttings in his locker. Every day.'

'You could take it to the sergeants' sector of the Federation – they'd protect you.'

'Or they could feel that someone on the accelerated promotion scheme might just be hoping to try someone else's desk for size.'

Rod paused while the waiter removed the soup bowls,

then suggested, 'ACC in charge of Support Services? Or whatever the job title is these days!'

'With all due respect, being an Assistant Chief Constable doesn't exactly predispose you against hierarchies. More locker problems, I'd have thought.'

'Welfare officer?'

She shook her head. 'No. What I ought to do, Rod, as one of my colleagues has made abundantly clear—'

'So other people are aware of the problem?'

'Everyone in the Squad, I'd have thought. What I ought to do is have a woman-to-woman talk with her. I would if I'd come to the problem . . .' She hesitated. But she could say it to Rod. 'If I'd come fresh to the squad, as it were.'

'You're saying that you two have a history? I didn't know that.' Rod stopped to smile as a waiter topped up their glasses.

'For no apparent reason. We simply never have got on.'

He checked that neighbouring diners couldn't overhear. But the tables were widely spaced, and he continued, dropping his voice anyway, 'You know how quickly you and Graham Harvey became friends?'

She hesitated: last time they'd spoken about her and Graham's friendship – when they were, quite simply, friends – Rod had chosen to tell her that a pair of gloves she'd thought lost lurked in Graham's desk. She'd no idea whether he guessed the present situation – she hoped and prayed he didn't – but her reaction then must have been sufficient to warn him against scoring any more cheap points.

'Yes,' she said neutrally.

'Rumour has it that she and Graham were an item years back. But he went back to his wife.'

Kate had heard the same rumour. The arrival of their main course spared her having to say anything.

'So she might well hold that against you,' Rod continued. 'Has she said anything about you and Graham?'

She took a risk. 'To my face? I don't know about behind my back. To me, though, no more than she's said about you and me. Pretty efficient, the rumour machine, isn't it? Which is another reason I couldn't come to you to discuss her problems. And why I'm talking to you in absolute confidence. I hope.'

He smiled. 'Can you think otherwise? Let's discuss this again later: it's a shame to waste wonderful food by talking shop. Now, try some of this Kang Pet Kung.'

'Provided you try some of my Kai Preo Waan.'

'Who could resist?'

At this point, the lights flickered, there was a simultaneous thunderclap so loud their glasses seemed to rock, and the storm Rod had predicted well and truly arrived.

It had not abated an hour later. By now they and their fellow guests had succumbed to weather watching from the restaurant's front window. As well they might. The manhole covers had blown, and the High Street was awash with floodwater. Any cars made huge bow-waves, leaving curling wakes. Rod's car was only twenty yards away, but they'd have been soaked to the skin in half that distance. In any case, to open the restaurant door would be to admit the floodwaters.

She could feel him leaning closer: could feel the warmth of his arm through his shirt. She shifted slightly. If only she'd been with Graham, they could have paddled to the car, arms round each other under the inadequate umbrella, falling into each others' wet arms as they reached safety. But even as she fantasised, she knew that Graham would never behave like that. He wasn't, was he, a man for shedding inhibitions.

The rain stopped as quickly as it had started. Another cup of coffee and the pavement was passable. Rod made no attempt to touch her, either in the car or as he saw her to her doorstep.

To the accompaniment of water dripping from roofs, from gutters, even from the leaves of her tiny new clematis, he coughed. 'Kate. I behaved intolerably when – when . . . I can tell you don't want to start again where we left off. And I can't blame you.'

She said nothing, but regarded him steadily in the light from the streetlamp.

'What I'd like – what I'd very much like – is for us to become friends again. Just friends, OK? And do things friends do. And if – if your feelings changed – then maybe . . .'

'There'd be a hell of a lot of gossip,' she said crisply.

'I know. Which is why I'd like us to do nice public things. Straightaway. To show we're not afraid to be seen together. Like you and Colin.'

'Not quite the same,' she laughed.

'No. But you know what I mean. In fact, let's start next week. I know you like art: I've got tickets for a private view at the Ikon Gallery. How about that?'

Kate nodded. 'That'd be good.'

But as she closed the door behind him she collapsed in giggles. Somehow she didn't expect too many of her police colleagues to crowd into a gallery best known for its obscure conceptual art installations.

'You've made a complete dog's breakfast of it, as far as I can see. Fancy letting the scrote bugger off like that,' Lizzie exclaimed first thing the following morning. She shook her splayed hands, raising her eyes heavenwards. 'God grant me patience.'

Kate added her silent prayer. 'He'll be back tomorrow, ma'am. Thursday, according to his neighbour, is his day for travelling.'

'*His day for travelling*, is it? And I suppose you know where he travels to?'

'Not yet, ma'am. But I will when I talk to him tomorrow.'

'Don't tell me: Friday is his day for coming home.'

'I hope so. Though now he no longer has to look after Mrs Barr he may be tempted to spend more time away from home. But he'll be back. He loves the garden, you see.' Even to her own ears Kate was sounding fey. She added, infusing irony into her voice, 'Not to mention the valuable wine and other untold riches in the butler's pantry.'

'The moment he returns, you wheel him in for questioning: right? Meanwhile,' Lizzie added with an ominous smile, 'although today is Thursday, you aren't travelling anywhere. How do you propose to occupy your time, Sergeant?'

'Superintendent Neville wishes to see me at some point this morning, ma'am. And I thought I might set about notifying the Foreign Office that we have two witnesses on foreign soil from whom we may need statements.'

'What the hell for? Oh, your *commission interrogative* or whatever it's called.'

Kate, whose French was decidedly GCSE full stop, though it might be *commission rogatoire*, but wouldn't have placed any bets on it, especially in the present circumstances.

'Well, you can forget all about that. Takes bloody months to go through official channels. There are ways round that. For a start, get on the bloody phone to the witnesses.'

'But—'

'That's how I do it, Power. And that's how you do it. Now.'

Kate stood up. 'Ma'am.'

'And don't even think about contacting the FO. They're the last people you want to involve. That's an order, Power.'

'Ma'am.'

✽

'So you can see, Rod, why I can't ask after her health,' Kate said, sipping some of his wonderful coffee. She'd told him nothing of the details of her most recent run-in with Lizzie, just the general tenor.

'I still think you ought to. Next to her you're the senior woman in the squad. You've seen her change. You're a decent, concerned human being. QED.'

'Or, more likely, RIP. OK, Rod. I'll try. But I'll have to pick my moment very carefully. If it goes pear-shaped, our working relationship goes pear-shaped too. And I'm in the middle of an intriguing case.'

'And I, I'm afraid, am on the verge of a far from intriguing meeting. Redeployment of already overstretched resources to comply with the latest government initiative. Kate,' he added, rising as she did, 'remember that my door is always open. And Kate – I'm glad we're friends again.'

'So am I,' she said. And meant it.


If Kate's French was limited, her Portuguese was non-existent. At least her German was reasonable, thanks to her father's brief relationship with Astrid, a woman involved in the marketing of Bosch products. The two women had got on so unexpectedly well that, even though Astrid and her father parted company quite quickly, Kate had still been invited to stay in Cologne a couple of times.

Even as she dialled International Directory Enquiries, Kate was scratching her head about why Mrs Barr had chosen witnesses from so far afield. Not Mrs Barr, of course. Max Cornfield had chosen the witnesses because his friends were the only people to visit the house. So why had he chosen such conveniently inaccessible friends? Horowitz was living on the Algarve, and Steiner in Berlin.

More to the point, why hadn't she asked him that very question when she had the chance? Because she wanted him to be innocent, that's why. Cursing herself for her laxness, her lack of professionalism, her downright stupidity, she dialled the first number.

Her German skills were hardly exercised. Dr Steiner spoke immaculate English. If he were taken aback at being addressed by an English policewoman, he did not show it. Yes, he had witnessed Mrs Barr's will. He'd been in Birmingham at the time to attend a chess convention at the National Exhibition Centre, and it had been natural for Max to invite him over.

'We go back years, Sergeant Power. Forty, fifty years. I always visit when I'm in the UK. Naturally.'

He would be only too delighted to send her a sample of his handwriting – why not, she suggested, an account of the occasion the will was witnessed – and yes, he was right-handed.

All she got of Mr Horowitz was his answering machine. She left a message, asking for the same handwritten account, and an indication of with which hand he wrote it. And prayed it was the left.

# Chapter Twelve

Nearly eleven it might be when Kate came home, but Zenia was putting out her black sacks of rubbish for the following morning's collection.

Zenia eyed the racquet: 'You look very sporty.'

'Yes: tennis with the girls. Plus a balti.' Tonight Midge and Lorraine had roped in a man as an honorary girl, a middle-aged probation officer who made up in cunning what he lacked in speed about the court.

'Any message for my Rafe?' Zenia asked quizzically.

Kate shook her head. 'Not yet. I seem to have an old flame flickering round me,' she added with a grimace.

Zenia's eyes widened. 'Come and have a last drop of Joseph's punch and tell me all about it. Come on, otherwise I shall have to finish it on my own.'

'I'd love to.' Perhaps she could talk about Lizzie too. Kate shouldered her sports bag into Zenia's hall. 'So long as you remind me to put my own rubbish out.'

'Thing is,' Zenia said, ushering her through into the kitchen, 'I could do with some advice too. About – about my Royston.'

Royston! He was the one person about whom Kate and Zenia never spoke. He'd got in with a bad set, and was currently in youth custody.

'I don't want him coming back here, Kate. He'll be in with the wrong sort before you can say knife – oh, God—' Her face crumpled and she turned away. Royston had been put away for stabbing Kate.

Kate put her arms round her and waited.

Zenia sniffed. 'It should be you getting upset, not me.' She straightened. 'But it's not because of you I don't want him coming back here. Nor because of what the neighbours will say. It's – it's the school and the boys he was with and – what chance does he have?'

'What's the alternative?'

'My brother would have him. The one in Canada. I don't want him going back home to my mum: she'll just spoil him and let him run loose and it'll be worse than if he's here.'

'What does Joseph think?'

'Him! He's got this wonderful idea that if I gave up work I could be here for him. But Royston needs a man's hand. And it'd make more sense for Joseph to give up work than me.'

'Have you talked to Royston?'

'Not yet. I can't talk to him, Kate, you know? I go and visit him and we talk about all sorts of things, but I can't talk to him about . . . You see . . .'

Kate had always thought Zenia a strong woman, the sort she could turn to herself. But there was no doubt that

Zenia's crisis was worse than hers, so she let her talk on. Problem sons, cracks in what had seemed a perfect marriage – what *did* Joseph see in this woman at work? And what should she do about this sexy administrator at the hospital? Kate's life was calm itself compared to Zenia's.

There was no doubt that when Lizzie was out of the office, everyone breathed more easily. Knowing in her bones her journey was in vain, Kate had set out bright and early to haul Max Cornfield in, tangling with evil jams and having to fight to get out of his drive when she'd established that no one was home. Perhaps she was simply too early. Wherever his travels took him, he had to get back from them, and if he relied on the railways, maybe lunchtime was a more reasonable ETA. Anyway, back at Lloyd House she could while the morning away quite profitably making phone calls for Derek, who was showing signs of going under.

'What are you going to do about Cornfield?' he asked, boiling a kettle for a mid-morning coffee.

'Try to talk to him this afternoon. Thanks. Not at his place but here. Perhaps it'll give the proceedings a bit more seriousness.'

'Scare him into admitting things?'

'Assuming he's got things to admit. Tell you what, Derek, you haven't got a spare half-hour yourself, have you? I – I like the guy, see. I don't see him as a scrote. It's quite clear he was the only person in the world to care for the old biddy. He admits to having written the will for her. His buddy in Germany has explained to my satisfaction how he came to witness the signature. But we've got this evidence from the handwriting expert—'

Derek shook his head. 'We've got this *opinion* from the expert.'

'You're right. Let's hear what Cornfield's got to say. But it'd stiffen my resolve no end to have you sitting in on the interview.'

He pulled his chin. 'I'd rather see this set-up for myself. Let's talk to him out there, shall we? If things look really sticky for him, we can easily wheel him in here. And, like you, I don't like prejudging folk as scrotes.'

'Lizzie said to talk to him here,' she admitted.

'Lizzie's not here. Any idea where she might be, incidentally?'

'No one seems to know.'

'Lizzie?' Tammy popped her head round the door. 'Anyone got any milk? The thing is, no one knows when she'll be back. Sick leave?'

'No phone call,' Derek said. 'And it was pre-booked, apparently.'

Tammy grinned. 'There are enough detectives in the building; we should be able to sniff it out!'

Kate shook her head firmly. 'Ours to do or die, ours not to find out why. No, let's leave it. There's something wrong with her and making her the object of gossip isn't going to help.'

Tammy raised mocking eyebrows. 'I wouldn't have

thought you'd be on her side, not after all the stick you've had to take from her.'

Kate poured some milk into a clean mug, and held out what was left in the packet. 'Is this enough? Thing is, Tammy, that's precisely why I don't want to ferret round in Lizzie's life. I've been the subject of gossip before now, and it isn't much fun. And if that makes me sound horribly pious, I'm sorry, but so be it.'

Derek had his eyebrows up now. 'Come on, nothing wrong with a harmless chinwag between friends.'

'Nothing at all. But that's not the same as poking around for something to chinwag about.'

Tammy exchanged a glance with Derek, took the milk and, with an ostentatious shrug, left the room.

'That was a bit head girl, wasn't it?' he said, after a moment. 'These rumours about you and that superintendent of yours getting you down, are they? Joke, Kate, Joke! But for your information, it was Lizzie who told Tammy.'

Kate produced what she hoped was an off-hand nod. 'I'm sure she knew there was nothing to gossip about: we're mates, Rod and I. We had a meal the other night and we're off to a private view next week.' Jesus, what had Lizzie said about her and Graham? Enough, no doubt. But it was too much of a risk to ask Derek — wasn't it? Or should she go on the offensive? 'I dare say she's told Tammy about me and Stephen from the museum and me and my tennis coach—'

'Hang on: I thought he was awaiting trial.'

'My new, even sexier coach. Pity he's on his honeymoon

at the moment. And who else? Well, I had a meeting with Graham Harvey the other day, and there's always my neighbour's gorgeous cousin.' By now, her dander was well and truly up. 'And I'll tell you what, Derek, if you and I are seen leaving the building together this afternoon, that'll be something else for Tammy to tell Lizzie, won't it?'

Derek raised his hands in surrender. 'Point taken.' He gave a rueful smile, then his face became serious. 'Maybe you don't want to know that, Kate, but you were right about one of those names.' He dropped his voice. 'They say that's why you had to leave Steelhouse Lane. They say you and Graham Harvey were having it off.'

'Graham *and* Rod! My goodness, I *do* get around, don't I?' All the swear words she'd ever known were battering at her skull, but she mustn't let any of them out. 'Better make sure you're wearing a chastity belt this afternoon, Derek, that's all I can say.'

*Damned if you do, damned if you don't.* Kate stared at her reflection in the mirror in the loo. Did she tackle Lizzie about these rumours or let them die the death? On the whole, since morally she could hardly deny them, whatever she wanted to do professionally, the latter seemed the better option. But that didn't mean she didn't want to yell the place down. A good loud scream here would be a good option. Some china to smash. Christ in heaven, what could she do?

What was that book she'd read at school? *The Scarlet*

*Letter?* That was it. She looked at the front of her blouse: it might almost be emblazoned with a big red A for Adultery. Oh, she and Rod had indulged in a harmless bit of fornication, but, her relationship with Graham must be adultery. Violating the seventh commandment. No wonder the poor man was feeling so guilty. He wasn't making love to her so much as breaking one of his religious tenets. And, of course, deceiving his wife, however unpleasant that woman might be.

What if he couldn't hack it any longer?

What if he broke it off?

Tammy came in, humming brightly. They exchanged a smile through the mirror.

'You all right, Kate? You're ever so pale.' Tammy came closer and peered.

'Last night's girls' night balti,' Kate said. 'Lorraine made us go to a new place.' She had to shut up. There was nothing like gabbling out redundant information to arouse suspicion.

'You sure?'

Was it sympathy or curiosity?

She pulled a face. 'No. Come to think of it it might have been the Caribbean punch afterwards. It goes down like silk but—'

'Then you stand up and you find your legs knotted together. Yes, I had some at one of Cary Grant's parties. Doing well on that TV programme, isn't he?'

Was there an edge to Tammy's voice? If there was, she must ignore that too.

'The one my old gaffer used to call *Grass on your Neighbour*?' she asked. 'Well, he's very bright, very good-looking.' And she'd be very happy for her name to be linked to Cary's. Rarely could there have been less electricity between two people supposedly out for a date.

'I thought they wanted you to front it.'

*Just because you're paranoid, Kate, it doesn't mean they're not out to get you.* 'Not to my knowledge. No, Cary does it very well. There's only one person I'd like to see on it more, as a matter of fact: young Fatima back in my old squad.' She peered closely at the mirror. 'You're right, a bit of make-up wouldn't hurt, would it?'

Max Cornfield was busy with a spade and wheelbarrow when they pulled up outside his house. He smiled at Kate, but was clearly disconcerted when Derek joined her.

'This is a colleague of mine, Mr Cornfield,' she said. 'Detective Constable Baker.'

Cornfield removed a leather gardening glove and shook his hand. He turned sadly to Kate. 'Clearly you haven't come to discuss my gardening plans. You have found something seriously wrong with the will? Shall we discuss it over a cold drink? There's iced coffee in the fridge.'

He ushered them through into the kitchen, and then thought better of it: 'The garden would be much more pleasant, or do you prefer not to discuss serious matters in the open air?'

Kate shot a sideways glance at Derek. 'You may prefer our talk to be confidential.'

'The garden is completely private. If you care to go through, Sergeant, I'll bring the tray.'

It would do no harm for Derek to see the garden, anyway – not to mention the junk stacked in the conservatory. She watched his eyebrows rise and fall, his lips purse in a silent whistle.

'I'd murder for a garden like this,' he said.

'The trouble is,' Kate asked quietly, 'did he?'


'So what is wrong with the will?' Cornfield demanded, as well he might.

'Probably just one or two technicalities,' Derek said easily.

Kate nodded. 'What we'd find helpful is if you'd tell us how the will came to be written.'

Cornfield shrugged. 'I told you. She was a very sick old woman and I begged her to discuss it with a solicitor. Then, one afternoon – I suppose it was only three or four days before she died, Sergeant . . . One afternoon, she said, "We have to do it now." "But we have no witnesses," I said.'

'So how did you find the witnesses?'

'Friends of mine. I'm sure I told you. We play chess.'

'Via the Internet,' Kate interjected for Derek's benefit.

Derek said, 'You can't have virtual witnesses, sir.'

For the first time he looked irritated. 'They were in

Birmingham for a chess convention, Constable. I suggested them to Mrs Barr, who agreed.'

'You didn't think of simply asking the neighbours?'

'Mrs Barr was a very . . . She knew her own mind, Constable. She emphatically did not want the neighbours to know her business.'

'But any witnesses——'

'My colleagues are very distinguished men in their own fields. She thought that they would bring discretion to their task.'

Kate shook her head. 'But they wouldn't have to know what was in the will itself. All they had to do was witness signatures.'

Cornfield shook his head. 'Part of Mrs Barr's eccentricity involved her dictating the will in the presence of the witnesses. So they would know.' He stood up, spreading his hands. 'I make her sound like a monster. She wasn't. I asked her doctor if she was in sound mind. You can check with him.'

'We will,' Derek said, the two syllables surprisingly menacing.

'So what exactly happened when she made her will?' Kate asked, glad that Cornfield himself had given her a lead.

'I – we . . . it was difficult. She didn't want to receive men in her bedroom. I half-supported, half-carried her down the stairs. Then in her wheelchair to the living room. I wrote down the will at her dictation. She signed it. It was witnessed. My friends returned to their chess. They wanted me to go with them but the whole business had distressed her unimaginably. How I got her back upstairs I'll never know. I sat with her holding her hand long into the night. She barely regained consciousness after that.' His face seemed to become older before their eyes. He brushed away tears. 'She was my friend, Sergeant. I cared for her. Would I wish her any harm?'

Kate flicked a glance at Derek. 'Who mentioned harm, Mr Cornfield?'

'She was so distressed – by the knowledge that she was dying. A will is an intimation of mortality, isn't it? She'd put it off as long as she could. It was only because she didn't want her children to benefit by her death that she consented to make a will at all. And I believe making it killed her.' He stood. Looking wildly round the garden. 'Officer, I killed her as surely as if I'd put my hands round her throat and squeezed.'

Derek was on his feet. 'Sit down, sir. Try not to upset yourself. All we want is the facts, remember.'

'And now you have them!' He pushed away from Derek. 'Please – can't you leave me to grieve?'

'You must have been very close,' Kate observed.

'Close! The family accuse me of having seduced her. We were friends, Sergeant, with all that the word implies. Now, for the love of God, leave me alone.'

'We'll leave you to mourn as soon as we can, Max,' Kate said. 'But I need to know one more thing. I understand you're never at home on Thursdays. Can you tell me where you go?'

'As if this is relevant! Sergeant, I went about my

employer's business. Now I go about mine. Mrs Barr had properties in various parts of the country. They were let. I travel round to each in turn to make sure it's being properly maintained.'

Derek frowned. 'I'd have thought that this was the responsibility of the estate agent managing them.'

'Tell me, Constable, have you ever entrusted property to an estate agent in that way? No. I thought not.'

'Where are the properties?' Kate asked.

'If you bear with me five minutes I will furnish you with a list.' Sighing resignedly, he pulled himself to his feet and headed into the house, returning before Derek had time to have more than a tiny gloat at the garden.

# Chapter Thirteen

Weekends were designed for couples. There was no doubt about that. There were couples in Sainsbury's; couples at the hardware-cum-garden centre in York Road, where Kate found a proliferation of unusual plants and some enthusiastic advice; couples parking cars so tightly in Worksop Road she was afraid she'd never get her car back in after her trip to Cassie's residential home, where there were couples visiting their oldies.

And that was the height of her weekend social life. Midge was seeing a new man, Lorraine going back to her mother's. Joseph and Zenia – still, despite all the pressures, a couple – waved her goodbye as, shoving a weekend case in the car, they manoeuvred it carefully out of a space suddenly too short.

She took a cup of tea into the garden and stared at the evidence that the slug bait had been working. If she felt like this at eleven-thirty on a Saturday morning, how would she be feeling at eleven-thirty on Sunday evening?

*

JUDITH CUTLER

The answer was, when the time came, not much better. Her house and garden might have won cleanliness and tidiness competitions; she'd got through two novels, one frivolous and one improving, and two Sunday broadsheets, and seen not a soul to talk to, Cassie apart. What a sad life. Pathetic. And nothing she could do to change it until she took her whole life, including Graham's part in it, in hand. Nonsense. Of course there were things she could do. She could buy a bike and explore the areas where a car was inappropriate. She could learn to swim, study a foreign language – any or all the things agony aunts advised. But she knew that whatever she happened to be doing, she would drop it the moment Graham phoned her to say he could come round.

The realisation stung. Look at her: even without make-up, even with an embarrassing toothpaste moustache, even with her hair crying out for a trim, she wasn't a bad-looking woman. She pulled herself up straight. Her figure was a taut classic ten. It ought to be: she hadn't hit thirty yet. But she would – any week now. Thirty was the time when women felt nesty, when the biological clock was ticking so loudly that it was almost audible.

Was that what was the matter with her, that she wanted a baby?

Surely not. She'd seen enough of Robin's children to know that children involved levels of devotion and patience she was fairly sure she couldn't aspire to.

*No more*, said an insistent voice she wished she could

silence once and for all, *than you freely give Graham, who has far less reason than a child to be demanding and selfish.*


Kate was in work early, if not bright, hoping against rational hope that Steiner would have replied quickly. Even if he had, however, any letter would have to come via Deutsches Bundespost, the Royal Mail and then the vagaries of the police post room. On mature reflection, a bit of decent pessimism was called for, wasn't it? Pessimism augmented, moreover, by the knowledge that Lizzie was back, and that she and Derek had defied her orders to bring Cornfield in. Just at the moment, however, it wasn't Kate but Tammy who was getting a bollocking. What might prevent Kate getting one would be a visit to Mrs Duncton. It was good practice, after all, to keep the public informed about cases in which they were involved. And Kate had a great desire to see where Mrs Duncton lived.

'I was just about, Sergeant,' Mrs Duncton announced when Kate phoned her, 'to complain to your superior officers regarding the lack of information on the progress of my case.'

So Kate drove out to Four Oaks with very little love in her heart. Even amongst other impressive houses, the Duncton residence was impressive: a big detached house, probably nineteen-fifties, set well back from the road. Kate parked carefully, nodding and smiling at an elderly man with a wheelbarrow. A gardener? Or Mrs D's elderly husband? Whoever it was, he nodded back with every appearance of uninterest, more preoccupied with dealing with minute aberrations from the orderly norms of drive and lawn.

On her own territory – thickly carpeted, well-uphol-stered territory – Mrs Duncton was far more gracious than Kate would have expected. When Kate exclaimed at the pottery on a display stand, she became charm itself.

'That's Ruskin,' she said. 'A local potter.'

Kate was ready to take his address. Some of this she had to have. 'He's still alive then?'

'Oh, no. Can't you tell from the style, Sergeant? Nineteen hundred to about nineteen thirty. The factory tried to emulate Chinese techniques of glazing and firing. This one,' she pointed to the vase Kate had particularly admired, 'is what they call high-fired. Taylor—'

'Taylor?'

'J Howson Taylor: the factory owner. He named his pottery after John Ruskin. Taylor was trying to achieve *sang de boeuf*. See all these wonderful reds and purples?'

Kate spread her hands. 'It's absolutely wonderful!'

'And worth a great deal too. A collector's item. My husband often says it should be in a museum.'

'That's your husband out there?'

'Possibly.'

*Possibly?* Wouldn't you know?

'Now, you were punctilious about offering me refresh-ment, Sergeant, and at this time of morning I always have a cup of tea. May I offer you one?'

'That would be very kind.'

'The sun seems to be coming out: shall we go into the garden?' Mrs Duncton opened the patio door and pointed to a hardwood table and set of chairs. They didn't need a price tag for Kate, fresh from garden-bench buying herself, to know that they were very expensive. Kate sat with her back to the house so that she could check out the rest of the garden. For neatness it surpassed hers; for size and landscaping it rivalled Mrs Barr's.

The tea came in china cups, but the biscuits were shop bought.

Delicately trying to avoid giving Mrs Duncton too much information, Kate outlined her progress so far. She mentioned the forensic graphologist's need to see the original will, and made more of her efforts to get hold of it than they deserved. But she kept quiet about Sam Kennedy's suspicions.

'I gather,' she said, taking a risk and a custard cream, 'that you've spoken to your brother about the will.'

'Stupid man. Just because he doesn't need any more money . . . Well, I'm glad you've taken no notice of him. Personal feelings shouldn't enter into the matter when a crime has been committed.'

Mrs Duncton's words bullied their way into Kate's ears all the way back to base. Lizzie, to whom Derek had obviously already confessed their sin of omission, repeated the same words more or less verbatim. Perhaps she had already vented her anger on Derek. No one could have called her friendly exactly, but at least there was less overt hostility than of late.

'What next?' Lizzie demanded.

'Sift through the rest of the in-tray while I wait for a response from our two witnesses,' Kate said. 'There's lots of routine stuff I can do for Derek. And Tammy may need a partner; she's ready to make an arrest.'

'Oh, yes. The Heath case. No, I'll go out there with her. Tell you what you should do. You should take a look at some of those properties Mrs Barr supposedly left Cornfield. See what they add up to.'

'By his own admission, a very great deal. With respect, though, Gaffer, much as I'd like a trip to the seaside, isn't it a bit premature to whiz off anywhere till we've got some hard evidence against the guy? Harder evidence, at any rate.'

'Who said anything about the seaside?'

'Torquay; Frinton; Scarborough,' Kate enumerated them on her fingers. 'Inland, Cheltenham, Harrogate, Hampstead. All nice places, but all a bit far afield. What I planned to do was check them through the Land Registry and with the local councils – find out their council tax rating and so on.'

Lizzie raised her eyes heavenwards. 'You mean you haven't done that already? What planet are you on?'

'There's no argument about them, though, Gaffer. Cornfield admits they're worth millions.'

Lizzie hesitated for a second, her face clouding with

doubt. Had it really penetrated that Kate was doing her best? Whatever she might have been about to concede, however, was interrupted by the phone.

'Who? Yes, absolutely. As soon as—' Whatever it was that someone wanted, she flapped Kate away with a backward waft of her hand.

Kate had reached Hampstead on her list of phone enquiries about Mrs Barr's houses and was humming along to more interminable phone music when there was a light tap and Rod Neville's face appeared round the office door. Kate wasn't sure whether to cut the call and stand up or wave an informal hand. He sauntered across to the kettle and hunted for a clean mug. Informality was in order then. Derek, arms full of files, stopped dead as he crossed the threshold. Try as she might to concentrate on the person who'd at long last consented to pick up the phone at the other end, Kate watched the interplay between the men. It seemed that coffee was in order for all three of them. However, the information she got from the phone startled her back to the matter in hand. Mrs Barr's Hampstead properties were in the highest two council tax bands.

Rod passed her her mug and pulled a chair up, sitting astride it. Shirtsleeves, no tie. My goodness, was this the informal approach or what?

'Kate, I've just been sent a couple of comps for an antiques fair at the National Exhibition Centre. Are you interested? Starts Thursday, but runs through till Sunday.'

Antiques! A chance to pick up some furniture to replace that damaged in the fire! She beamed.

'Do I take that as a yes?'

'Not so much a yes as a yes please. But it had better be the weekend, Rod – we're quite busy here.'

'Fine.' He fished out his electronic organiser, which he held up, grimacing. 'Present from my mother so I've got to learn how to use it. Which is better, Saturday or Sunday? Actually, Saturday would be better for me.'

'Saturday it shall be, then.'

He grinned – unbuttoned indeed. 'I'll pick you up from your house about ten-thirty, then – always assuming I can fight my way into that car park you call a road.' He waved and was gone.

Which allowed Derek's eyebrows to return to their normal position.

'I told you we were mates,' Kate said. 'Meanwhile, have you any idea just how much Max Cornfield may be worth now?'

He whistled. 'That's a hell of an incentive to forge a will, isn't it?'


Kate slumped against the lift wall as the doors closed. She pulled herself up quickly as they opened again. Lizzie. Great: she'd probably get a bollocking for going home only an hour after she was supposed to.

As she braced herself, however, she realised that she

hadn't been the only one straightening her shoulders. Lizzie had looked limp as a rag doll. Her redhead's pale skin was white.

On impulse Kate said, 'Fancy a quick half, Gaffer?'

She might have overshot. Lizzie's lips tightened. Then she managed a half-smile. 'You know, I just might. Yes, that'd be good.'

They'd left the building and were halfway to the pub before she spoke again. 'It really gets to you, this heat, doesn't it? Especially at night.'

'Trouble sleeping?' Kate risked.

'In spades. The heat,' she repeated, as if to reassure herself.

'Have you tried—'

'I don't take pills, Power. Not for trivial things like that. They're addictive.'

'So's not sleeping. Been there, Gaffer, got a collection of T-shirts. Tell you what, when things got bad with the fire and everything, someone put me on to some homeopathic sleeping tablets, guaranteed non-addictive.'

'Who are you trying to kid?'

'Well,' Kate said, as mildly as she could, 'I'm not taking them now. Honestly, you can't afford to miss your sleep, not in a job like yours.'

'There's always a stiff whisky,' Lizzie said, closing the door firmly on the discussion.

So what could they talk about? Kate ran various possibilities through her mind. In the end she decided to make a pre-emptive strike. She could tell Lizzie about Rod, before rumour told Lizzie about Rod. At least there'd be a modicum of truth in her version.

If Lizzie were listening, she didn't show it. She managed an abstracted nod, and didn't seem to register Kate's offer of a drink. At last, settling down at an outside table with white wine for two, Kate said as delicately as she could, against the noise of a city rush-hour, 'Lizzie, you've not been looking yourself recently. Are you sure you're all right?'

'I told you. I'm not sleeping. I'm getting by on two or three hours at most. How do you expect me to look?'

Kate swallowed and tried again. 'Usually there's something worrying people when they can't sleep.'

Lizzie downed the wine in one gulp. 'I appreciate your interest, Kate, but there really is nothing wrong with me that a good night's sleep won't put right. Now, I've just remembered I need to pick up some food. So I'll be off.'

Kate would have one last try. 'My fridge is pretty empty, too. How about we find a pizza or something?'

'Honestly, Kate! I told you, I have to go and shop. I'll see you in the morning.'

More slowly, Kate finished her drink. On impulse she used her mobile phone to page her answerphone. Yes! Graham might manage to get round at about eight.

She got home at seven-fifty. And spent the rest of the evening on her own.

# Chapter Fourteen

*Dear Sergeant Power,* Dr Steiner's letter ran, *I hope this provides you with all the handwriting you need. I was asked by my good friend Max Cornfield to witness the signature of Mrs Sylvia Hermione Barr. Rather to my surprise, despite his urgings even at the eleventh hour that she should employ a solicitor, Mrs Barr dictated to Max her will, which was then duly witnessed. Mrs Barr was by now too distressed for Max to contemplate leaving her to fulfil the evening engagement we had planned.*

Derek, who was reading over Kate's shoulder, said, 'To my untutored eye, his handwriting corresponds with the will signature.'

'It should do. It's not with Steiner's moniker we have the problem, remember. It's Leon Horowitz's. And there's something I don't like about this letter.'

Derek picked it up. 'Such as what?'

'Such as the very terse account of the signing. No mention of Horowitz at all. Jesus,' Kate sighed, 'what if Steiner and Cornfield have cooked up a nice little conspiracy between them?'

Derek snorted. 'For God's sake, Kate, if you're on to the problem this quickly, it should be a piece of cake! You should be dancing on the desk, not looking as if you'd like to hide under it.'

She opened her mouth to tell him that Cornfield deserved his money. But shut it again. As Mrs Duncton had pointed out, her feeling had nothing to do with the law.

'Let's see what Horowitz's letter says, shall we?'

'Always assuming he sends one, of course.'

'How long will you give him?'

'Another twenty-four hours at least. I've no idea how good the Portuguese postal system is, but I'd bet the German one would be better. If I don't hear anything by tomorrow noon, I'll phone him again – just to jog his memory,' she added grimly. 'Meanwhile, what's new in the in-tray?'

Despite Derek's huge groan, there was nothing so urgent that she had to cancel a lunch-time hair appointment she'd managed to fix after that long Sunday evening stare in the mirror. She was staring again, now, at Guiseppe, the stylist, shearing swathes from the back.

'Not too much,' she urged.

'Sorry?' His accent was more Midlands than Milan.

If only he didn't have the radio going full blast he might be able to hear. My God, this must be what happened when you grew old. You complained about loud music. She hesitated. Perhaps it was the quality of the music, which would surely have been naff even when it was new, which it certainly wasn't now. Still, that was perhaps what local radio listeners liked.

'Not too much,' she repeated.

'Signorina, this is so *ageing*,' he said, grabbing the rest and pulling it out of sight. 'Look, this is your jawbone again, and look — if I trim this — your cheekbones are back.'

So they were.

'What,' she began slowly, 'if I were to consider some colour?'

'You can consider all you like, but it couldn't be today. I've got an appointment list this long.' None the less he paused to consider, holding her hair to the light and letting it fall again. 'Have you ever thought of a nice red tint?'

The news jingle spared him an unfairly pungent reply. And then a news item.

Her stomach clenched. 'Forget the colour. How soon can you get me out of here?'

It was a further ten minutes before she could sprint back to work. By then, the headline had made the newspaper vendors' boards:

## FOUR OAKS WOMAN DEAD
## IN FRENZIED ATTACK

'Don't ask me how I knew. I just did,' she told a highly sceptical Lizzie.

'You're telling me that out of all the women in the

Midlands you intuited that it would be one who gave you tea that would be killed. Come on, Kate.'

'At least my intuition's been backed by hard facts,' she said tartly. 'Mavis Duncton, née Barr, preferring to be called Maeve, is dead. And I can offer the investigating team ready gift-wrapped two nice suspects, plus possible motivation.'

'Who's running the MIT? Or is it called something else this week?'

'I've an idea it might have changed from a murder investigation team to a murder investigation unit, or it might just have changed back again.'

Lizzie managed what seemed to be a genuinely comradely grin. 'All these bloody initials,' she said. 'I always used to say we ought to have a handbook saying what they stood for. Trouble is, it would be out of date in a week.'

'Oh, less. So – MIT or MIU or whatever – shall I pop along and give them chapter and verse?'

The quality of Lizzie's grin changed perceptibly. 'Why not? Tell you what, though, Power. Keep your hands off Neville's prick.'

Was it supposed to be a joke? If she didn't laugh was it because she didn't have a sense of humour?

'Oh,' she said, as off-hand as she could, 'I prefer to keep my prick-feeling for after hours. Don't you?'

'That's not what I heard.'

'Then you heard wrong, ma'am. And I'd like to make a formal request that you check the origins of any gossip before you pass it on.' She turned on her heel and walked out.

*

Rod was on the phone when Kate opened his office door. Smiling, he waved her to a chair, while he carried on talking and making the occasional note. Kate took deep breaths and looked at the pictures on the wall: he'd brought them from his Steelhouse Lane office. With a bit of luck her pulse would have returned to normal by the time he could switch his attention to her.

He cut the call and came round the desk, half sitting on it while he spoke. 'You look upset. Lizzie?'

'That's neither here nor there at the moment, Rod. I just want to know who's in charge of the team dealing with the Duncton death. I've got information they should have.' She faltered. Why on earth hadn't she simply asked his secretary?

'She's been having another go at you, hasn't she?' he asked, reaching back for a file as he spoke. 'There you are. Dave Allen. No jokes about his name and being a comedian. The incident room's already up and running in Sutton. Dave'll be glad to see you. Do you want to be seconded on to his team? He's not exactly mob-handed, and it'd get you out of Fraud for a bit. Out of Lizzie's fire.'

She shook her head. 'Thanks for the offer, but no. A, I want to stick with the case I'm on, and B, she'd see it as a victory. I tried to talk to her last night. Rod, there is something wrong, I'm sure of it, but she clammed as soon as I tried to press her.'

'I'm glad you tried, anyway.'

She smiled, and made for the door.

The phone rang. He picked up the handset but covered it immediately. 'Kate, your hair looks really good!' he whispered.

They exchanged a friendly wave, and she was on her way to Sutton Coldfield.

However busy he undoubtedly was, DCI Dave Allen gave her a friendly wave as she peered round the incident room door. He was about fifty, his figure sagging into a paunch. His eyebrows were already caterpillaring into a tired old man's furrows. But his smile lit up his face.

'Two possible leads, I gather,' he said with no preamble. 'Shoot. I've tickets booked for my holiday and I'd hate to have to cancel.'

'Only possibles.' Perhaps her desire to get out of Lizzie's orbit for the afternoon had inflated their importance. She's got a brother who loathes her and she may not have endeared herself to her late mother's man of all work.' She could have phoned, radioed, e-mailed, for God's sake, but she'd come out all this way. OK, she'd brought photocopies of all the relevant interview transcripts, could chew over likelihoods and problems, but truly she didn't need to be here. Despite what she'd said to Rod, yes, perhaps Lizzie's harassment was getting to her.

At any rate, it was good to be back in the bustle of an active inquiry, as opposed to the quiet, almost studious environment of the office she shared with Derek.

'I've got to out to the scene again in five minutes. Care to come?' Dave asked. 'Another pair of eyes, and all that.'

*Yes, yes, yes!* 'If I can be of any use,' she said, cautiously.

'My wedding anniversary in Mauritius tells me *any* extra help would be worth having. And you can fill me in on these suspects as we go.'

The whole caboodle was waiting for them: more police cars than anyone working in Fraud could imagine, a couple of vans, two big private cars and the news media, plus yards of police tape and – already – a couple of sheaves of flowers. The neighbourhood was too middle-class for hordes to be out rubbernecking, but blinds and net curtains were certainly a-twitch.

Mrs Duncton had died messily in her kitchen. Her blood had splattered all her immaculate Hygena units, trickled down the window, seeped under the back door. Some bone and brains around, too, on the newspapers spread, for some reason, all over the floor.

'Have you found the murder weapon yet?'

He shook his head. 'We're still at the no-stone-unturned stage. It'll help when the path. tells us what we're looking for. A bit more specific than hard and heavy, anyway. No sign of any forced entry, by the way. Looks as if she let in her killer. She might even have been making him a cup of tea. The bastard.' He swallowed hard, adding, as he ushered her quickly outside into the garden, 'Could either of your suspects have done this?'

'One's a retired doctor, so you'd have thought he might

be a bit more scientific. The other looked after a crazy old woman for years without laying a finger on her. But it'd be nice to check their alibis.' She breathed deeply to get the smell of blood from her nostrils.

'Motivation?'

'As far as her doctor brother was concerned, she was more anxious, I'd have thought, to kill him. But who can tell with dysfunctional families?'

'And the other one?'

Kate looked soberly back at the bloodstains on the window. Could the gentle, courteous, bereft Max Cornfield have done such a thing? 'Well,' she said, recalling Mrs Duncton's words, 'it was she who got between him and about twelve million quid.'

'I'd say that was a motive.'

They walked silently down to the bottom of the garden, turning back to look at the house. Dave sniffed deeply. Then snorted.

'Good clean country air my arse. What's the pong?'

Kate pointed. 'Could be the compost heap. Or maybe that lot – manure of some sort. They took their gardening very seriously. Which reminds me. Her husband. How did he take it?'

'Gibbering. Practically certifiable. Heavily sedated. Poor man found her. Tried mouth-to-mouth, he says. Covered in her blood. The forensic people have his clothes, incidentally, just in case he killed her first and found her second, if you see what I mean.'

Kate saw. 'How old is he? What does he look like? You

see, I saw this oddball I took to be the gardener. But Mrs
D was so off-hand he could have been a husband she'd just
had a row with.'

'Or simply not be on speaking terms with,' he amended.
'They certainly had separate bedrooms. We've checked —
not a photo lying around of them as a couple. Come to
think of it, no photos lying around full stop. Makes a house
a home, having pictures of the family, doesn't it? All your
loved ones.'

Kate nodded. Not a lot of chance her having a photo of
Graham anywhere. And there'd be nothing like a photo
of Robin on her bedside table to make Graham lose his
erection.

'We could organise it so you could get a quick shuftie
of the bloke in hospital, medics permitting, of course,'
Dave continued, 'in case the gardener and husband are one
and the same. Talk to Jane McCallum when we get back to
the nick.'

They started walking slowly back.

'Anyone else in the frame?' Kate asked. 'I know I drank
tea with the woman, but we never got on to the intimacies
of family and friends. Did she have children?'

'Not to my knowledge.'

Kate slapped the side of her head. 'There was an
estranged sister. What was her name?' She snapped her
fingers. 'Something as old-fashioned as Mavis, which is
what Mrs Duncton was called before she changed it to
Maeve. Edna. That's it. And she was about four years older
than Maeve. The person you really need to talk to, Dave,

about the Barr family is none other than suspect number two, Mrs Barr's handyman.'

He nodded, making a note. 'Do you fancy talking to him about this Edna?'

'In general or in the context of this crime?'

'Let me think about that one.' He looked at his watch and speeded up.

'Gaffer, have you time for me to have a look at the house?'

He looked again. 'If you take more than three minutes you'll have to hitch a lift back.'

'No problem. You've got enough cars out there.'

'You Fraud people; always whinging about not having transport . . .'

By common consent, they turned away from the back door walking round to the front of the house. A uniformed constable half-saluted and pushed it open for them.

'Anything out of place?' Dave asked, as she stared round the hall.

She shook her head. 'Strange, I hardly registered this when I came to talk to her. She whisked me into the living room. Have the SOCOs finished in there yet?'

He put his head round the door, then waved her in, standing arms akimbo while she looked round.

'Where did you stand, where did you sit?' he prompted her anxiously.

'She'd have done better without help. Biting her lip, she sat down on the sofa she'd sat on before. She blinked, looking around, closing her eyes to his glances at his watch, her ears to the sound he made sucking his teeth.

'Did you find any pottery lying around, Gaffer?'

'Pottery?'

'She had a valuable piece of something called Ruskin: it used to be in the middle of that shelf.' She pointed to the display shelves. 'It was lovely: about a foot tall, purple and red. *Sang de boeuf* she called it.'

'*Sang* – doesn't that mean blood? We've got enough of that in the kitchen!'

'But no shards?'

He shook his head: 'Apparently not. But with all the smears and everything, someone— Hell, Power, are you suggesting he whacked her with a vase?'

'Or did the mysterious "he" whack her with something else: surely a vase wouldn't on its own make the sort of mess in there?' She jerked her head towards the kitchen. 'And then he steals the pot?' She shook her head doubtfully. 'I know she said it ought to be in a museum, but would that make it valuable enough to steal?'

'You tell me, Power. Trouble is, if it is, it wouldn't half widen the list of possible suspects, wouldn't it?'


But it wouldn't be left to supposition. SOCO would get on to it. Bins would be searched, the pathologist consulted. Not just any pathologist, of course. Her old friend Pat the Path, he of the motorcycle collection, which had now started to spread from the huge room in which he'd kept them into a purpose-built centrally-heated garage. She could phone him up and pick his brain. She could even suggest a meal. That would be an evening satisfactorily filled.

On the way back Dave talked about his daughter's degree, his forthcoming anniversary, all the cheerful domesticity anyone could crave. Despite the afternoon free from Lizzie's attacks, despite the sense that she'd done well and was for a change appreciated by a boss, Kate was biting her lip in misery as Dave pulled up alongside her car.

She felt him looking at her.

'Come on, lass. Come and have a cup of tea with the team. No matter how tough you are, no matter how many times you've seen worse before, it always gets to you, doesn't it? Tell you what, I've got this supply of biscuits I keep for just such a day as this. And when you look a bit brighter, Jane'll fix for you to visit Mr Duncton.'

The red light was pulsing on her answerphone when she got home. Graham? But even as she reached for the play-button, she hesitated. What if he promised to come and then didn't turn up again? She couldn't wait in all evening on the off-chance.

She could. Worse, she would.

No, nothing from Graham, not even an apology for letting her down. But one from Rod.

'I hear you've so impressed Dave Allen that he'd like to co-opt you on to his team, pro tem at least. Are you quite sure you wouldn't like me to say yes?'

# Chapter Fifteen

Should she accept Rod's offer? It would take her away from Lizzie, sure, but it would also take her away from Graham: the long hours of overtime on a murder inquiry weren't conducive to snatched early evening meetings. If only she could phone him, talk it through with him. Even as she lay awake worrying, she hated herself. This was her job, the one she wanted to do, the one she was good at. It ought to outweigh the demands of even such a dear lover as Graham. After all, she told herself sadly, his job, not to mention his marriage, always took precedence over their time together.

At three she pulled herself out of bed. No, not the whisky she desperately wanted, but some of the homeo-pathic tablets she'd recommended to Lizzie.

They worked so well that she was still asleep when the phone rang at seven. It was Dave Allen, telling her that he'd officially requested her services, as long as their two cases were linked. She could meet Jane McCallum at the University hospital, the one to which Mr Duncton had finally been admitted, at eight. OK?

OK indeed. She'd rarely showered more quickly, and ate

her breakfast at the wheel. Two main roads separated Kings Heath from the west of the city; fortunately she'd be going against or across the flow of rush-hour traffic. But – spineless as it seemed – it was good to have had the decision taken out of her hands. Even if the first thing she was likely to get was a bollocking for not having found the approximate value of that vase. If anyone would know, of course, it might well be Rod. Which should she phone: his home, his office or his mobile number? Given the sort of man he was, the second seemed possible. She pulled over and tapped.

He answered second ring. Even at that time he must have someone with him, responding to her cheery, 'Morning Gaffer,' with a formal, but still very cordial, 'Good morning, Sergeant: can I call you back?'

'On my mobile,' she said.

His call came through while she was parking at the hospital and smarting at having to pay a fee.

'*Sang de boeuf* Ruskin? How big?'

At least he knew what she was talking about, which was more than she did. She gave him the approximate dimensions.

'You're probably talking about three k.,' he said. 'Give or take five hundred.'

'Not worth killing anyone for,' she said, disappointed.

'I wouldn't have thought so,' he agreed. 'Though there are fanatics. Do you really like it? There'll be some at the

NEC on Saturday.' He sounded as excited as a schoolboy.

She responded in kind. 'That's great. But tell you what, Rod, if you want to see some more lovely stuff, make an excuse to drop round at the Dunctons' house.'

'I may well. What time will you be there?'

*Careful, Kate!* 'Depends when Dave Allen sends me there. He seems a good bloke, Rod.'

'One of the best. A good old-fashioned copper. I'd better go—'

'Before you do,' she cut in, 'let me just say this. Thanks for – sorting this out.'

'My pleasure,' he said, as if he meant it.


There was no pleasure in the brief visit to Mr Duncton, who lay on his back apparently seeing nothing in a side ward. The only sign of life was the tears trickling slowly from his blank eyes. She wasn't authorised to ask any questions, and it was clear he was in no state to make rational responses.

Jane McCallum, a chubby but spruce young black woman with a strong accent she cheerfully declared to be from Dudley, nodded sadly as they walked side by side into the already warm sunshine. 'Poor old bastard. Finding your wife like that. Now, sixty-four thousand dollar question, Kate – gardener or not?'

'Gardener, Jane. And the sad thing is I don't reckon he had all his marbles when I saw him the other day. It's about time to access his medical records, if you ask me.'

'You're not suggesting he did it?' Jane looked genuinely shocked.

'To be entirely honest with you, I'd rather it were him than either of the other possible suspects. And it'd make Dave's holiday look a lot safer if it weren't some batty burglar. I'll get uniform on to the records.' She fished out her phone and dialled. 'There. That's that sorted. Now, what's on for the rest of the day?'

'Hasn't anyone told you? God, they don't let the grass grow, do they. We're straight off to talk to your two: the brother and the handyman, right?'

Kate nodded. 'In any special order?'

'You're the gaffer.'

'I know Mrs Duncton had a row with her brother. What about him first? He lives out Tamworth way.'

'Nice day for a run in the country. What about your car? Do you want to drop it back at the nick or leave it here?'

'I'm not leaving it here,' Kate said positively. 'I'd need a mortgage to retrieve it.'


'My God,' Kate said, as Jane pulled over on to Dr Barton's drive. 'Wouldn't you just die for a house like that?' It was, as Barton had said, a perfect Queen Anne in warm red brick.

'Are we talking mortgage or gift here?'

'Oh, if you had to worry about paying the mortgage, you couldn't afford to live here. Tell you what, Jane, this is the best-heeled family I've ever come across. Where do you reckon they got their loot from?'

'God knows. And he's not telling me, either.'

'Maybe the good doctor will,' Kate said grimly. 'Let's see, shall we?'

No one would have suspected when Kate introduced Jane that Dr Barton was anything other than delighted to see them both, though he tempered his enthusiasm with a decent sigh. 'I suppose you've come to talk about poor Maeve's death. Do step inside.'

Smiling sympathetically, Kate looked about her. If she had a hall as elegant as this she sure as hell wouldn't leave books or ugly piles of paper on each stair tread.

'My filing system,' Barton said. 'I have a project in mind . . . a book. One always intends to write when one retires, but then finds there's even less time than when one was working.'

'That's what everyone says,' Jane agreed. 'The main thing is to live long enough to enjoy your retirement.'

'Quite.'

The hall itself was perfectly tidy except for a suitcase-on-wheels tucked behind a side-table, but the sun-filled sitting room had two or three heaps of paper on the floor.

'I must say, I found the whole process distinctly upsetting. I saw some very unpleasant sights in my medical career, but – dear me . . . Most distressing. Most.'

'I'm sorry you had to be involved, Dr Barton,' Jane said, pesonifying sympathy and understanding. 'But we did need next of kin—'

'And unless you find the missing Edna, I am of course that.'

There was something in his intonation that intrigued Kate. 'The missing Edna,' she prompted.

'It's a long story. Why don't you two ladies sit down and I'll make some coffee?'

Jane nodded. 'That would be very kind.'

But neither woman sat. Jane looked out of the window, while Kate was drawn to the plates and jugs on a battered-looking cupboard.

'You're admiring my majolica ware,' Barton said, returning with a laden tray which he placed on a law table.

'Of course! I thought I knew it from somewhere. The Uffizi? No, the Bargello.'

He nodded with approval. 'Mine are later than that, of course. But still a little early for the house, as is the court cupboard.' He came and stroked it lightly. 'One of the bonuses of a bachelor existence, Sergeant. One can spend any money that comes one's way exactly as one wants to. Please, do sit down.'

Jane looked around her. 'It's quite a big house for one person,' she said mildly, as she arranged her skirt.

So why did that comment irritate him? There was no doubt that there was a compression of the mouth, of the nose. But he said nothing, pouring coffee from a silver pot into delicate china cups. More silverware for the sugar and milk. Kate was tempted to take sugar for the sheer pleasure of using those delicate little tongs.

'Your late sister and her Ruskin collection, you and this

lovely majolica ware — what does Edna collect, Dr Barton?'

He raised an elegant eyebrow. 'In the days when she still lived in the family home, men. Very much in the plural. With the knowledge I have now, I'd say she was a nymphomaniac. In those days my mother simply described her as man-mad and showed her the door. A little' he sighed, 'before she showed me the same door. However, I had qualifications to earn a good living, which I fear poor Edna didn't — unless you count a pneumatic body as a career asset, which she may well have done.'

*Pneumatic!* His sister? She must tread carefully here. 'Your break with your family was sufficiently final for you to change your surname.'

He nodded. 'But I had the incentive of that legacy, remember.'

'Did you at that point seek a reconciliation with Edna? You had something in common, after all. A row with your mother, being thrown out.'

He shifted uneasily. 'It wasn't quite as straightforward as that, Sergeant. A medical — an ethical — problem was involved in my name change, too. If you care to check the records you'll find an . . . indiscretion with a patient. It was forty years ago. My record since, may I add, is entirely unblemished. But no, I never liked either of my sisters sufficiently to seek one out or maintain much more than decent contact with the other.'

'You mean Christmas and birthdays, that sort of thing?' Jane asked.

He nodded.

'A little more than that, surely,' Kate put in. 'After all, you were in contact over the will, were you not? And you had a disagreement. You tried to curb her interference.'

'I believe in fair play, Sergeant. What happened was this: Max let both of us know – he's a decent punctilious man, Sergeant! – when mother was dying, and then when she died. He told us about the will, in due course. Maeve acted on her own initiative. When she told me I was appalled. Without Max, mother would have been sectioned years ago. Without Max, there would be no family fortune to squabble about. He did everything a highly paid PA would have done, plus one hell of a lot more. Nurse, gardener, estate manager. Max. All, as far as I can tell, without a penny of salary.'

Both women whistled.

Kate set her cup aside. 'Did I hear you correctly? No salary?'

'Payment in kind. Food, shelter, in the early days. They had this strange devotion, Sergeant. I never asked what was at the bottom of it, but they were like this,' he crossed his fingers, 'from day one. So, as I said to you the other day, Max is entitled to whatever he gets.'

'Even if it's in the region of millions?' Kate asked. 'Several millions?'

'Were it a king's ransom,' he said. He allowed himself a glance at his watch.

'Would your other sister think that?'

He raised eyes and hands heavenwards. 'How on earth would she know? I can assure you I haven't told her, because

I couldn't, and I'm positive that Maeve wouldn't because if Maeve didn't want Max to get it she sure as hell wouldn't have wanted Edna to get her claws on it.' He looked much less covertly at his watch.

Jane caught Kate's eye. 'Are we taking up too much of your time, sir?'

'It's just that I do have to get to the airport. A holiday in—'

'Have you had it booked long, sir?'

His mouth and nose tightened again. 'An impulse. After the distress.'

'Of course,' Kate commiserated. 'The trouble is, sir, in the middle of a murder inquiry it's best if those involved – the family and so on – remain where we can reach them easily. Sometimes there's even the formality of handing over a passport.'

'Are you saying I can't go, Sergeant?'

She smiled. 'I think my boss might find it suspicious if you suddenly flit the country on a surprise holiday, don't you?'

'Not a happy bunny,' Jane observed, heading for the A453. 'Mind you, I wouldn't be if someone stopped me nipping off to the South of France. The sun, the blue skies, the sea.'

Kate rolled down the window, wafting in what little coolness there was. 'The only thing we're missing as far as I can see is the sea. Mind you, you're right. I don't think it'll be any consolation to him that weather's better here than it is in Nice, according to the papers.' She fanned herself. 'Days like this, it's better to be plain clothes than uniform, isn't it?'

'Tell me any day when it isn't. Now, our friend Max, next – right?'

'Right. Tell me,' Kate added thoughtfully, 'did you notice anything when he was talking about his family?'

'Should I have done?'

'Maybe not. But it's a funny thing; neither he nor his sister ever mentions their father. The one who provided all the dosh. There's a story there. Maybe we should ask Max.'

Jane looked at her sideways. 'I thought we were supposed to be asking Max much more important things.'


'My whereabouts yesterday? Where do you expect me to be in such weather, but in my garden? I've made a good start: come and see the progress.' He ushered them along the gloomy hall straight through the conservatory into the garden.

Jane stopped short, blinking. 'Hey, it's like a bloody park!'

Max raised an amused eyebrow at her accent. 'See, I've cut down those old sycamores. Needed to before they fell, really. And that patch where it was covered in brambles. All gone.'

'You'll have the cats in there.' Kate pointed at the fine tilth. She sniffed.

'Ah, you've come to tell me I've been breaking the law.

At least, a bye-law. I know, Sergeant, I know. No garden bonfires. But what could I do with it all?' He kicked some of the ash. 'I started with several bundles of newspapers, then added some wood, then . . . then Mrs Barr's bedding. Then more wood, and then the brambles!'

'What time did you start it?' Kate asked.

He narrowed his eyes questioningly. 'About two, maybe.'

'What did you do earlier in the day?' Jane asked.

Arms spread, he laughed. 'I told you; I had my therapy. I cut, I saw, I hack. And then I get rid of everything.'

Kate froze: that was an ambiguous sentence if she'd ever heard one. 'I suppose none of the neighbours saw you – *could* see you? You didn't go out to the shops at all?'

'Sergeant, something tells me this is about more than whether I needed fresh milk. Oh, it's that will, that bloody will again. I tell you, I wish she'd never made it, and if she had, I'd put it straight on the bloody fire!'

Jane reached out a restraining arm, but Kate shook her head.

'I'm sorry, ladies. For nearly fifty years I've been as quiet as a lamb. And suddenly for no reason I lose my temper and . . . please forgive me.'

Kate nodded, turning to lead the way back to the house. She sat on the garden bench.

'So you were here in the garden all morning. But no one could see you.'

'They'd have heard me. They'd have heard me, Sergeant. All that – you don't do it quietly.' He held her gaze. 'I have a feeling you're trying to tell me bad news.'

'Someone's died, I'm afraid.'

He shook his head impatiently. 'You don't send two police officers to tell an old man someone's died. You don't ask for an alibi because someone's died.'

'You do if they've been killed, Mr Cornfield,' Jane said.

He jumped as if he'd forgotten she was there. He spoke to Kate. 'Who's been killed?'

'Mrs Barr's daughter,' she replied quietly.

He turned to her eyes wide with disbelief. 'An alibi . . . Killing . . . Why on earth would I want to kill Maeve Duncton?'

# Chapter Sixteen

'Thank goodness for DNA and all the rest of the SOCOs' tricks,' Dave Allen said, breathing pickled onion at them over his half of mild. 'It's just a matter of time before they come up with the answers. Meanwhile, you're convinced that this Cornfield guy was surprised by the news.'

'Surprised. Shocked. Disconcerted.'

'OK, Power, spare us the thesaurus. I get the picture. Jane?'

'Yeah, gobsmacked, Gaffer. Plus of course, he must have some sort of alibi, assuming he's telling the truth. He must have made such a racket with his deforestation that someone would have heard him, even if they didn't actually see him. A day like yesterday, there must have been loads of people wandering round their gardens. That old biddy that lives next door, for instance.'

'Mrs Hamilton. Yes, I'll pop round again on my way home,' Kate said. 'Plus people in the offices and consulting rooms along the street. And I bet the council logged half a dozen complaints the moment the fire was lit.'

'No takers,' Dave laughed. 'Another half, ladies? No, I

suppose you shouldn't, not really.' He gathered the glasses and toddled off to the bar.

Kate shifted in her seat. 'A bit laid back, all this,' she said quietly, 'considering we're in the middle of a murder inquiry.'

'You mean you'd rather be dashing round like a blue-arsed fly getting stomach ulcers?'

'Yes, frankly.'

'Well, I'll go to the bottom of our stairs! They told us you lot from the Met were workaholic masochists. No, this is how *this* team works, Kate. You'll just have to stick a gera-nium in your hat and get on with it. Each day he'll take a couple of us down the boozer and hear what we've been up to. That way he gets to know us and makes sure we have a break. Mind you, he'll phone at the weirdest times and expect a sensible answer. That's his way. Oh, and he's dead keen on pork scratchings.'

Kate wasn't about to argue about the weird hours phone calls. And she didn't think she'd argue about the team-building, either.

'Do you reckon this Cornfield knew that Mrs Duncton had snitched on him about the will?' Allen asked, plonking himself down again and slinging crisps on to the table.

'Thanks, Gaffer. He might have guessed, but neither of us enlightened him,' Jane said. 'Not a very big field, I suppose. Her or her brother.'

'He might think it's to do with the courts, on the other hand – you know, random checks on handwritten wills: that sort of thing.' Allen drank deeply. 'Ah, good drop of mild, this. Banks's. Have this down south, do they, Kate?'

'What,' she asked, laughing, 'do you think keeps me up here? The mild, of course! That,' she added more seriously, 'and the Ruskin pottery, of course. That vase that's missing – it could be worth about three thousand.'

'You're joking! All that for a bit of a pot! But it doesn't seem valuable enough to crack someone over the head for.' He raised his glass. 'Good quick work, though, Kate.'

She'd never known how to accept compliments. 'That's what they teach you up here in Brum.'

'Jesus! Brum! That's a foreign country,' Jane said. 'We'm both from the Black Country, our kid, and don't you forget it!'

The chirrup of Allen's mobile phone cut short their laughter. Eyebrows down – eyebrows up once more. And back down. Mouth compressed and relaxed by turns. Oh, yes, there was news, wasn't there?

'Right,' Allen said, stowing the phone. 'They've found summat I'd like you to see, me wench.'

The accent he'd dropped into wasn't quite Jane's Dudley but it wasn't Brum, either. One of these days she'd have to sort out this Black Country business.

'What sort of summat?' she asked, as he drained his glass in one swig and got to his feet.

'Wait and see,' he said. 'Jane – see you back at the incident room – right?'

He slung Kate his car keys. 'Don't like driving when I need to think,' he said. 'Don't like talking overmuch, either, so don't be offended, my wench.'

*

Allen led Kate straight to the bottom of the garden, where the smell from the compost heap was riper than ever. How the SOCOs stomached it, she'd no idea, but they were systematically turning it over and riddling it. She squatted beside a pile of shards. It was all too clear what they'd found.

Almost immediately she was joined by another figure, altogether too tall and lithe to be Allen.

'It must have been beautiful,' Rod said almost reverently. 'Look at those colours.'

'It was,' she said. She outlined the original shape with her hands. 'Simply lovely.'

'Hang on, you two,' Allen said, sounding outraged. 'That could be our murder weapon. It smashed a woman's head in. You sound sorrier for the bloody vase than for the woman.'

They straightened, simultaneously.

Rod nodded. 'Any sign of bloodstains? Other . . . matter?'

So Rod was in his never-apologise-never-explain mode, was he? Fair enough. She'd take her lead from him. And, incidentally, remain silent till spoken to.

One of the SOCOs broke off what she was doing and pointed with a gloved finger. 'There — and there. There's more than enough for the lab. And they might like a look at this poker too.'

'Poker? In these days of central heating?' Dave asked.

'She had one of those gas fires that look like coal fires. And – yes – wrought iron fire-irons,' Kate said.

The three police officers turned back towards the house.

'So it wasn't robbery,' Allen observed heavily. 'Well,' he added, brightening, 'at least we're back to a narrower field. Maybe my holiday's looking safer.'

'So whom do you see in the frame?' Rod asked.

'The brother, who stands to pick up an extra six million quid or so and, according to Power, here, was ready to do a quick flit. Sorry, this is Kate Power, on loan from Fraud. And you'll have gathered, Kate, that this is our Big Cheese – Superintendent Neville.'

Rod smiled easily. 'Oh, we've worked together before. So, the brother or . . . ?'

'Again according to Kate, the husband's lying in a hospital bed staring at nothing crying his eyes out.'

'Out of his mind with guilt? A simple domestic, then?'

'Could be out of his mind with grief, of course. Or – and we're trying to access his medical records – just plain and simple out of his mind. What do you think, Kate?'

She awarded Allen more brownie points for being a good boss. 'I have this comic-grotesque scenario, sir. She's a very house-proud woman; you can see that. And she's got this pottery she thinks the world of. And a husband she doesn't acknowledge in conversation.'

'Or in bed, apparently,' Allen interjected. 'Two very separate bedrooms. Even two separate bathrooms, would you believe? OK, carry on.'

'Now,' she said slowly, 'say she's just cleaned her kitchen floor and she's done what my great-aunt used to do if she was in a real hurry; she's put down newspaper to protect it—'

'Which is what we found. Covered in blood,' Allen confirmed.

'And say he wanders in from the garden and makes a mess somewhere—'

'SOCO will have lifted any prints from the carpets,' Rod observed. 'OK. I'm with you so far. She tells him off and he grabs what she values and whacks her with it. And then tries to revive her.'

'He *says*,' Allen corrected him. 'But if he was cunning enough to hide that pot-thing and the poker, he might have been cunning enough to think of that as an explanation. Forgetting, of course, splatter marks. Kate, get the lab to speed things up.'

Rod would just have to do without her for the conducted tour of the house. She'd gone four or five yards when he called her back. 'Kate, could you spare me five minutes before you dash off? There's a problem back at Lloyd House,' he told Allen. 'I've an idea Fraud want her back.'

'Tell them to take a running jump,' Allen said. 'We need her here. I've got my anniversary to worry about, and their pieces of paper'll wait. In the meantime, I'll get on to the lab while you two chafe the fat.'

A sudden gust of wind enveloped them in compost smells.

'Maybe we could talk somewhere else?' Rod asked. 'The house, maybe? Dave, you may want to be in on this.'

'You know my views. And Power can show you the crime scene and such as well as I can. Don't forget Duncton's medical file, though, Kate. Or Cornfield's neighbours.'

'Gaffer!' She sketched a half-salute, which he waved away, scuttling to his car, tapping his phone as he went.

'Enjoying yourself?' Rod asked, with a quizzical, amused smile.

'A bit chastened when Dave said that stuff about valuing the vase more than Mrs D. Thing is, Rod, it's true. She was a greedy, ungrateful woman, and the world may well be a better place without her. The vase was perfect and unique and I'm missing it already!'

'What's the other stuff like?'

'It's in here, in the living room.'

He walked straight over to the display shelves, snorting. 'Why on earth didn't he choose that dreadful orange thing to clock her with?'

Kate joined him, running her eyes across the collection. 'It's a funny mixture, isn't it? Half ugly, the rest stunning.'

'Exactly what I said last time I was at the Brohan Museum, you know, in Berlin. Half the *jugendstil* and art deco I can barely live without, the other half I certainly couldn't live with. I wonder who that little beauty will end up with.' He pointed to a delicate turquoise bowl. 'Look, you can almost see through it! And the shape!'

'The rich brother, I suppose. Unless he done it. I don't think he'll like it – not his period.' She explained about the

177

majolica. 'And if he did, there's always the missing sister, Edna.'

'Do I know about her?'

'She left home over thirty years ago and no one's seen hide or hair of her since. Dave reckons we shouldn't break into a sweat finding her until we're sure the husband didn't do it.'

'How do you feel about that?'

'Makes sense. I don't know what the house-to-house had thrown up yet, of course. If a mysterious woman's been prowling round here it would certainly make life more interesting.'

'Shall we look at the rest of the place while we're here? After you.' They peered into the dining room, big but almost dwarfed by heavy oak furniture. 'What they're doing now, the dealers,' he said, 'is stripping off this stain, so it looks like wood again, and then waxing it.'

'What does it look like?'

'To my mind, heavy oak furniture stripped down and waxed! No, I'm sure we all have our favourite periods, and I'm afraid twentieth century Scottish baronial isn't mine. OK, shall we head upstairs?'

There might originally have been four bedrooms, plus a boxroom. But it looked as if the boxroom had been converted into a bathroom some time in the sixties. Cramped and full of avocado fittings, it was almost certainly the one Mr Duncton used. Mrs Duncton's was newly fitted so not a pipe showed, the cupboards full of skin preparations.

'All very expensive,' Kate said. 'Nice thick towels, too — better quality than those in his. Oh, what a sad relationship. Surely everything points to his having done it.' She caught his eye and grinned. 'Though I'll not close my mind to a mysterious woman who learns — somehow — about the loot her siblings may inherit and decides to claim her share. But it's all a bit iffy and dodgy and presupposes she knows the will's being contested.'

'Was Mrs Duncton the sort of woman to phone her up — always assuming she knew where she was — to gloat?'

'Would you? Wouldn't you just keep quiet and hope she never got wind of it? And the money was by no means in Mrs D's hands. We're still waiting a reply from one of the witnesses, by the way. I'll check into Lloyd House before I come out here tomorrow, provided it's OK with Dave. It might have got there by now.'

They started down the stairs.

'How's Lizzie?' she ventured.

'Who can tell? I heard her in full throat myself this morning administering a rare trimming to some hapless soul. Ben, I think.'

'Whose name is Derek.'

'So why does she call him Ben?'

'A joke. Derives, I gather, from when there was another guy called Bill in the team. But seems to be joke no more, not as far as Derek's concerned.'

'Hmm. I take it someone has pointed this out?'

'Yes. Me. Rod, this is just gossip, and I don't like gossip. Having been the subject of it.'

'You and Graham, you mean. These things—'

'Me and you, actually,' she said flatly. 'So it was a bit hard to deny categorically. Anyway, being tête-à-tête like this won't help our cause.'

'But we're friends!' he objected. Well, even detective superintendents could no doubt be naïve over some things.

'So you're going to put a notice in the *Police Gazette*: Rod and Kate are just good friends?'

He turned to her with an intensity that took her breath away. 'If ever you let us be more than that, nothing would give me more pleasure than to put an ad in the bloody *Times*.' He stopped, listening to voices in the hall below. 'Now, was there anything interesting in the third bedroom?' he asked, raising his voice to a more public level. 'I'm beginning to feel like Bluebeard.' He pushed open the last door.

Kate peered with him. 'I suppose you'd call it the guest room, but it's not exactly inviting, is it? All this blue paint ... Plenty of bed-time reading though.' She wandered over to the shelves that covered one wall. 'And,' she added, 'books to look at, too. Rod! Look at this!'

Rod drove her and her find back to the incident room, staying to join the team in a coffee, though up to his standard it definitely was not.

'So there we are, ladies and gentlemen – photographs of the whole Barr tribe, plus this character here who may be a suspect too,' he announced with a flourish.

Dave Allen donned reading glasses and peered closely. 'So that's Maeve — or rather, Mavis. So that must be . . . ?' He turned to Kate.

'That's Michael, the one we intercepted in mid-flit. And that must be Edna.'

'Look at those eyes,' Rod put in. 'A bit of a goer, I'd have thought. Or . . . I'm not sure. She looks . . . knowing. But vulnerable.'

Kate said, 'She may be both — according to her brother, she's a nymphomaniac who was shown the door. This young man here—'

'The drop-dead gorgeous one?' Jane asked. 'God, that's never Max Cornfield, is it? Hey, it is, too. And is this Mr Duncton? Poor ferrety-faced little git. Which leaves this couple here.'

'I suppose they must be Mrs Barr and her late un-lamented husband.'

Rod had taken another album and was turning the pages slowly. 'There are quite a lot of gaps in this, as if some have been removed. See? And someone's been cut off this one. Black sheep syndrome, I suppose. You know,' he added, laughing, 'I could almost wish that none of our existing suspects could possibly have done it. It'd be interesting to see what's happened to Edna of the come-to-bed eyes.'

Kate parked outside the Dunctons' GP's surgery, wondering if she dared leave the car windows open enough to maintain at least a minimal current of air. After all, it was an extremely couth neighbourhood. But there was car theft in even the most couth areas, so she resigned herself to getting back into an oven. Or what about the sun-roof? Yes, she could leave that open a crack.

She started with a receptionist: could she see either the practice manager or Mr and Mrs Duncton's GP? The receptionist, for whom the adjective stereotypical might have been coined, responded with an implacable wall of non-cooperation. But Kate had dealt with receptionists before: a very public display of her ID generally worked wonders.

As it – oh, so coincidentally – happened, Dr Smallwood, the Dunctons' doctor, just happened to have a cancellation, and Kate was ushered in. Not used to GPs who didn't look up, let alone get up, when she entered the room, she was immediately prejudiced against him. And against whichever medical school had let him loose on the world without teaching him manners: weren't they supposed to be high on the curriculum, these days?

'Good afternoon,' she said crisply, laying the ID ostentatiously between them. 'I wish to talk to you about Mr and Mrs Duncton.'

She was rewarded with a minimalist glance. 'Who are you – their daughter or something?' His gaze returned to the file he was perusing.

What was this rumour about people with Scots accents sounding more intelligent than the rest of the UK?

'I'm not aware that they have a daughter. Didn't your receptionist tell you that I'm a detective sergeant from

West Midlands Police? I'm one of a team investigating Mrs Duncton's death.'

This time he looked up properly. Indeed, furtively. 'Is there a problem?'

'Only inasmuch as someone appears to have killed her. Now, what I would like to do is ask if I might have access to Mr Duncton's medical record – you'll be aware that he's in the psychiatric unit of the Queen Elizabeth Hospital?'

Furtive was replaced by hostile. 'You'll be aware of the proper procedure. Your solicitor will approach the court with a request, which we will respond to.'

She sighed, a hot, tired, late-afternoon sigh. 'Is that really necessary, Doctor? We're talking a murder inquiry here. It's a matter of eliminating people from our enquiries.'

He put his fingers together in a steeple of smug self-satisfaction and shook his well-groomed head.

'Did you know the couple well?' She tried not to grit her teeth; he was, after all, within his rights.

'They've been patients at this practice – let me see . . .' He tapped his computer. 'Oh, some fifteen years now. They became nominally my patients when Dr Morgan left us. Murder?' he asked, at long last.

If she offered him a titbit would it help thaw him? 'Murder. A blow to the head. It's possible she disturbed a burglar.'

'So why do you want Mr Duncton's records?'

'It's possible she didn't.' She turned on her dimpled smile. 'So you can see why I need to look at his medical history.'

'No, I can't. Patient confidentiality, Miss — er. We have to respect patient confidentiality.'

'Well, your patient's currently dosed to the eyeballs, staring at the ceiling and weeping silently. And another one is on a mortuary slab.' She winced at her melodrama, but pressed on. 'It would help us, Doctor Smallwood, to check Mrs Duncton's file too.'

'I can't see why.'

Neither, at the moment, could Kate, but she wasn't going to be outdone for cussedness. 'Procedure,' she said briefly. And, come to think of it, there was just a chance that Mrs Duncton had mentioned any possible oddities in her husband's behaviour. Yes. Where had her brain been? 'So if I might take it? I'll receipt it appropriately, of course.'

The car was baking. It was a pity about the open sun-roof. With precise, almost scientific accuracy, a bird had splodged prolifically right in the centre of the driving-seat.

# Chapter Seventeen

Kate had been pleased that she had her own car to take her back to her part of the city. Rod was getting altogether too intense for her comfort. He seemed sublimely unaware of not just how deeply he'd hurt her before but also of the pressure any resumption of the relationship might put on her. Even if Graham weren't in the frame, she wasn't sure she wanted Rod again. And between him and Graham, there was no choice.

Was there?

Not certainly, if Graham had been free. Not, perhaps, if he could have spared her even a little more of his life than he did at the moment. On impulse, she pulled over to page her answerphone. Nothing.

No, professional women didn't cry just because their boyfriends didn't ring them, especially professional women about to talk to potential witnesses. Right. Back into the traffic, which was so heavy she parked without hesitation on Mrs Hamilton's drive.

Edward barked when she pressed the bell. Then he stopped abruptly, and she fancied she could hear his feet scuttering off. Nothing else. She rang again. This time Edward barked with increasing urgency. Soon he was barking right by the letter flap. She peered through. He barked, and then made a little scurry away. When she did nothing, he did it again, and again. Suddenly, she felt sick. He was trying to tell her something. There was only one thing to do, wasn't there?

'Kate: I am sure we are wrong to do this,' Max Cornfield said, watching her pumping the old lady's chest. 'She wouldn't want—'

'Just shut the fuck up and go and see if there's any sign of that bloody paramedic!'

Mrs Hamilton lay in the shade of Mrs Barr's Leylandii hedge, a cup of still warm tea beside her. There was a pulse, now, just about, but Kate knew she needed hospital treatment immediately if she were to have any chance. Now she paused for breath, however, she wondered if Max were right – that Mrs Hamilton wouldn't want to be pulled back to live the life of an invalid. Or worse.

Or maybe better, of course. It'd surely take more than one seizure or heart attack or whatever to lay this woman low.

She was glad, all the same, to be relieved of any further part in the proceedings. Max, running, brought the paramedics into the garden. Edward came back with him, whimpering and trying to lick the old lady's face, only to be elbowed aside.

Max took his collar. 'Come on, old boy. Come with Max and help me pack mother's case. Come on.'

Off they went. Kate didn't argue. Nor was she surprised when he returned a couple of minutes later with an overnight bag, a polythene bag containing bottles and bubble packs of pills, and an address book.

'She showed me where everything was,' he said quietly. 'These are the numbers to phone, Kate. Can I go with her?' he asked one of the paramedics. 'Until her family come, that is. This is her regular medication, by the way.' He handed it over. 'Is there time for me to go and lock up my house?'

'So long as it isn't Fort Knox.'

He went back the way they'd come in – over ladders he'd propped either side of the fence – and was waiting in the road by the time they'd carried the old lady through.

'Let me just set her burglar alarm and lock the door,' he said. 'I'll have to leave Edward in the garden, then he'll come and stay with me till . . . till everything's sorted out.'

No, a man like this couldn't have smashed a Ruskin vase over Mrs Duncton's skull, could he?

But it would be a long time – if ever – before Mrs Hamilton could provide him with an alibi. Or deny him one, of course. Meanwhile, she'd better follow the ambulance to Selly Oak Hospital, this time, where she sat in the car park, working through the list of phone numbers Max had provided.

She'd almost finished – Mrs Hamilton's relatives were widely spread, and all seemed grateful that Max Cornfield was on the scene – when there was an incoming call.

'Kate?' Graham asked cautiously, as if they might be overheard.

'Yes!' He'd hear the delight in her voice.

'It looks as if I may have a free hour or two. Can I come round?'

'Oh, Graham.' She explained.

'Can't you leave everything to this Cornfield guy? It's been so long, Kate.'

The pleading in his voice was almost irresistible. 'I'll go and see what's happening. I'll ring you back.'

She sprinted to A&E. Cornfield was sitting knees together, hands in lap. His eyes lowered, he might have been praying. Perhaps he was. It took him valuable seconds to register Kate's presence.

'Her grandson's on his way from Worcester,' she said. 'And a nephew from Leicester. But they can't be here till seven-thirty, eight.'

'I'll wait here for them,' he said. 'They're good boys, Giles and Martin. They've got copies of her living will. For my own sake,' he smiled ruefully, 'I'm glad you resuscitated her. She's a good neighbour. But she may not thank you.'

'Will she live to thank me – or otherwise?'

He shrugged sadly. 'They won't say either way. But if she lives, she'll need more support than she's been getting. And Edward will certainly need a home for a while. So it looks as if I can kiss my travelling goodbye.'

'Travelling?' she repeated sharply.

'For the last forty odd years I've been nowhere. Seen no

paintings, heard no music, basked only in the sun that chose to shine in the garden. There is a lot of world out there, Kate, and I want to see as much of it as I can before I too need resuscitating!'

She sat down and looked him straight in the eye. 'You do realise you mustn't attempt to go anywhere until both Mrs Duncton's murder and the will business have been cleared up. Anywhere.'

'But tomorrow I'm supposed to go to Cheltenham.'

'Yes. Thursday's your day for travelling.'

'You'd be surprised how lackadaisical letting agents can be – failing to inspect roofs and woodwork, for instance . . .' He tailed off, as if aware that he was talking for talking's sake. He smiled ruefully at Kate. 'I'm sure the irony that I maintain properties in distant cities to the highest of standards while living in a house on the verge of rack and ruin will not have escaped you. I used to pretend to Mrs Barr that her rents were much lower than they were so I could pay for repairs. And she had so much in the bank a little harmless deception is something I can sleep with.'

She nodded. It all made eminent sense. 'But you mustn't go anywhere without letting me know.' She gave him as many phone numbers as she could think of: Fraud, the incident room, her mobile.

'And failure to phone you would result in?'

'Probably your arrest.'

'I see. You are taking this seriously.'

'We always take murder seriously. And you're one of several people involved in the inquiry.'

'I see.' He bit his lip.

Now what? She couldn't just leave him waiting here. She was the one in charge, for God's sake. But Graham wanted her, and she wanted Graham. The only chance they'd had to be together and this must crop up. It wasn't as if she could do anything. It wasn't as if Mrs Hamilton would have wanted her around, even if she'd recognised her. But she couldn't, try as she might, allow herself to leave the old lady with only a possible killer for company.

For the first time she noticed how Cornfield was trembling. She laid her hand on his. 'Let me get you a coffee. You look as if you need one.'

He nodded. 'I've known her so long. Such a lady, Kate, such a lady. She's been unwell for so long, but refused to let go.'

She got the coffee and then buttonholed one of the staff. No reason why she shouldn't assert a little authority, in the form of her police ID, to find how things were going. And then felt horribly like Maeve Duncton, prodding people already overtaxed and under-resourced. And – in the case of the doctor, Karen Cammish, a houseman according to her badge, who crawled over to see her – overtired to the nth degree.

The prognosis – both short and long term – was hardly encouraging. Mrs Hamilton was old and frail – tell her something new! – and either shock or exertion could tip the balance of a very weak heart.

'Shock? You mean someone making her jump?'

Cammish shrugged. 'Could be anything. It could just

stop of its own accord. That's what happens when you're eighty-six.' She turned to go.

'I'm asking a very serious question, here. Could someone deliberately have tried to scare her to death?'

'D'you mean did someone try to kill her?'

'Exactly that.'

Cammish's eyes opened wide, perhaps for the first time that day. 'That's a very serious allegation.'

'Not an allegation. A question.'

The young woman shifted uneasily. Kate felt guilty about putting her on the spot, but didn't drop her gaze.

'I think you should ask the cardiologist,' Cammish said at last.

'And where is he or she?'

'Left about an hour ago. Look, I've got patients to see to.'

'Of course you have. And I'll talk to the cardiologist. Thanks.'

Another little job for the following day. She pestered the reception staff again till she got the consultant's name and his probable arrival time, and now – now she could step outside again and reach for her mobile. It was a perfect evening for lovers, wasn't it, the air still and warm, ideal for sitting in the garden lingering over a post-coital glass of wine. And she was going to have to tell Graham that she had to stay where she was until she could run Max home.

At least he understood, said he did anyway, even if he didn't sound convinced. And he'd even promised to call back every half-hour as long as the coast was clear – he couldn't risk Kate calling when his wife had returned. But she'd sensed a hint of resentment that she didn't put him first. Well, that was no doubt what his wife had done all these years: accommodated shift work, watched dinners ruined by sudden overtime, sewed extra stripes on his shirts. And weren't mistresses supposed to be even more accommodating?

Not that she was a mistress, she told herself crossly. They were lovers, equals in this relationship. Weren't they?

It was time to get back to Max. He'd drunk the coffee, and disposed of the cup, and was now sitting exactly as he was before. As she sat down, he managed a bleak smile.

'All these ladies,' he said. 'Mrs Barr and Maeve dead, and now Mrs Hamilton lying here helpless. Are you not afraid to sit down beside me, Miss Power, lest something dreadful happens to you?'

Dave Allen said something similar when she phoned him from outside Mrs Hamilton's house to report on her evening's activities and to suggest she postponed interviewing other potential witnesses till the following morning.

'Kiss of death material, this guy. Watch yourself, young Kate. Until you've got those witnesses, at least!'

Hating herself, knowing there'd be nothing, she checked for messages. No, nothing from Graham. Nothing for it but to turn for home. She felt so dismal that she didn't even stop off at the chippie for her favourite chicken tikka in a naan. A whisky, that was what she wanted. A whisky and a sandwich, and maybe not even the sandwich.

She'd just finished the first glass, and the second sat beside her elbow, encouraging her through the paperwork, when the front doorbell rang.

My God, it couldn't be, could it? Not Graham! Please God, let it be Graham.

She flew to answer it.

# Chapter Eighteen

'You were expecting your man, weren't you?' Zenia asked, standing in the dusk on Kate's doorstep. 'Poor Kate, the way your face fell when you saw it was only me.'

Kate made no attempt to deny it. 'Come along in. I've just broached the whisky bottle.'

'Oh, no, not spirits, thanks. They're fine in punch but not on their own. No way.' Zenia headed into the living room and sat down in a way that belied her next words. 'Now, I won't keep you. I can see you're busy. But my cousin's having this party and—'

'We're talking your cousin Rafe – the gorgeous one?'

'We are. Can I tell him you'll come?'

'I've got a man, Zenia.'

'You've got this much of a man.' Zenia spread index finger and thumb. 'That much only. You need the whole of a man, Kate.'

'We love each other.'

'So why was I on your doorstep, not him? And why you got the whisky and just the one glass?' Her accent slipped from slightly Brummie towards distinctly patois. 'You give my Rafe a chance, girl — he give you a better time all the time.' She dropped her voice and leaned closer. 'Tell you what, girl: the little you see of your married man, you could see both him and Rafe: Rafe'd never know the difference. And since when did anyone notice a slice off a cut loaf?'

'I couldn't . . . be . . . unfaithful to him.'

Zenia exploded with laughter. 'You mean you can't fuck with anyone else while you're waiting for him? Get real, girl, you think he doesn't fuck his wife?'

'I gather— I don't think she likes—'

'So he's just coming to you for a quick poke. God, girl, doesn't that make you feel a teeny bit like a whore?'

Kate stood up fiercely. Then she subsided. 'I love him.'

'And maybe he love you. But I don't see him here.' Zenia knelt beside her and hugged her. 'Oh, Kate: someone have to say these hard things. And seem to me that someone's me.'

The early phone call the next morning came not from Dave but from Derek to tell her that there was a letter on her desk with a foreign stamp. So instead of zapping straight across the city to Sutton Coldfield and the incident room, she joined the city centre chaos instead. As soon as she could, she phoned Dave Allen to explain and apologise. If she was expecting a howl of complaint, she didn't get it.

'I meant what I told you last night,' he said. 'Two women dead, a third at death's door. It's all beginning to

look a bit Harold Shipman, isn't it? You want to watch
yourself.'

'I will, Gaffer. Tell you what, checking this new will
stuff back here will take some time. Plus I want to decipher
what Mrs Duncton's GP laughingly calls handwriting. We
don't have Mr D's file, however.' She explained.

'Bloody hell. Don't these people realise we're trying to
find a killer?'

'Apparently not.'

'I'll get someone on to it. Sounds as if you're a bit busy.'

'Just a bit. While you're at it, Gaffer, is there any chance
of a bit of uniform support checking house to house round
Cornfield's place? Some of the houses have been divided
into offices or consulting rooms. Not to mention someone
talking to the cardiologist treating Mrs H.' She gave his
name and clinic hours.

'Your wish is my command,' he said. 'What time will
you be in?'

'As soon as I've chewed my next move over with DI
King,' she said. 'I've an idea, though, Gaffer, that someone
may be taking a couple of trips abroad, very soon.'


'And that someone is you, Power,' Lizzie said, ten minutes
later, from her side of an overflowing desk. 'Look, I've told
you: we don't fart around waiting for Foreign Office
permission. I draw up a flowery letter on best headed
paper asking in the most complicated English I can
manage for the esteemed co-operation in the matter of

whatever it is. It's always worked for me. Every time.'

Kate braced her legs. 'With due respect, Gaffer, I'd rather go through the proper channels.'

'This is an order, Power. We're so under-strength I'd welcome that *Big Issue* seller down there in the squad and they go and bloody pull you out. Oh, it's a case of what Rod Neville wants, Rod Neville gets. And don't say I didn't warn you next time he tries to get his hands in your knickers. Which you've certainly got in a twist over this will business.' Lizzie laughed. 'Now, you're on your own as far as Portugal's concerned, but, as it happens, I've got this old mate in Berlin. We had a bit of a fling when I was younger, between you and me. I'll give him a buzz. Get him to meet you off the plane at Tegel, go with you to interview this Steiner guy and take you back to Tegel. Shouldn't take you more than a day.' The laugh became a cackle. 'Though I wouldn't blame you if you wanted to take twenty-four hours so long as you didn't try to swing hotel expenses. If you want to fuck Jo, Kate, fuck him with my blessing, only do it in his flat.'

She was hardly out of Lizzie's office – seething at the thought of being bequeathed anyone's ex, but particularly Lizzie's – when Rod called her from down the corridor.

'Kate! Kate Power! Have you got a minute?'

Sergeants tended, didn't they, to have a minute for a superintendent. Kate stopped short, and walked back towards him.

'Dave Allen tells me there's been a development on the

will front. Can you brief me? Let's go down to my room. I might be able to organise some coffee.'

She had an idea that he was scrutinising her rather more closely than she'd have preferred after a particularly bad night, against which the homeopathic pills had been almost useless. They walked in silence to his office. A casual observer might have thought he was taking her back there for a bollocking. The way he ushered her in, pulling up a chair for her, however, was more social than business, as was the way he poured and handed her coffee. Again she was aware of his scrutiny.

'So what's the latest?' he asked.

'We've just had the second of the two handwriting samples I wanted,' she began, 'from Max Cornfield's friends. Neither of them, incidentally, gives an adequate account of how the signing took place. So we may have conspiracy to defraud. Worse, even to my eyes one signature at the bottom of the will doesn't seem quite the same as the one on the specimen one that's just arrived. Leon Horowitz's. And – though this may not make much sense without an explanation – he says he's right-handed. I'm talking to a forensic handwriting expert at eleven. If she thinks there's anything fishy, then I need to talk to both witnesses to compare their accounts of the will signing itself. One of whom hangs out in Berlin, the other in the Algarve. So Lizzie's told me to pack a bag. She's talking about tomorrow, if I can get a flight. Which may affect our plans for Saturday. Sorry.'

'We can always make it Sunday,' he said dismissively.

'Lizzie's dealing with all the Foreign Office red tape, I take it?'

She tried to avoid his scrutiny. 'Sure: everything's in her hands.'

'It always used to take ages,' he said doubtfully. 'Maybe there's some euro-fast-track these days.'

'If Lizzie can find it, she'll be on it,' she laughed.

'Are you OK about flying?' he asked suddenly.

'Sure. Why?'

'Because — more coffee? No? Because you look quite washed out. As if you didn't sleep last night, to be frank. Kate, if something's worrying you, you would tell me, wouldn't you? As a friend?' Concern was written all over his fine features. 'It's more than just Lizzie, isn't it?' he added, very gently.

'I'm fine, honestly.' The last things she wanted were kindness and sympathy. Maybe that was why Lizzie kept fending hers off. 'Things are beginning to look pretty bleak for Max Cornfield, though.'

'You don't want to nail him if he's killed three women?'

'If I thought for one second he had, there'd be no one keener than me.'


Sam Kennedy could make time to look at the new sample of handwriting between ten and half-past. So Kate had a chance to sit in the quiet of her office to read through Mrs Duncton's medical file, which seemed, now she came to think of it, remarkably thin for a woman of her age. No wonder. All it contained was a print-out of her recent prescriptions. Bloody Smallwood. That was why he'd handed it over with so little protest!

She reached for the phone.

The receptionist informed her that the doctor didn't take phone calls during surgery hours.

'In that case I'll speak to the practice manager.'

'The practice manager is in a meeting.'

'Interrupt the meeting, then.'

'The meeting, Sergeant, is in London.'

Kate said, very politely, 'In that case I must speak to Doctor Smallwood. Now.'

'But he's with a patient.'

'I don't care if he's conducting a gynaecological examination of the Queen Mother. I want to talk to him now. Or both he and you, madam, will be discussing the consequences of wasting police time. With a magistrate.'

She was put through.

'I don't know what game you think you're playing, sir,' she told Smallwood, 'but it's a very stupid one. When I ask for a patient's file I expect a full set of notes in date order. And I shall be expecting to find it waiting for me when I come into the surgery in one hour's time.'

'My good woman—'

What century did the man think he was in? 'In one hour, Doctor,' she said flatly, and put down the phone. Thank goodness for the Dr Kennedys of this world.

*

'I would say,' Sam Kennedy said, peering at the magnified will, 'that it is likely that the person who wrote the will forged Horowitz's signature. And more so since you tell me that Horowitz is right-handed, it makes it even more likely.' She smiled. 'Want to have a look? Look, this is the will version, this the new one.'

Kate nodded. 'Oh, yes. It's those striations you told me about. They go in a different direction on Horowitz's sample signature.'

'And the quality of line is much better. When you write the same name every day, you don't have to think about it. If you're writing someone else's signature from memory – he didn't even have it to hand to copy, presumably? – then the line fades and deepens where you'd expect uniformity. See?'

'Yes.'

'You don't sound very pleased,' Sam said accusingly.

'I'd much rather everything had been completely legal and above-board. I'm going to have to ask a nice man some nasty questions. And maybe get him sent down.'

Sam stared. 'How can someone be a nice man and do a wicked thing like this?'

It might, of course, be even more serious, mightn't it? If you could forge a will bringing you millions of pounds, there was always a chance – as Lizzie and even the late Maeve Duncton had pointed out – that you might have killed the person making the will. But not, surely to goodness, not if you were Max Cornfield.

Kate pulled herself straight, managed a smile. 'So it

looks as if I may be popping off to Berlin soon.'

'Lucky you. You don't want someone to carry your bags? No? Tell you what, why don't you meet up with my bloke? He could show you bits of Berlin the tourists don't get to see.'

'That'd be great, though I suspect I shall fly back the same day.' Yes, someone's current lover would be nicer than someone's discard.

Stopping long enough to collect a thick file from a receptionist who contrived to be both cowed and surly, Kate headed briskly back to Sutton Coldfield and the incident room.

Dave Allen greeted her with a cheery wave, and her news with an enveloping handshake. 'Well done, excellent news. So we can fry the bugger on toast for that at least.'

'At least?'

'Yes, the bleeder seems to have an alibi for the morning Mrs D was killed. At least two office workers saw him, three neighbours heard him and there were indeed three calls to the council complaining about the smoke from his bonfire. Not even the same three neighbours, as it happens: two of those complaining say they wouldn't have if they'd known it was that nice Mr Cornfield's fire. So unless we can break the alibi — and believe me, that's number one priority at the moment — it'll be hard to pin *that* murder on him at least.'

'That murder?' she repeated. 'Who else?' As if she didn't

know. 'Mrs Hamilton – has she . . . is she . . . ?'

'Mrs Ha— Oh, the old lady in Selly Oak. No, she's OK, or she was when we checked with the consultant this morning. He says her heart's simply wearing out. It's been bad for years and years, he says. Something making her jump could have caused problems, but so could an exciting passage in a book – and she was in the middle of a Dick Francis. All bloody inconclusive. Why don't you sit down? You make the place untidy hovering around like that.'

Kate said nothing. She had a nasty suspicion what was coming next. If she'd thought it, every other decent cop would have thought it.

Dave raised a finger. 'So it's up to you: if you can get a couple of nice incriminating statements from his buddies, then what we'll do is apply to the Home Office to have Mrs Barr exhumed. Despite what her GP said.'

'GP?'

'Yes, Lizzie King got on to him this morning. She said you hadn't got round to it for some reason, so she'd get him sorted. Have I said the wrong thing?'

Opening and shutting her mouth in disbelief wouldn't help. 'Since when has DI King been involved in the case, sir?'

He slapped his desk. 'Oh, for crying out loud! *DI* King? *Sir*? You're not coming the prima donna, are you?'

'I wasn't aware of her involvement, that's all.' She forced herself to relax. Putting Dave's back up was hardly the way to help the case. 'I suppose – where did this exhumation idea come from, Gaffer? Lizzie?'

'That's neither here nor there.'

It was the first time she'd seen Dave bluster.

'Gaffer, you may think I'm off my head, but may I suggest something that may save us all a lot of time and effort? I think we should haul Cornfield in and simply talk to him.'

'And you suppose he'll sit down and tell us he's killed her! Come on, Kate!' He shook his head, more in sorrow, she thought, than anger.

She bit her lip. 'He's not a young man. He's in a very emotional state, especially after yesterday, and he may just want to get things off his chest. It's not even a particularly high-risk strategy. The evidence will still be there waiting for us if he denies it, won't it?'

He looked at her for several seconds, pulling his lip. At last he said, 'OK, Power. If that's what you think, what are you waiting for? Go, go, go!'

'Only one thing, Gaffer,' she said, smiling ruefully, 'today's his day for travelling. He's down in Cheltenham at the moment.'

# Chapter Nineteen

If Dave Allen had wanted to scream and shout, he showed commendable restraint, merely dismissing Kate to do the most tedious tasks he could find – reading Mrs Duncton's file and running to earth the missing sister, Edna. She was just leaving the incident room, tail between her legs, when he called her grudgingly back.

'Do you want to work with Jane McCallum again?' he asked. 'Two heads being better than one?'

She smiled, and then, seeing the kindliness in his eyes, allowed her smile to deepen and her dimples to appear.

'Hey,' he said, diving into Black Country again, 'you'm a real bonny wench when you do that. If I wasn't going to have my silver anniversary, I swear I'd be round this desk and joining the rest of the blokes sniffing after you. Tell you what, though, chick,' he dropped his voice confidentially, so she had to return to his desk, 'you want to keep away from us married ones.'

She started. 'What the hell—?'

'You look like a bloody terrier, all stiff-legged,' he said mildly. 'Sit down, wench. I've hit some nerve, haven't I? I only meant to have a bit of a joke, like. And at my expense, too.'

She sat reluctantly, but said nothing. Had she over-reacted? It might well be that it was just possible for Lizzie to have five minutes' conversation without spreading muck, of course.

'You got some fellow giving you grief?' he asked, kindly enough. 'I haven't heard anything and I don't want to. But I'll tell you something for nothing. Married men stay married. You want to get yourself one of your own.' He smiled again. 'I'll tell you summat else, an' all. A pretty wench like you should only have to knock and they'll come out of the bleeding woodwork. Now, get on with the job, and no more letting suspects go off to bloody Cheltenham. Oh,' he called her back, 'you'll find young Zain Khan's real hot stuff when it comes to deciphering medics' scrawls, and he's got a bit of a dodgy foot at the moment. You could do a lot worse than ask him to cast his beadies over that there file. That way we'll get him back to his cricket a bit sooner and convince him he's being useful. What d'you think?'

'If you really want to know, Gaffer,' she said. 'I think you're a boss in a million.'

'Thank God for computers and computer records,' Jane said, sitting down at her keyboard and easing her skirt by running a finger round the waistband. 'It's no good, is it – this last half stone'll have to come off. It was Crete that fixed me. I always thought salad would be slimming . . .'

It wouldn't be kind to point out that it was what came
with the salad that counted: who could resist feta and olives
anyway?

NCIS, national health, national insurance, DVLA: any
one of those could have a record of the missing Edna. But
none did, not by her maiden name. So, while Kate checked
and rechecked house-to-house statements for any details of
strange women that might make a coherent picture, Jane
continued her trawl through name changes by deed poll
and by marriage. By one o'clock they'd come up with
nothing.

'Disappeared off the face of the earth – our bit of earth,
at least,' Kate told Dave Allen, as he stopped by their
corner. 'And I've got a short blonde woman about five foot
ten, with a dark mop of hair who looks as if she sells
double-glazing or might be on the game. Such goings on in
sunny Sutton.'

'So what next?' He looked at her very steadily. 'I know
you don't like the idea of your Cornfield being a serial
killer, but . . .'

'Come on, Gaffer, Michael Barton said she left home,
not that she disappeared at the same time Max Cornfield
was digging a trench for his runner beans!'

'Talk to Barton again. Precise details. And did I hear
you say you'd checked his alibi?'

'You didn't.' She checked a pile of paperwork. 'But the
DC taking his statement the afternoon he ID'd his sister
did. Said he was – hang on – shopping in Lichfield at the

time. And he had till receipts with the time of transaction on them. And there's nothing in these,' she tapped the pile she'd been working through, 'to indicate the presence in this neck of the woods of any man between fifty and seventy at the relevant time. But it'd be nice to put him under a bit of pressure too: shall Jane and I bring him down here?' She wasn't unaware of her reluctance to pull Cornfield in under similar circumstances: yes, she'd been letting her standards slip, hadn't she? Why had she been so lax with him?

'That means a double journey, and we're supposed to be watching our petrol budget. No, you talk to him out there. You can always wheel him in if he wants to make a sudden confession! Tell me, Kate,' he added, bringing up a chair and sitting down with a sigh, 'why does young Lizzie want you to hare round Europe when a simple phone call might do?'

'More serious, Gaffer, than that. Neither man mentions the presence of the other when he talks about witnessing the will. I've got the strongest suspicion that Horowitz wasn't actually there. The question, to my mind, is really not whether Cornfield bumped off any of these women, but whether he persuaded Steiner to become his accomplice in taking over twelve million quid.'

'Conspiracy. OK. Do you really want a couple of days jetting round Europe?'

She grinned. 'Wouldn't say no. And even if I did phone, to be fair, if either of them said anything incriminating, I'd have to go off with my *commission rogatoire* and a friendly foreign cop and talk to them, wouldn't I?'

He dropped his voice. 'Don't tell anyone I said this, but Lizzie has been known to cut corners. And it isn't her that comes to grief. Remember that chick.' He patted her arm. 'Now,' he said, raising his voice to include Jane, 'would you wenches like a bite down the pub before you go and talk to the good doctor? I could just fancy a plate of chips.'

'So long as I can phone the hospital first,' Kate said. 'I'd like to know how the old lady's doing.'

Which was not particularly well. The young man at the other end of the phone didn't seem overly concerned. My God, what if they thought she was too old to resuscitate if she had another attack?

'Remember she's a key witness in a murder inquiry,' she told him. 'And we prefer our witnesses alive.'

Dr Barton's case still stood ostentatiously in his elegant hall. Suave had slipped to peevish by the time they'd explained their mission, and he made no offer of tea or coffee as he showed them into the same room as before. Nor did he invite them to sit down.

'This preoccupation with the prodigal sister,' he said. 'I can't understand it.'

'Dr Barton,' Kate said carefully, 'it can't have escaped your notice that if the will is overturned you and your sister stand to inherit a considerable amount of money. The least we can do is tell her the good news.'

'I told you, I've no desire to challenge the will. That was Maeve's idea. Now she's dead, surely—'

'Once the law discovers an element of doubt about anything, it can't just stop in mid-process.'

'You mean there *is* an irregularity? My God! But – for goodness' sake – I told you, there's no doubt whatsoever in my mind that my mother would have wanted him to have everything. Or that he deserved everything. So what was wrong?'

Kate withdrew behind the sort of official tone and language Rod would have deplored. 'I'm not in a position to reveal any details, sir. But we do need to determine your sister's whereabouts if we can. Now, if we might just ask you a few more questions? May we sit down?'

He nodded, as if still too stunned to do proper honours, collapsing into a chair himself. Jane sat out of his immediate sight-line and produced her notebook.

'Now, would you simply tell us the circumstances in which Edna left home? A family row?' Kate prompted him. 'A row over a boyfriend? That sort of thing.'

Barton stared at one of the majolica plates, as if it might guide him.

'Dr Barton? What caused her to leave?'

He shrugged. 'I suspect that the man with whom my mother found her in bed – actually *in flagrante* – was Max Cornfield. The blue-eyed boy. An alternative could have been my father. And believe me I don't discount that. My father was the most evil, disgusting—' He pulled himself awkwardly from his chair and made for the window. Kate could see his shoulders move as he took a deep breath. God knew, she could do with a deep breath herself: what a family! Barton faced the window as he spoke. 'My father bullied and buggered me; he bullied and fucked my sisters; he bullied and fucked my mother. Forgive me if I use such crude verbs. Another would do, cleaner but no less explicit. Rape. He raped all of us from time to time. Maybe even Max. It doesn't take a great psychiatrist to work out why I prefer a bachelor existence, Maeve married a total nonentity whom she bullied unmercifully and Edna – and this is pure supposition – embarked on a search for a loving and gentle man.' He turned, going to stand by the court cupboard.

'And your mother?' Imagine what that woman had been through. No wonder she was on the weird side of eccentric.

'Found a focus for her affection in Max. What else developed between them who knows.' At last he looked at her. 'Has he told you yet? No, I thought not. I tell you again, ladies, that Max Cornfield should have every last dime. And I'll tell you something else: if he has done anything wrong and the inheritance reverts to me – and to Edna, if she's still alive – then I'll give him my share. I hold you to witness. Yes, Constable, write it down.' His voice cracking, he pointed a quivering finger. 'Go on: I insist. Write it down: Michael Barton promises to give anything he inherits from his mother to Max Cornfield. There. And I'll sign it and you can both witness it.'

Kate made herself say quietly, 'Now, sir, let's just get back to business—'

'Not until we've all signed. I insist. I demand – give me that damned notebook!'

Jane flashed a desperate glance at Kate, who nodded. Surely it wouldn't do any harm to humour the man? Three solemn signatures were recorded, plus the time and date. Barton fumbled in the cupboard for whisky. He sank half a tumbler neat, only as he set down the glass turning to the women with the bottle raised in invitation.

If only she could have a double!

But Kate shook her head for both of them. Pitching her voice as low and calm as she could, she said, 'Now, Dr Barton, we were talking about the date of Edna's departure. Month and year. Even the year would be a starting point.'

As if his outburst had drained him, he said, 'Maeve used to keep the family records. Yes, you should run some photos to earth. When they no longer include Edna—'

'They're not dated, Dr Barton, or we could have used them as a starting point.'

'Oh, surely you women can get a good idea from the clothes.'

'Come on. *You* must have more accurate touchstones. How old would you have been, for instance?'

'Oh,' he said pettishly, 'I suppose it might have been while I was away at medical school. I'd have been in my early twenties. And I'd already left the bosom of the family. There'd be nothing to link it to, not in my memory.'

'A sister disappears and you've nothing to link it to in your memory! Don't give me that, Dr Barton. When was it in relation, say, to your father's death?'

'I can't even remember which year he died.'

'Your amnesia seems a little unusual, Dr Barton.'

'Oh, I can remember the season. Winter. I was shivering in my digs in Nottingham when the news came through. Snow on the ground. The campus lake had frozen over. So it was that hard winter, in those days when we had hard winters. Early sixties. Anyway,' he demanded, 'I'm sure you'd be able to find his death certificate on some computer file if you really wanted to know.'

So Max Cornfield knew the year of Barr's death, but his own son couldn't – or wouldn't – be precise.

Kate confined herself to a noncommital nod, but kept her eyes on him. 'And your sister left at this time? Before or after your father's death?' There was a flicker of anxiety there, she would swear it. 'Dr Barton?'

'I've really no idea. I was away, remember. And I told you we were never close.'

'But you know enough about the circumstances to tell me precisely why your mother threw her out. Did your mother know about your father's assaults on you all, by the way?'

'I can't believe she didn't. I truly can't. But she never – I can't remember her ever . . .' He gathered himself up to his full height. 'Officer, I can't believe this is of any relevance in an enquiry into a trivial irregularity in an old woman's will. I have answered your questions with considerable patience and would now like you to leave.'

'Of course, sir,' she said easily. 'I'm sorry we've had to ask questions which have dragged up unpleasant memories. Just one last question. Thinking back now, where would you think your sister might have gone? Did she ever – you know how young people do – threaten to run away to a particular place to be with a special person?'

He seemed to be making a genuine effort. 'One of them was in love with Cliff Richard, the other with Adam Faith. I can't remember which, off hand.' He managed a rueful smile. 'So I can't even tell you she might have run away to be with Elvis Presley, can I?'

'No flesh and blood special men—'

'I've told you, Edna thought every man was special enough to take into her bed the first time she met him. Why not let her go, Sergeant?' He snorted. 'If what you say about the will is correct, I should imagine there'll be more than a modicum of publicity. That might produce precisely the information you want.'


Max Cornfield said more or less the same thing when Kate and Jane picked him up at seven that evening. He'd clearly been eating when they'd rung the doorbell, and Kate saw no reason why he shouldn't be allowed to finish his meal. It was the sort familiar to all solo-eaters, if an up-market version: salad, with so many different types of leaves it almost certainly came from a bag, a baked potato, steak and a glass of red wine. Edward lay by the stove, apparently too well-mannered to purloin the steak he was eyeing. Jane was on her knees in a flash, cooing with delight.

'I wish I could invite you to join me,' Cornfield began.

'Not at all. Enjoy your meal,' Kate smiled. She wished she didn't have to add, *it may be the last you enjoy for some time* under her breath. 'Did you have a good day in Cheltenham?'

'The usual. I took the opportunity of a quiet train journey to check her share portfolio against current prices. I think you'll agree her broker did her proud.'

'Broker? I'd have thought she'd want to do it herself.'

'She lost sharply one year. That was when I suggested a little expertise might not come amiss.' He addressed himself to the rest of his meal, mopping the juices from the meat – he preferred his steak on the rare side – with a chunk of baguette. 'I was going to have the rest of this with some cheese,' he said. 'But it can wait. I don't want to keep you waiting any longer.' He got up to put his plate and glass in the sink. 'There. Now, ladies, how may I help you?'

'There are a number of things we need to talk to you about, Mr Cornfield,' Kate told him, feeling like Judas. 'So we'd like you to come along with us to the police station.'

He shook his head. 'I don't understand.'

She kept her face blank.

'I may be gone some time?' he quoted with a vestige of a smile. 'Well, I'd better make sure Edward has the quickest of visits to the garden. At his age his bladder . . . If you're in a hurry, perhaps you'd be kind enough to open that tin for him. This is his bowl. And he can have those scraps from my plate.'

He was so relaxed, wasn't he? Innocence personified. As if he hadn't a care in the world. Was that how he'd survived, an island of sanity in that bizarre family? By being innocent? Unless, and Kate reminded herself fiercely of the evidence mounting against him, apart from being a manservant to put the admirable Crichton to shame, he was a consummate actor as well.

As for herself, she'd be glad to take a back seat in the forthcoming interview: it would be nice to see what other, less partial officers made of him.

# Chapter Twenty

'You're probably much better at interviewing than I am these days, Kate,' Dave Allen said, binning a crisp packet and the cling-film from a baguette, 'because people in my position don't get as much practice as those of you further down the pecking order. But if you think a change of bowler would be useful, then of course I'll sit in. Tell you what, send young Jane off home. And the others. Neville wants overtime down and morale up. So long as I get my leave, I'm not arguing. Here – while you're doing that, get me a KitKat or something, will you?'

Dave was still swallowing the last crumb when they went into the interview room where Max Cornfield was waiting. If he was surprised when Max stood up and offered a hand, he showed no signs of it, shaking hands and smiling cordially as he introduced himself. He even explained the tape recording system as if it were some tedious routine, rather than a vital means of preserving tamper-proof evidence.

When they were all seated, he began, 'Well, Max – it is all right to call you Max, is it? We're in the middle of a murder inquiry at the moment, as you know, and one lead we have to pursue is that of the missing Barr sister, Edna. Now, her brother — Michael, is it — seems delightfully vague about when and why she left Birmingham and has no idea, he says, where she might be now. Kate here reckons you know more about the family than he does, which is why we want you to look at a couple of photos and then tell us what you know. First of all (DCI Allen is showing Mr Cornfield a photograph from an album found at Mrs Duncton's house), could you confirm who these people are?'

A smile of recognition and then a frown. 'Oh, it's the Barr children: Michael, Edna and Mavis-Maeve. That's Mrs Barr. But look, someone's cut off this edge.' He showed them. 'I should imagine it is Mr Barr who has been removed.'

'You don't sound surprised,' Dave observed. He told the recorder, 'Mr Cornfield is shaking his head.'

'I've told Kate — Sergeant Power — that none of the family got on well with Mr Barr. He made a great deal of money but created enormous unhappiness with his bullying and overbearing ways.'

'How did he get on with you, personally?' Kate asked.

'I kept largely out of his way. It wasn't difficult. My work in the garden was done during the day. I retired to my quarters as soon as the evening meal was over if we ate without him. If by chance he was home, I kept out of the way till it was time for me to wash up. I'd reheat the left-overs then.'

'Left-overs?' Kate wrinkled her nose.

'Oh, it was understood by the family that they would leave a portion for me. And we weren't so fussy about food being fresh from the microwave as we are now,' he added with an ironic smile. 'You'd put everything on a plate, cover it with another plate, and put it in the oven or over a saucepan of boiling water.'

Dave clearly wanted to cut short the little history of domestic economy. 'OK. Bullying and overbearing. Anything else?'

'Isn't that enough?'

'In what way did he bully? Verbally? Physically?'

'Mostly verbally, Chief Inspector. Though I did end up on more than one occasion at the old Accident Hospital.'

Kate asked, 'What about the others? Did they end up in Casualty?'

'I'm sure the hospital records would show that Mrs Barr fell downstairs on more than one occasion. And that she and doors supposedly had a magnetic attraction for each other. Michael had tried to intervene on more than one occasion, I gather. That was why he went away to school — to be out of the way.'

'And Maeve and Edna?' she prompted.

For the first time he lowered his eyes. Then, breathing deeply, he straightened. 'If either were alive, I would tell you to ask them. But since Maeve is no more, and I truly think Edna must be dead by now, I will tell you that I believe he — abused them.'

'Sexually?' Dave asked quietly. 'Mr Cornfield is nodding,' he added.

Aware she was heading towards difficult territory, Kate asked, 'Did – did their mother know?'

'There were some subjects upon which we never touched. Ever.' He sliced his hands in a gesture of complete finality.

'You lived there for nigh-on fifty years and you never discussed it?' Dave demanded, but not unkindly. It seemed as if he too were falling under Cornfield's gentle spell. But then he leaned forward, full of latent aggression. Kate was glad she'd turned to him. 'Tell me, Max – you eat scraps from her table, you sleep in a garage, you don't get any pay: why the hell did you stay? What was your relationship with the family? And especially, what was your relationship with Mrs Barr?'

Whatever reaction either of them might have expected, it wouldn't have been the one they got. Cornfield leaned back in his chair, tipping it on to its back legs, and smiling, though his eyes were filmed with tears. 'Is either of you a musician? Chief Inspector? Kate?' He pulled the chair upright. 'Kate, you have pianist's hands. Have you ever played Brahms? And Schumann?'

She was about to nod when she remembered the tape recorder. 'I've played both. Why do you ask?'

'Did you study them, as well as play?'

'Not in depth,' she admitted cautiously.

'Would you mind telling me what Sergeant Power's musical habits have got to do with Mrs Barr?' Dave asked, no longer sounding patient.

'Brahms went to live as a young man in the Schumann household, when Schumann was still sane. He and Clara, who was nine years older than he, became lifelong friends. They influenced each other enormously. Schumann died insane, and Clara mourned him for ever. She and Brahms, despite many rumours that they were lovers, never married. Brahms loved other women: that's well documented. But when Clara died, he lost his will to live, and survived her by only six months.'

'Are you saying that you and Mrs Barr were the Brahms and Clara Schumann of Edgbaston?'

'In some ways. Our relationship was deep and complex and enduring, Chief Inspector. Just like theirs. But like theirs, it will never be more than a matter of gossip and speculation. Were we employer and employee? Were we lovers? Were we purely friends? You won't find out from me. I promised her that. I am a man who keeps his promises.'

Kate was moved and exasperated in equal measures. She heard Dave swallowing hard.

One of them had to break the silence. 'What other promises did you make?' she asked, her voice over-loud, almost harsh. 'About the children and their father, for instance?'

He flinched. 'What sort of promises?'

'You tell me.' She didn't know what she was on to, but she was on to something.

'I don't know what you mean.'

'Promises not to tell anyone anything about Edna's

sudden departure. Round about the time her father died.'

'I wish I knew what you were talking about. Edna was
– a very difficult young woman. She had certain – needs –
which distressed her family.'

Dave frowned. 'What sort of needs?' He sounded
genuinely curious.

'Does it matter now? This is all in the past. She may be
a respectable married woman, may be a grandmother living
in Bognor.'

'Do nymphomaniacs become respectable grandmothers
living in Bognor?' Kate asked.

His head jerked up. 'Nymphomaniac?'

'According to her brother,' she said levelly. 'He believes
her mother found her *in flagrante delicto* with someone. Was
that someone you?'

He stood up, eyes blazing. 'How dare you? How dare
you?'

'Calm down, Max,' Dave said. 'It was a simple enough
question, and you can choose whether or not to answer it.
No? Shall I ask you another question: was the man in question her father? (Mr Cornfield is nodding.) So was that why
she left home in such a hurry?'

Max took so long to reply she thought he might be
preparing a lie. 'Yes. It was clearly necessary to separate the
two. She went abroad. I had friends, contacts. We pulled
in some favours.'

'Why did no one simply inform the police? Men aren't
allowed to abuse their daughters.'

'Chief Inspector, you're old enough to remember the

mores of the time. There was Mr Barr, a respected member of the community, handing over dollops of his considerable wealth to all the best charities. And there was his far from respectable daughter. Who would accept her word over his? No, it was better as it was.'

'But he died, Max. Why didn't she come back then?'

'Who can say? I can give you the address I took her to. I have nothing more recent.'

'Address *you took her to?*' Kate repeated.

'Of course. Who else could Mrs Barr rely on to escort her, see her settled?'

'Where did you escort her to?'

'Berlin,' he said. 'I took her to Berlin.'

'To your friend Steiner?'

'No, no. And before you ask, he has tried to find her. Berlin, Kate, when it was occupied. How many soldiers would be able to resist a pretty girl? She may not be in Bognor, but in Nice or Miami. I hope she is.'

'Hmm.' Dave sounded as if he were reflecting on the frailty of mankind. Then lightly, casually, almost as if he were offering a cup of tea, he asked, 'Why did you forge Mrs Barr's will, Max?'

If Kate had seen it on TV, in a movie, she'd have gasped aloud in admiration. As it was, her eyes were glued on Max.

'Forge it? I told your sergeant the circumstances. I wrote it down to Mrs Barr's dictation. She insisted. Hasn't Dr Steiner told you that? He told me you'd phoned him.'

'Tell me the circumstances,' Dave suggested. 'Exactly what happened?'

'Almost word for word what he told me, and very much what Steiner said. But no direct mention of Horowitz,' Kate said, as she and Allen left the interview room to give Cornfield a breather. They sent a constable in with coffee, while they retired to the canteen.

'And do you believe him?'

'Not any more. I think I may know how to crack him, Gaffer, but I need to catch him unawares, even more than you did. Can you leave it to me?'

He stirred extra sugar into his drinking chocolate. 'Don't see why not.' He looked at his watch. 'What say we give him five more minutes – just long enough to go over his gardening alibi again – and then you pounce?'

She sipped her mineral water, wrinkling her nose as a bubble tickled. 'No. I've got to do that when I run him home. But I'll tell you what, Gaffer, I think we're going to have to talk to him again anyway. That Edna business. And the death of her father. There's something that adds up to more than four, if you see what I mean. A medical student. A brutal father. A heart attack. A sudden disappearance. What do you make that?'

'Nearer five than four, that's what I'd make it. Five being unnatural death. Shit! All I wanted was a nice, straightforward domestic so I could wrap it up and go on my hols in peace.'

*

Kate brought the car to a gentle halt in front of Mrs Barr's house. To her alarm there were lights on in two of the upper rooms.

'A timer device,' Max said, laconically.

She turned to him. 'I'm sorry to be putting you through all this grief about Edna. But she could be a suspect, you see.'

'Even less likely than me,' he said bitterly.

'Quite. But don't let my boss hear me say that.' She got out of the car with him. 'Another lovely evening.'

He peered at his watch under the streetlight. 'I had hoped to see Mrs Hamilton.' He left the implicit rebuke hanging in the air.

'Tomorrow might be better – she's still very poorly.'

'She'd want to see me – to hear about Edward.'

'Of course.' She set off up his drive, just like a young man seeing his date home. 'What are your plans for this weekend?' All very calm, comradely even. And she banked on his returning too to their easier conversations.

'If I can't start on my world tour,' he said, managing a smile, 'I shall stay in the garden. Time enough when the autumn comes to work on clearing the house. And you? Will you be seeing a young man?'

'Oh no,' she said, feeling a complete louse, 'I'm off to Portugal this weekend.'

'Portugal?'

'Yes. To the Algarve. Any messages for your old friend Mr Horowitz? It's him I'm going to see.'

✻

Lying had never been Kate's favourite technique, but she hoped it would be justified on this occasion. Ideally, Max would have pre-empted her next sentence with a swift confession. As it was, she thought she might have to wait till the following morning. Perhaps even a last minute call as she was about to board a plane. That is, of course, if a plane journey materialised. All he had done, however, was to wish her a pleasant journey.

Nearly home now. Chaos outside Edgbaston cricket ground: God, not an accident! No. Supporters pouring from the ground after a day-night game. From their faces, the local team — what did they call themselves? The Bears? — might have won. She'd never quite got the hang of cricket, perhaps because it was supposed to be a three-dimensional game of chess, another game she'd never mastered. She wondered idly if Max would pass Lord Tebbit's cricket test for immigrants, who, according to the Noble Lord, could only be considered truly integrated when they supported England, not their country of origin, in test matches. Certainly Lizzie's fancy pretence of a *commission rogatoire* wouldn't pass any test; there was something inherently displeasing about using a spoof to catch a forgery, not to mention the probable fall-out when the ploy was discovered. Not, of course, that it would be Lizzie who carried the can, not if what Dave Allen said were true.

Despite her horror of grassing, she was deeply tempted to phone Rod and lay the whole thing before him. He wouldn't mind being phoned even at this time of night; nearly eleven. Her stomach sank: that was more than could be said of Graham. Had he tried to reach her tonight? Not on her mobile, that was for sure. And no, not on her answerphone either. Damn him, didn't he know how much she needed to hear his voice? Three words — *I love you* — would be enough. She'd make them enough. Would have to make them enough.

Just as she'd have to make the sad contents of her fridge enough. Bread sandwich seemed to be top of the menu. What about turning out for a last minute take-away balti or fish and chips?

Altogether too much effort.

Sardines on toast: that was a possibility, if only there were sardines, which there were not. The heel of cheese was no better worth than a trip to the wormery. Heavens, there was a woman in her eighties out in Selly Oak Hospital who cared enough for herself to make not just biscuits but *langue de chat* biscuits for herself. And here she was, hale and hearty and not capable of knocking the most elementary snack together. Kate reached for the whisky.

And put it back again. Popping bread into the toaster, she reached for a pencil and paper. Tomorrow's shopping list would be a revelation.

# Chapter Twenty-One

Kate was contemplating what Aunt Cassie would no doubt have condemned at the ultimate dereliction of house-keeping duty — a breakfast McMuffin on the way into work — when the phone rang: Dave Allen was calling a breakfast meeting of the squad.

She was greeted by wonderful smells: Dave had orga-nised two piles of sandwiches, bacon and sausage. 'Staff morale,' he muttered as an aside.

He reported to the group what he and Kate had managed to extract from Cornfield; then others reported on their progress so far. Zain Khan's was the most interesting: he'd managed, as he modestly said, to decipher some of Mrs Duncton's file. Apart from her varicose veins and her irri-table bowels, what had caused her some concern was the state of her husband's health.

'Time and again we get her saying he's moody — there's even a hint or two he may have knocked her about. Still no path report. Bastards are busy. Kate, you and Jane to my office, please, soon as you've fed your faces.'

Which was quite an urgent order from Dave.

The flipchart was already in position, with Rod writing something on the bottom of the Ken Barr sheet. What he was adding was a large £ sign, followed by a couple of others and three question marks.

'That's what it comes down to, isn't it? The budget's already overstretched (when will the public learn we can't afford for them to go on killing each other?); we're pushing everything we can out from the centre; more bobbies on the beat; better clear-up figures. And now what may or not have been a murder a generation ago. Dave, what are your feelings?'

'I'd rather hear what the two wenches who've talked to the brother have to say. Jane?'

More brownie points for him.

'He's bloody rich. Loaded. I've never seen a house like his without having to pay a fiver to get in. But that doesn't mean as how he had to kill his old man to get it. Kate was saying he had this legacy provided he changed his name.'

'But then he said he'd changed it after some medical scandal, didn't he?'

'And he had his bag packed to take him abroad. Now, if he was a medic, wouldn't he have access to drugs? He could slip his dad a few, make it look like natural causes.' Her face fell. 'Except he was in Nottingham at the time.'

'No reason why he shouldn't have given them to his sister and got her to do the dirty,' Kate said. 'And then Max

Cornfield was there to get her out of the country. However,' she added, more soberly, 'we haven't checked his medical records, assuming they still exist, or the evidence presented to the inquest.'

'Which may indicate that Barr had a long-standing condition and was simply a heart attack waiting to happen,' Dave concluded for them. 'Tell you what, Gaffer, why don't we get Jane here to sort out the historical stuff, as it were, while Kate goes back to Fraud and sorts out the will business.'

Even as she nodded her agreement, Kate's stomach sank. Back to Fraud meant back to Lizzie. Back to the dubious *commission rogatoire*. And back to the constant bad temper and barrage of innuendo.

'Come on, our kid,' Jane said, putting a hand on Kate's shoulder, 'you look as if you've lost half a crown and found a rusty button.'

'I never did like paperwork,' Kate said, managing a pale smile.

'But you've nearly finished, and the more you've done, the glummer you've got. You come down the canteen: you could do with a breather, by the looks of things.'

Kate's smile was more positive. 'That'd be great. My shout.'

Jane dug in her purse. 'It may have to be an' all — I'm clean out till I've been to the hole in the wall. Funny,' she continued, as they fell into step, 'the ways this job changes your life. Like forgetting to buy milk or pick up the dry-cleaning or whatever. Makes a difference if you've got a good boss, of course. I mean, Dave works the socks off us when we've got a panic on, but he does understand about breathing time – like those trips to the pub you were so sniffy about.'

'I was wrong there. Freely admit it. I wish I could stay in this squad, to be honest.'

'But you're a high-flyer!'

'It's all very well flying high, but you never know what you're going to land in, do you? Sometimes it's a nice spot like this, others it's a shit-heap.'

'You reckon Fraud's a shit-heap, do you?' Jane asked, pushing open the canteen door.

'I didn't say that at all,' Kate laughed. Hell! Why did Jane have to raise her voice at that point? Talk about walls and bloody ears! 'Tea or coffee?'

'Well, why do you want to stay with us, then? Coffee, please.'

'Less paperwork,' she said. 'And trials that don't go on for years, and evidence the jury can understand, and a proper sentence for the scrote at the end of it all. For God's sake, we see people who've ruined more lives than a serial killer ending up with just a couple of years in the library of an open prison. Nick a car radio in Handsworth, you get six onths. Nick millions of pounds no one can actually see, and you may even get off scot-free if the jury can't follow the rows of figures.'

Jane snorted. 'Careful how you get down.'

'Get—? Oh, off my soap-box, you mean. Sorry. How about sitting over there, away from the TV?' She paid for the drinks and headed towards an isolated table.

'Thing is,' Jane said, sitting down, 'they say that that DI's a bugger to work with. King, whatever her name is,' she added, in another stage whisper. Damn Dudley and its carrying voices.

'Come on, Jane, being a woman in the service is tough enough without other women bitching about you. We're all in the same spot — bikes or dykes, whatever. Now, what are you up to this weekend?' This loyalty was getting to be a strain.

'Looking at houses, that's me and my boyfriend. Party tomorrow night. If this weather holds, we're off to Wales on Sunday. What about yourself?'

Kate could have kicked herself: this was going to be a worse topic of conversation than the last. 'If a phone call I've got to make back in Fraud comes up with the answer I'm expecting, I may have to fly out to Portugal. Or Germany. Otherwise there's something at the NEC I might go to.' And suddenly her heart lifted. No, she wasn't going to have a weekend entirely on her own, after all. But it sank again. Rod would be the last person Graham would want her to spend time with. A terrible though struck her: she might not tell him.

*

'It's all right,' Derek greeted her, 'you can breathe freely. 'Lizzie's not in. Some meeting somewhere. So we're not sure whether she'll be back or not.'

Kate slung her bag on to her desk. On impulse she phoned the hospital for news about Mrs Hamilton. She was conscious and might be moved from Intensive Care the following day. But family visitors were all that would be allowed for a few more days.

'Her neighbour's very keen to see her,' Kate said neutrally. 'The one who brought her in and who's looking after her dog.'

'We'll have to see,' said the voice. 'As I told him when he phoned.'

One phone call seemed to lead to another. She found herself dialling Leon Horowitz.

'I need to talk to you in more detail about the will you witnessed,' she said. 'Will you be at home early next week?'

'What sort of detail?'

'Just the order in which things happened,' she said. 'I'll be accompanied by a colleague from the Portuguese police, of course, so your statement will have legal validity. So you will be there next week?'

'It's hard to say,' he began.

'Oh, Mr Horowitz, the sooner this is done the better. After all, Mr Cornfield won't be able to claim his legacy till all formalities are complete.' She gave him her number. 'I'll be flying out specially,' she added, 'so if you do have any last minute changes of plan, I'd be very grateful if you let me know.'

Then a similar call to Mr Steiner. And another to the travel agency the police used. Yes, it looked as if she'd be jetting round Europe. Suddenly she was tired of not knowing – she wanted to pounce.

# Chapter Twenty-Two

It was love, wasn't it? It was definitely love that filled Rod's eyes. Not for her, not at this moment, anyway. But for something he'd run to earth after long, hot hours searching at the Antiques Fair at the NEC. Kate had never seen so much old or beautiful — sometimes old and beautiful — stuff gathered together in one place. It was almost as if the National Trust were having a car-boot sale. At last, hot and thirsty, they were about to call a halt for lunch when they saw it — Kate first, as it happened. A Ruskin vase, the cousin of the one used to smash Mrs Duncton's skull. It was certainly very lovely, a comfortable, almost peasant-ish shape, but sleek and sophisticated, and obviously infinitely desirable. But it wasn't, as far as Kate was concerned, as lovely as the weapon had been. Too much red, not enough purple. It cost roughly what Rod had valued the murder weapon at.

'Far too much of an extravagance,' he said firmly.

But he could hardly tear himself from it.

'Why don't we just walk along this aisle and then come

back?' Kate asked quietly. 'If it's still here, you should have it. If it isn't, it wasn't meant.'

'Is that the logic,' he asked, 'you employ when you're at work?'

'Are you supposed to use logic? I thought it was all intuition and creativity; especially the paperwork. Anyway, we agreed: the first one to talk shop would pay for drinks.'

They exchanged a grin, neither the sort full of sexual challenge or promise, nor the easy one of long-standing friends. Something in between.

'On the other hand,' she said, catching his backward glance, and deciding to take a risk, 'now that work has been mentioned, with the sort of salary you must be on, why the hell shouldn't you indulge yourself? Go on, while it's still there!'

He turned, but stopped: 'If I do, will you – if you see something you fancy?'

It was the only way to put him out of his misery. She nodded, dawdling behind as he headed back to the stall, already fishing for his wallet.

'Now for something for you,' he declared, leaving the dealer to pack his vase. 'A real hard look for that furniture.'

Most of what they'd seen so far had been much too grand for her front room, which was, after all, homely to the point of small. Too grand and too old: however much she was attracted to Georgian or Regency furniture – and she found she was, deeply, despite the price tags – she knew that she ought to have late, unpretentious Victorian.

'Does it make sense to get chairs before choosing a table?'

'If they're those chairs there, yes.' He pointed to a set of four, whose upholstery happened to tone with her carpet. 'Pretty little balloon backs. Nice to get four like that. Six would cost you an arm and a leg.'

'But I need six.'

'You could get carvers for the head and the foot. Come on, how many sets of six have you seen so far?'

'Plenty, but none in my insurance company's price range!'

They celebrated their purchases — they'd collect everything when they were ready to leave — with a sandwich lunch. Kate would never have imagined Rod doing anything so human as peeling the halves apart and peering with disdain at the contents, clustered as if for company's sake, at the centre and never venturing near the edges. But then, she'd never have imagined him buying that vase. What she did suspect was that he wanted to buy her something. He kept drifting towards jewellery counters; she drifted, with at least equal purpose, away. No. No intimate gifts. It was bad enough being here and enjoying his company without having thought about Graham for three or four hours. Once having thought about him, however, she couldn't get him out of her mind: what would he have made of an event like this? His home décor had been unobtrusive to the point of bland: she'd blamed his wife for that, but perhaps, compared with Rod's, weren't his clothes a little on the ordinary side? But what was style, when he was the man she loved?

The funny thing was, when Rod had unpacked her chairs and driven away, she'd almost have liked to call him back to suggest a meal together. Nothing special, but . . .

No. It was best as it was. Wasn't it?

But Saturday night, that was, always had been, the worst night to spend on your own. Thank goodness, she thought, her face in a wry smile, for Aunt Cassie.

'Flying? You mean flying? In a plane?' Aunt Cassie clutched both her wrists in panic. The grip was firmer than Kate would have expected.

Kate was about to crack some joke about not having any wings when she looked more closely at the old woman's face. There was real fear there, real panic. 'It's safe, Cassie,' she said. 'Quite safe. Honestly.'

'Quite safe? All those people dying in China last week and you're telling me it's safe?'

'According to this article in the paper the other day, you're less likely to die in a plane crash than to die of a donkey kick.'

'Oh, trust the papers to say something stupid like that! How many donkeys do you see in Kings Heath, you tell me that.'

'For that matter, how many plane crashes do you get over Kings Heath? Come on, Cassie: you know I'm much more likely to get killed crossing the High Street than I am flying to Berlin.'

'Did you say, "flying to Berlin"?' Graham's voice asked. He stood in the open doorway, and then stepped in, closing the door behind him. As always, he went straight over to Cassie, taking her hand and kissing her cheek.

Without being asked, Kate poured three G and T's. She passed Cassie hers, but Graham stepped towards her, apparently to reach for his glass but in face to take her hand and press it against his crutch. His cock pulsed: he looked her straight in the eye.

'I've got two hours to spare,' he mouthed, before walking to the window and saying over his shoulder to Cassie, 'I'm surprised you're not out there having another barbecue tonight; it's a lovely evening.' He downed his gin in one surprising gulp.

'We could do with some rain,' Cassie said. 'Freshen the place up a bit. And this heat . . . All you young people in your nothings. Look at Kate, here. I'd never have thought of showing the world my tummy button like that.'

Kate laughed: 'I bet you did the equivalent.' Her eyes sought Graham's. She tapped her watch and raised five fingers.

Nodding, he went back to Cassie. 'I'd best be off,' he said.

'But you've only been here two minutes.'

'Mustn't make Mrs Nelmes jealous.'

'But you haven't heard about Kate and this flying busi-ness. I want you to stop it. You're her boss.'

'Not any more. She got too much of a handful for me.'
He kissed her again, then turned to Kate, kissing her hard
on the lips. 'At your house,' he whispered.

'My regards to Mrs Nelmes,' Cassie said. 'Now, young
Kate, how d'you feel about a nice game of whist? We're one
short tonight. Old Trev's only been and popped his clogs.'

How could you be as casual about death when you were
that close to it yourself? 'Trev?' How soon could she
escape?

'I told you. The one who can never remember what
trumps are.'

'Well, I can't manage it tonight, I'm afraid. In fact, I
must dash, I've got my washing and ironing to do.'

'Isn't tomorrow good enough for that?'

Poor old woman. Pleading with Graham, now with her.
But she hardened her heart. 'Packing tomorrow,' she said.
'I'll call in as soon as I get back.'

'I want you to phone the people here,' Cassie wailed.
'Soon as you get to Berlin. And then when you get to wherever it is. You'll be killed in a crash, I know you will. And
then who'll look after me?'


Usually Graham parked his car round the corner. Tonight it
was in front of her house. God, what a risk! What if his wife,
or Rod—? She shooed him away to park more discreetly,
leaving her front door on the latch while she ran upstairs,
shedding clothes as she went. Her bra arranged itself into an
arrow shape through her open bedroom doorway. It was a

game she'd played with Robin, but Graham would never know it was second-hand. He had another, unspoken, fantasy: that he was the first man in her life. It was not her function to initiate anything, but to respond to him, which she did, with absolute willingness. But the pretence had been difficult to maintain when he had bouts – not rare – of impotence. That, at least, wasn't a problem tonight. He entered into the spirit of things, taking her with gusto.

If she turned her head, she could watch him in the wardrobe mirror: see his cock plunging into her, see the thrust of his buttocks, his thighs. She had almost as much pleasure in that as in the sex act itself. When he had come, and had rolled off, stripping off the condom and dropping it by the bed – she'd cured him of his habit of dashing straight to the bathroom to flush away his guilt – she ran her hands over the parts she'd looked at so lovingly before. Perhaps he might do the same to her.

But he was pulling himself on to his elbow, reaching for his glasses. Was it they that changed his voice?

'So what's this about Berlin?'

'Chasing a witness in a fraud case. Then on to Portugal to talk to another. The sun, the wine, the food – oh, it's a hard life! I suppose you couldn't discover a case to take you there too?'

'Are you sure you can justify the expense?'

What was the matter with him? 'Not my decision. In fact, I rather voted against it. Lizzie's idea.' Could she risk it? 'I'm afraid she may be cutting corners over the paperwork.'

'She's a good cop,' he said, which didn't seem to be an answer to anything.

And felt like a criticism. Not good, if you believed that Lizzie and he had once been such serious lovers that he'd gone back to his wife. Not just stayed with her: gone back to her.

'Life's too short to talk about work,' she suggested. Any moment now, he'd decide he had to go, and she didn't want Lizzie to be their final topic of conversation. How crazy, to hate his relationship with a past lover more than she hated that with his wife. But what she feared, so much she found herself shivering, what she really feared, was that he would drop her not for his wife but for Lizzie – after all, he never spoke of the poor Flavia with half the enthusiasm he reserved for Lizzie. She swallowed hard: he'd never speak of her, Kate, with that enthusiasm, would he? Couldn't. Not while they were secret lovers, and almost certainly not afterwards. And she wanted his praise more than she'd ever wanted anyone's, even her father's: wanted his praise for her work, and now, yes, now for her body and her sexiness and desirability. She wanted to hear that she was his best lover, with the loveliest body.

What she did hear was a quiet sigh as he turned over and reached for his watch.

# Chapter Twenty-Three

If Birmingham had been hot and almost airless, when Kate stepped off the disconcertingly small plane at Tegel, she found Berlin even hotter, and what little air there so thick she could have cut it up and taken it out in chunks. Her lightweight suit was already a crumpled mess; her shoes felt exceptionally full of foot. She strap-hung on the airport link bus to the city, her nose close to the plain-clothes armpit of Jo, Lizzie's ex, who had been wished on her willy-nilly. Since he'd pocketed what Kate still suspected was dodgy paperwork without comment, perhaps she shouldn't regret the absence of Sam's partner. Jo — short for Johannes, and therefore pronounced *Yo* — had greeted her with courtesy but markedly little enthusiasm. He'd be a little older than Graham, but was already fleshing out a little around the midriff, and markedly about the jaw. From time to time he'd smooth a broad hand across his pale thinning hair. He lurked behind impenetrable shades.

'We'll get the U-bahn straight out to Gneisenaustrasse,' he said, in English so perfect Kate decided not to embarrass either of them with her German. 'That's in Kreuzberg.

We'll find somewhere to get a coffee. Maybe an *imbiss* for some lunch — you've put your watch forward?'

Kate nodded. So long as she could have a long, cold drink, she could tackle anything. But she suspected Jo was the sort of man to put work first.

Their conversation was no more than tepid. Maybe Jo wasn't by nature an affable man. He barely responded to her favourable comments about the U-bahn, or her unfavourable ones about its graffiti. Her German wasn't up to translating the terse advice he offered to a beggar working their carriage: whatever it was, it seemed to be taken rapidly to heart. Kate glanced at him as he spoke: without the sinister dark glasses maybe he'd be reassuringly normal.

At last they emerged into the sunlight of a suburb, right, as it happened, in the middle of a street, a broad thoroughfare with plane trees down the central reservation as well as the pavement. They waited obediently for the pedestrian signal to cross an entirely clear road. At a tiny café, old men — Turkish, by the looks of them — drank coffee and stared disconsolately at a profusion of vegetables glossy with freshness spilling out from the equally tiny shop next door. A couple of women scurried past, swathed from top to toe in black. As always, Kate found the effect disconcerting, as disconcerting as Jo's mirror glasses.

'Hmph,' Jo said. 'You get this in Birmingham? This ethnic crap?'

'Yes, some women have started to wear their faces entirely covered, even their eyes.'

'What I say is: when in Rome . . .'

If pushed, that might have been what Kate confessed to feeling. But she was so offended at hearing it said so brutally she pushed all her more liberal ideals to the fore. 'If it's their religion,' she began.

'Religion? Pah! It's all political. Left here.'

Schleiermacherstrasse. Some sort of playground – yes, there was a school there, too – occupied the far side of the road. Theirs had more shops – one displaying patently second-hand items that must have been trashy even when new – and a couple of restaurants, one Indian, one Turkish. The smell of food still hung over the pavement. If only she wasn't so thirsty.

'You mentioned coffee,' she said. 'It's been a long time since I had a drink.'

'Why didn't you say?' He perched his briefcase on one knee and produced a bottle of mineral water. He swigged and then offered it to her.

Was there any etiquette about wiping it before she drank? She did anyway, wiping it again before returning it to him. 'Thanks. That's better.'

He stowed it, then produced something else. Sun block. 'Who'd have a bald spot?' he asked, with the first genuine grin he'd managed so far. 'So we don't forget when we come out,' he added, rubbing the lotion in vigorously.

'We've all got noses,' she said, accepting the bottle.

'True.' He checked she'd fastened the lid before putting the bottle back. 'There you are: Steiner, Dr Joseph.' He pointed to a name on the entry-phone before applying a finger to it. He took the tube and shoved it in his pocket as the buzzer sounded. 'So you talk and I listen?'

'Fine. And when you take his German statement, you talk and I listen.'

Inside were wide marble stairs; true, after the first flight they became stone.

'Built to last,' he said, shoving the shades into his breast pocket – yes, he looked remarkably ordinary. 'About eighteen seventy, I'd say. Officers' flats, now converted into apartments, of course.'

'Barracks! A bit grand for barracks!'

'No. Not barracks. Flats. Not on the compound or whatever. Actually, my aunt used to live round the corner: accommodation for the officers' orderlies. Very inferior.' He produced another grin.

Neither had much breath for conversation by the time they'd reached the third floor. Someone had propped open all the stairwell windows, but the air was too exhausted to flow in or out.

'Ready?' he asked, his thumb ready for Steiner's bell.

'Ready.'

But when a door opened, it was to the apartment on the opposite side of the landing.

'Sergeant Power, I presume?' asked a lightly accented voice.

Kate spun round to be confronted by a double for an Old Testament prophet. No, his beard was too neatly trimmed, and his hair no more than a hangover from an earlier, more youthful style. But his bones were wonderful, an elegant jaw and cheekbones framing a pair of fine dark eyes that obscurely reminded her of Cassie, as did the age spots on the hands.

'That's right. You must be Dr Steiner.' They shook hands. 'And this is my colleague Inspector Rathman of the German police. He will take down your statement in German.'

'Oh, statements! I'll let you into my flat and then I must just finish feeding the rabbits. Unless you're keen on rabbits?'

Kate was suddenly very keen on rabbits, if, when it came to it, less keen on their smell in the confines of a flat. Carrots, lettuce: Dr Steiner had left a colander of food just inside the door. Rathman seemed to take to his allotted task, feeding guinea pigs to which he muttered German endearments, while Steiner tackled a couple of caged para-keets, whistling Bach to them.

'Who on earth keeps all these?' Kate demanded at last, standing, hands on hips, gazing at pens and cages and fish-tanks, all in an otherwise normal and possibly elegant sitting room.

'A lady who is lonely without them,' Steiner said, his voice dry with irony. 'All it remains for me to do now is feed the piranha.'

'The – the piranha?'

Steiner nodded in the direction of a high-walled tank, perhaps a foot wide and three feet long. It was occupied by nothing but a solitary fish so huge she wondered how it turned round. If the lady was lonely, what about this fish?

'I thought they were small fish,' she said, 'in big shoals.'

'Without the rest of their shoal, perhaps they grow. This one did. I suspect he grows large on redundant guinea-pig litters.' He paused to mist some foliage she'd only ever seen in a hothouse. 'There. And now you have met my neighbours, perhaps I might offer you my hospitality?'


Steiner's coffee was ambrosial, especially when served with tall glasses of iced water and the sort of biscuit that Sam Kennedy had offered her. They sat in what she suspected was a double cube of a living room, its proportions so good that all Kate wanted to do was stand by the open balcony doors and absorb them. One long wall was entirely covered with bookshelves, crammed with books in at least four languages.

Jo caught her eye and tapped his watch. She glanced at her own, which told her what her stomach didn't – that it was way past lunch-time.

Nodding, she smiled at Steiner, and fished her note-book from her bag. 'Now, Dr Steiner, I wonder if we might just put together your statement about the signing of Mrs Barr's will?'

He settled into a chair opposite her, moving aside a chess table the better to cross his ankles, his relaxed posture at variance with his unsmiling face. 'You have my account of the events. I sent it to you as soon as you asked me. I have nothing to add to that.' He reached for a file from the bookshelf behind him, fishing out three copies. Keeping one on his lap, he passed Rathman the others.

'I'd like to clarify just a couple of points, if I may,' Kate began. 'How did you come to be a witness? After all, you weren't a friend of Mrs Barr's.'

'I doubt if Mrs Barr had any friends by then, she was so cantankerous. What happened was that she decided that she must make her will that very day. Like that.' He snapped his fingers. 'I had arranged to meet my good friend Max that afternoon anyway, and he telephoned me to ask if I would come earlier to witness the will. It was as simple as that. I arrived at about two-thirty. She insisted on dictating the will, word by laborious word. I hadn't realised till then what a very sick woman she was. In fact, she was so distressed by the whole procedure that Max had to give up our evening engagement to stay with her.'

Nothing new there.

'The other witness was Mr Leon Horowitz: at what——'

'Yes, another old friend of Max's. We shared the same child and young manhood, Sergeant, all three of us. I've been an academic all my adult life, a not unsuccessful one, if I might say so, and Leon a distinguished gerontologist. Who can blame him for seeking the rich pickings to be had amongst the elderly inhabitants of the Algarve? But if any one of us had a wonderful future, I'd have predicted it for Max. Such a fine mind.' He sighed, a huge rib-cracking sigh. 'Who'd have thought he'd remain a general factotum all his life? Sergeant, have you seen that rat-hole he calls his room? A place like that when there is a mansion full of fine rooms . . .'

'Fine when they've been emptied and cleaned,' Kate agreed. 'Now, Mr Horowitz arrived at what time?'

'My dear Sergeant, it's all in here; everything I wish to say.' He flicked his copy of his account.

'It's singularly lacking in detail, Dr Steiner, if you don't mind my saying so. Indulge me a moment. I like to see how things really happened: a snapshot, as it were, of the event.'

He flicked the paper again. 'Here is your snapshot.'

'I think it might need some more time in the developing dish, then,' she said.

'I don't understand.'

'In which room did all this take place?'

'That dreadful living room. I remember thinking it was more a dying room than a living room.'

'My colleague here has never seen it. Could you tell him something about it?'

Steiner half turned, but with an air of humouring her. 'It is a dirty, ugly room, officer, half filled by a grand piano excruciatingly out of tune. Any one of the pictures on the wall might be sold and the proceeds keep a person modestly fed for a year. There may be windows at either end but it is dark as a cellar. A basement, at least.'

Jo nodded with apparent interest.

Kate continued: 'How did Mrs Barr get into the room?'

'In a wheelchair. Max had to carry her downstairs.'

'And you sat where?'

'The armchair nearest the piano.'

'And Mr Cornfield?'

'What does it matter where he sat?'

'At the table? Or did he sit in an armchair with a writing pad on his knee?'

'Sergeant, you are playing games with me. You know as well as I do there is no table for him to sit at. He sat in the other armchair.'

'And Mr Horowitz sat?'

'By a process of elimination, Sergeant, you can surely work out that anyone else in the room must have sat on the sofa.'

Ah! So she wasn't the only one playing games. 'Did Mr Horowitz sit on the sofa?'

'I thought you'd just established that.'

'What time did Mr Horowitz arrive?'

'I didn't check my watch.' He sounded pettish.

She was getting somewhere: she knew she was. 'He didn't arrive with you, then? Earlier or later?'

'Sergeant, I have said all I wish to say about the incident and wish you good-day.'

Kate reached for her bag, made all the moves that one would make to leave. But instead of standing, she fumbled in a side pocket, producing one of the photos from the Duncton albums, still in its official evidence bag.

'I wonder if you recognise this young woman, Dr Steiner?'

He looked as disconcerted as she'd hoped he would, fumbling on the bookshelf behind him for reading glasses, small as half-moons but more elegant. He took the photo, peering at it from a variety of distances. But that, as she realised, was another game.

'It must be that young friend of Max, the daughter of the Barr household. Now, whatever was her name? Not Mavis, she was the one who stayed at home. Edna. Why are you showing me this?'

'Because she didn't stay at home, did she?'

He smiled coldly. 'If you know, why do you ask me? Yes, Max will have told you about her. About her row with her vile and vicious father, about her escape here, about my providing her with accommodation. Because he is what I still think of as a gentleman, he will not have told you that she and I were briefly lovers, till she left me for a black American sergeant, whom she left for a French captain, whom she left for God knows whom. I have tried to trace her, he has tried to trace her. For all I know Inspector Rathman's colleagues have tried to trace her.' He bowed graciously towards Jo. 'But she has disappeared as completely as last winter's snow.'

Kate nodded. She was inclined to believe him, and would in any case be handing over the snapshot to Rathman before the day was over. 'Thank you. Now, Dr Steiner, Inspector Rathman would be happy if he could take a statement from you in German.'

'Why on earth should he?'

'It is customary to ask the witness to give an account in his or her native language.'

'Then there is absolutely no reason for the inspector to take a statement. My native language is Polish. As a young man I spoke Hungarian. Now I am also happy to speak English, French, Russian and German. I have given you a statement in English. Why should I want to make one in another language?'

'Because you've made a notable omission in your English version. You've omitted to say anything about the role of Mr Horowitz. Neither, Dr Steiner, have you told us that in the absence of Mr Horowitz, Mr Cornfield forged his signature.' She paused. He said nothing. 'And what I really need to know, Dr Steiner, is whether Mr Horowitz was ever meant to be there, or whether all along you and Mr Cornfield planned an elaborate fraud.' She stood up. 'How much did he promise you to keep your mouth shut, Dr Steiner? If he stands to gain twelve million pounds, I hope it was a very great deal.'

'We're obviously talking extradition here,' Jo said, placing a beer in the exact centre of the mat in front of her, 'if your suspicions are correct.'

'I hope they're not. I really, truly hope they're not.' She drank deeply.

When they'd left Steiner's flat, Jo had led her in the opposite direction from the U-bahn station, away from the *imbiss* he'd promised her. 'I think you deserve a decent meal,' he said, taking her elbow briefly to remind her she was looking the wrong way down a road. 'A stroll through this park, which as you can see has the benefit of a canal.'

'A canal! It's wide enough to be a river!' She leant over the parapet.

'No, it's not like your strange English waterways. Along here, we'll find just the place.'

They did. A perfect place. The awning covering the outside seats might have been wished in from Greece – a trellis covered with vines. Beer, chilled to perfection, water, ditto, and a fresh salad. Perfection. If she could just believe she'd ever get her shoes on again.

Fortified by a meal too late to be lunch, too early to be dinner, Jo became a more engaging companion, though she never felt as if he particularly liked her. They strolled round a market dominated by great discs of Turkish bread and more of those wonderful fresh vegetables, stopping at last in another café to sink another beer.

'Where are you staying?' he asked without preamble.

'In an Ibis not for from Tegel.'

His eyebrows suggested that while she could have done better, she could have done worse.

'And how do you propose to occupy yourself this evening?'

'By writing a watertight account of our interview with Steiner,' she said.

'And after that?'

'An appointment with my earplugs and sleeping mask.'

'Oh, come, Kate, Lizzie tells me you're not yet thirty. You must have more stamina than that. How about I collect you and we head for a bar?'

It was neither courtesy nor coyness that made her ask,

'Are you quite sure? I mean, I've taken a good deal of your time already, and—'

'Absolutely. I promised Lizzie I'd look after you.'

Hell. 'You have. You've fed and watered me and—'

'Tell me, do your expenses run to taxis, or shall we stroll back to the U-bahn?'

'I'm happy with the U-bahn.' But still not happy with the invitation, or the manner of it.

'If you're ready, we'll set off then. I'm afraid we find ourselves in the rush-hour.'

'I thought I'd stop off in the centre: melt some plastic in Ka De Weh.' Astrid had told her years ago that it was worth a pilgrimage.

Looking at his watch he shook his head. 'Window-shopping only, I'm afraid, by the time you get there. Now, give me that photo of yours. I'll photocopy it and return it to you tonight. Meanwhile, I'll write down for you the lines and the stations you'll need . . .'


'OranienburgerStrasse?' Kate asked, looking around her as they emerged from the car park: true to his word, he'd picked her up from her hotel. 'The name rings bells.'

'It is *the* area for clubs and pubs,' Jo said, again, she thought, with an edge to his voice. Maybe it was his normal inflection. But she wasn't convinced it was.

She scratched her head. 'Clubs wouldn't have come into any conversation with Astrid. The woman who might have become my stepmother.' She explained: he seemed mildly interested. 'So how would I know about it?'

He stared at her, unhelpful behind the shades he was still wearing, despite the deep dusk. Remembering was important, wasn't it? But he had already set them in motion, behind, as it happened, an exquisite young woman, dressed, unsuitably, perhaps, for the still baking weather, in an extravagantly cut Hamlet shirt and tight black trousers, atop high-heeled shoes. From time to time she'd toss back her blond mane. Except women didn't usually have bums as neat as that, nor shoulders as broad. But the face, under its glowing make-up, was surely female. Wasn't it?

At least there was no doubt about the gender of the next person to catch her eye. High heels, fishnets, a short skirt so full as to be a tutu – and a shock of black chest hair. Or the next, a young man sporting what an Elizabethan would have called a codpiece. She was jostled by others less defined: boys with breasts, women with male genitals bulging under tight jeans. The *kniepe* Jo drew her into was heaving with cross-dressers or transsexuals at various stages of their change. A couple on a tiny spotlit stage, a strong-shouldered man and a delicate young woman stripped inexpertly, their subsequent bored coupling suggesting that neither had been what they seemed.

It wasn't long before Jo disappeared on to what might have ben called the dance-floor if you were optimistic about such things. Kate neither knew for certain nor ultimately cared the sex or the sexuality of the person who was all over him like a rash. From time to time the shades would glint in her direction but she contrived as best she could not to be seen to be returning a glance. Cool, that was what she must be, however much she might be seething under-neath. Embarrassed? Not after her stint with the Met. Titillated? Not by the androgynous figure that tried to chat, then to touch her up. Jo and his partner disappeared from sight. The gents'? For a quick fuck? She shrugged, and tried to get another beer. It seemed she couldn't, not unless she became a member.

'I don't think I qualify,' she told the bar-person. She'd better make the dregs last. As long as she had a glass in her hand she had some semblance of justification for being here. But being a dry wallflower for much longer was so deeply unattractive she allowed herself to think in terms of five minutes more before she slipped out and found a taxi. Observing the human condition was much more fun if you had someone to share your observations with. And she felt vulnerable in a way she'd not felt since her early days in the force. Damn Jo and his clever ideas.

Jo reappeared a minute before her unspoken deadline.

'I need some air,' she yelled, pointing at the door and setting off, not caring whether he followed or not.

He did. 'You are not enjoying yourself?'

'On the contrary, I find it immensely entertaining and instructive.' She raised her hand at a slowly cruising cab. 'Only one thing taxes me.'

'Taxes?'

'Troubles my brain. Your purpose in bringing me here.' She opened the cab door. 'Something Lizzie said, was it?'

He took off his shades and bit an earpiece.

The driver asked something she didn't pick up – the accent, perhaps, from a different region. He repeated his question. Joe said something, ushering her in. To her amazement he followed, giving the driver directions.

'There's no need,' she said. 'And what about your car?'

He shrugged. No doubt the driver would bring him back. 'My behaviour was bad,' he said, his accent appearing for the first time that day.

'Unusual. But I'm sure there was a reason for it.' She fastened her seatbelt. Lizzie. That was the reason.

'I like irony,' he said. 'I like the irony that Oranienburg was once the administrative centre for the concentration camps. Populated extensively in their early days by gays. Ever visited them? No? And the street named after Oranienburg is as you see it. I relish the ironic connection.'

'And the ironic connection between me and that club? No, don't tell me. Lizzie,' she said. 'She must have said something.'

'She told me,' he said quietly, 'to make sure you got plenty of sex.'

'And do you want me to pass any message back?'

He shrugged. 'The message is in the medium.'

# Chapter Twenty-Four

Kate escaped from Faro airport at about eleven-thirty to find the overwhelming heat blessedly tempered by a strong breeze. She'd no idea what public transport would be like in the Algarve. Her only visit before had been on a low-budget family holiday to a cheap and cheerful resort where they'd baked themselves silly on the beach. So it seemed sensible to drive across from Faro to Lagos, which was where Leon Horowitz lived. It would be more flexible to hire a car, and cheap, too, but after the oddities of the previous evening, she thought that for once she'd rather simply be taken, and haggled what seemed a ridiculously low fare out to the west.

And the taxi was air-conditioned! OK, it was too late to rehabilitate her suit, but she felt better. She was too busy gaping at the scenery to begrudge the driver his part in the vehicle roulette of the main road: a game in which her father had briefly displayed a terrifying desire to participate. There were far more concrete excrescences jumbled along what she remembered as a lovely coastline: accommodation for all those pale Northerners keen to acquire melanoma of the skin as quickly as they could.

The intense light started to assuage the sourness she still felt after Jo's activities. It wasn't just the quick sex that had fired him up, she was sure of that. He'd almost certainly taken something – coke, she rather thought – while he was with the young man at the club. Grovelling with apologies for his ungentlemanly treatment of her, he was, he'd assured her, quite happy to fuck with her if she wanted – provided she promised not to tell Lizzie. It had taken her rather longer than she'd liked to convince him that such chivalrous activity was quite unnecessary. And that her silence on the whole episode was guaranteed, whether or not he liked it. She was angry not just with him – who would have liked any part of her treatment? – but with Lizzie for her part in it, even if she could hardly blame Lizzie for the way things turned out.

'There is much to see here in Lagos,' the policeman at the enquiry desk said. More perfect English to humiliate her. 'Enjoy the tourist sights while we read this document of yours. You know that we are twinned the city in Nigeria. You will find the old slave market, also a statue to Henry the Navigator and the museum well worth a visit.' In his way he was as impenetrable as Jo had been. Courteous, charming, and immovable. He would show Lizzie's shady letter to his superior, who was currently at lunch and who was the only person who could deal with it. No, they had no record whatsoever of Detective Inspector King's telephone call – did Kate know whether it had been in English or in Portuguese?

Kate only knew she was hungry. Was there somewhere close by where she could eat?

'Any one of the restaurants in the town.' And she could return at three.

Three! Did they take a siesta as well as a meal? And then she realised, as the heat engulfed her as she stepped into the street, a siesta was absolutely the most sensible option. No sun-hat, no sun block – she shouldn't be out in the open at all. At least she could remedy those omissions, even if she couldn't remedy those of that bloody *commission rogatoire*.

So she could enjoy an icy beer and wonderful chicken piri-piri in a street café, and wander down to the broad esplanade to bask in the shimmering views of the river and chic boats heading for the sea. If only Graham were there: Lagos was as full of couples as Kings Heath, and far more romantic to boot. The thought of him brought her to her feet. There must be some tiny gift she could take him, something to keep in his desk to show she'd thought of him. Nothing brazenly Portuguese lest anyone else see it. But something with quality, with style. Behind her was the town: she struck inland up steep steps to find a leather goods shop, full of delectable handbags and wallets. But she couldn't give him a wallet, could she? And suddenly she wanted nothing for herself, either, to remind her of a time when she missed him so painfully.

Almost shouting at herself for her stupidity, she drifted back to the main shopping area, to buy the naffest mug she could find – for herself. There: at least she'd done something touristy.


'And did you have an enjoyable lunch?' the desk sergeant – if that was his title – asked her.

'Very enjoyable, thank you. And did your superior—?'

'I regret he has been detained. Now, have you visited the slave market?'

'I have, and I've made the acquaintance of Henry the Navigator.' What an act of faith; to set sail in a tiny ship heading simply for the horizon.

He nodded, then beamed. 'The archaeological museum; have you visited that? There are extensive Roman remains, and some fascinating biological specimens: a dog with three eyes, a cat with two heads. Detective Sergeant, it is just a step across the street. May I suggest you cannot do better than to investigate that?'


Which was all she did investigate in Lagos: infinite numbers of fragments of Roman pottery, deposited rather than organised, wherever there seemed to be shelf-space, some fabulously embroidered church vestments, the church itself brilliant with gilded plasterwork, and some deformed animal foetuses, to which a smartly dressed young woman curator had specifically drawn her attention. As Luis da Ponte, the senior policeman fresh from his lunch explained, as he poured her coffee, 'Napoleon never conquered Portugal. His armies stormed across the rest of Europe, Senhorina Kate, but thanks to your forebears and mine, he never took our tiny country. So the Code Napoleonique does not, alas, operate. All the *commissions rogatoires* in the world would be inadequate to persuade me to let you interview Senhor Horowitz while he lives here. To see him, you will have to seek permission from your Foreign Minister, who will speak to our Internal Affairs Minister, who will speak to the Chief of Police and a team of lawyers to determine whether such permission will be given.' Luis smiled, his teeth white in one of the most handsome faces Kate had ever seen, dashes of white hair at his temples an additional artistic touch rather than a sign of ageing. Not that he was much more than thirty-five anyway. 'I am desolated. But we do not extradite even murder suspects unless all the paperwork is absolutely in order.'

Luis insisted on running her back to Faro himself, pointing out with pride and delight the new bridge at Portamao and various delights on the road. Since his car was air-conditioned and he found a radio station called Nostalgia, which played her father's favourites from the sixties, she didn't argue. He even phoned a tour courier friend to pull strings to get her on a flight the following day. Finally, having booked her into not the Ibis she'd planned but a smaller place he assured he would be altogether more pleasant he bought her a drink.

As he leaned forward to pass her olives, two thoughts occurred to her simultaneously. That it would be a delight to flirt your way into bed with such a gorgeous man, and that he was bound to be married.

And what, in any case, was she doing, imagining making love with anyone but Graham?

If Luis' courier friend hadn't told her to present herself at the airport an hour before the regular check-in time, if sea mist hadn't engulfed the airport creating delays, if there'd been somewhere to sit, somewhere to get a drink during what seemed an interminable wait – well, she probably still wouldn't have worked out the best way to frame her report on the previous two days' events. If she told the truth, no one would come out of it smelling of roses. If she told the whole truth, Lizzie in particular would stink of horse manure. Rod would be angry with Lizzie, maybe passing information to her line manager. But Rod would also be furious that Kate hadn't checked and double-checked what Lizzie was up to. Even Dave Allen had warned her about Lizzie's reputation for cutting corners, her underlings not herself carrying the inevitable can.

Meanwhile, she also had to plan her return to Birmingham. The courier had got her a flight, sure, but it was to Glasgow, not exactly the heart of England. Glasgow to Birmingham – what were the options?

'I expected you yesterday afternoon,' Lizzie observed coldly as Kate presented herself at eight on Thursday morning.

'Yesterday afternoon?'

'A day in Germany, a day in Portugal; that should have wrapped it up. Home yesterday morning.'

'There was fog on Faro,' Kate said flatly. 'And a signals failure on the railway line from Glasgow.'

'Fog? Oh, for God's sake, they've got radar and computers these days,' Lizzie objected.

Kate might have framed exactly the same opinions to fellow-queuers, but to hear the chief architect of all her woes express them pulled her to her feet. 'With respect, ma'am, you can't hold me personally responsible for the inability of technology to defeat ordinary weather. Or for Railtrack's problems. On the other hand, it seems to me that you are responsible for the major cock-up that prevented me from even talking to Leon Horowitz and thus wasted police time and a lot of taxpayers' money. Here is my report on the events. Feel free to doctor it as you wish to minimise your part in the disaster. So long as you don't falsely implicate me. Good morning, ma'am.'

She made the impressive exit such a line demanded. And then had to return. The noise she heard as she shut the door behind her was indisputably sobbing. Lizzie was in tears. So there was nothing for it, was there, but to turn round and go back in.

'A lump? What does your doctor say?' Kate passed Lizzie more tissues, squatting beside her and holding her spare hand. In her head, pennies were cascading down.

'He . . . Oh, he said it wasn't . . . But he wanted to be sure . . .'

'Quite right. So he's referred you to a consultant?'

'A clinic. I couldn't go. There was a policy meeting. So I couldn't go, could I? So they made another appointment, but there was a meeting with the DPP, so that had to go too.'

'Hang on, Lizzie: you're telling me you have a breast lump — and we all know what we think we've got if we find a lump — and you've not been to have it checked?' The woman was off her head.

'You know what it's like here. You can't just drop everything—'

'There are some things you have to drop everything for.'

'But these were important. And now the hospital people have written asking if I really want an appointment.'

So the stupid woman hadn't phoned to cancel; she'd simply not turned up. Kate swallowed the thought and said, 'And you've phoned up to say yes. Oh, come on, Lizzie. You have to go. The lump's still there, is it?'

Lizzie shook convulsively. 'I don't know. I'm too . . . too scared. What if it's bigger?'

What indeed? What if it were bigger and had spread? 'Do you want me to phone? Thing is, Lizzie, whatever date they offer, you're going, right? Even if the Chief Constable invited himself to tea, you'd still go. And I'll tell you why you'd still go — because I'll be going with you.'

# Chapter Twenty-Five

'You know what sticklers the Portuguese police are, Gaffer,' Kate told a tight-lipped Dave Allen later that morning. 'They even turned down France's request to extradite the bloke who was prime suspect in that student murder case, remember. A few words wrong, they won't co-operate.' It wasn't just her own back she was trying to protect, after all. If ever she'd seen a woman near the edge, that woman was Lizzie.

They were in his office, so no one could hear his words, but the glass walls made her bollocking something to avert the eyes from in comradely support or something to goggle at. At least he'd positioned his chair so even if they had the skills no one could lip-read. And he'd told her to sit, so his bulk hid her face.

'I like my officers to get all the words right, Power. Always.' He tapped her report, newly doctored after the meeting with Lizzie. 'What I don't like is the word fudge leaping out at me. That's what this document says to me. Fudge. It tells me that there's been a cock-up and that this is a cover-up. I don't like that.'

'Sorry, sir,' Kate hung her head.

'Farting around in the sun when your mates are sweating their rocks off trying to put a case together – it's not good enough.'

'No, sir.'

'And it's not just that you've cocked up, it's that you've wasted time and money on what you must have known would be a wild goose chase. I'm disappointed in you, my wench. Disappointed. And I can't say I won't say it in my report on the case, because I will. Any promotion to inspector: you can wave that goodbye for a bit.'

'Sir.'

He put on his glasses and started to read a file. Kate took the hint, and slipped out, shutting the door quietly behind her. She made herself sit down, made herself look busy. She'd expected no less, after all. And can-carrying was part of life's tatty tapestry. She was aware of glances, sympathetic or curious, but contrived to ignore them. Only a few minutes before the team meeting: at least no one would be looking at her then. Especially if she made sure she sat at the back. But she'd be ready, just in case. No, she wouldn't just look busy, she'd actually be busy for the next ten minutes.

At least Dave spared her a public bollocking. He was too busy up-dating. The psychiatrist in charge of Mr Duncton was demanding a court order before he'd release his medical file, so they'd simply got to wait for all the due processes. Mrs Hamilton was still alive, but her doctors hadn't let the police talk to her about anything. The medics' evidence about time of death wasn't good enough to break Cornfield's alibi. As for the possible Barr murder back in 1963, well, Jane had waded through all the paperwork, but there was nothing conclusive. There'd been a misadventure verdict at the inquest, the coroner having added a timely warning to all middle-aged men who took too little exercise and then fancied they could risk with impunity the exertion of digging snow. Barr's body had been cremated.

'All the same, it wouldn't do any harm to go and stir up Barton, maybe,' Jane added, glancing with sympathy at Kate, who grinned back gratefully.

Dave intercepted both looks, but nodded. 'Not a bad idea. And what has your trip thrown up, Power?' he added, without apparent irony.

She hoped her deep breath didn't show. 'Steiner refuses point-blank to say anything about Horowitz's presence or absence when the will was signed. Unfortunately, I cocked up on the documentation for Portugal, and the authorities declined to let me talk to Horowitz in person. Sorry, everyone.'

'Thought the bloody Common Market was supposed to make this sort of thing easy?'

'Too busy subsidising bloody French farmers . . .'

No, no one seemed to blame Kate too much. Though that might have had something to do with the cheap fags and chocs they'd be expecting.

'Anyway, I'd say,' she continued, against all her wishes, 'it's time to pull Cornfield in and suggest it's time he stopped playing chess with us. That's what he and Steiner are doing. I don't think either of them has ever lied about Horowitz's presence or absence – I just don't think either has ever told the whole truth.'

'You're sure of that?'

'Positive. But I've done an OHP acetate of both statements. May I?' Talk about toadying, but at least it showed something. She flicked on the OHP, focusing it on the wall. 'There: you see that Steiner gives a fairly detailed account of events, or at least his and Cornfield's part. But of Horowitz there is nothing.' She slid the first page of Cornfield's statement up. 'Here again there's plenty of circumstantial detail, but truly nothing to confirm – or deny – Horowitz' presence. And the graphologist indicates that there is sufficient evidence for her to say that whoever wrote down the will – and no one contests that that was Cornfield – also wrote what purports to be Horowitz' signature.'

Dave Allen permitted himself a grin: 'What are you waiting for, Kate? Go and wheel him in!'

She responded with a grim smile. 'Trouble is, Gaffer, Thursday is his day for travelling, remember. He promised me he wouldn't go anywhere without letting me know where he was off to. I paged my answerphone after you— a few minutes ago. He's in Hampstead – should be back about nine, he says. Can Jane and I make a little reception committee?'

'Hampstead, eh? Kate, I can't imagine him returning to anything less, can you? And while you're waiting, you and

Jane can go and have another word with Barton. Just to keep him on edge.'


They went nowhere till after Dave had treated them to lunch in yet another obscure pub. This one, promising though it may have been on the outside, offered very meagre fare — baps, that was all, and you could have poor cheese or worse ham, full-stop. Compare and contrast, Kate thought, with herring salad and chicken piri-piri. The food wasn't important, though, compared with the gesture. Dave might have chewed her ears off, but he bore no grudges. That was the message, which she received gratefully.

They emerged to find the clear sky filling with big fluffy clouds that threatened to become bigger but much less fluffy. It looked as though the heatwave would soon be over and in a dramatic fashion. The sky was almost brown by the time they reached Dr Barton's, a trick of the light making the house itself glow more redly than ever.

There was no sign of his car, and all the windows were shut.

'Sorry for the wild goose chase,' Jane said.

'Maybe he hasn't gone far. Let's have a look-see, shall we?' She got out, a sudden gust of wind whipping her skirt against her legs.

When, as predicted, there was no response, Kate peered through the letter-box, which was so small that countless posties and leafleters must have cursed it. She could see very little except the suitcase. At least he'd taken their advice.

But she felt uneasy, and led the way to the front window, making hand tunnels to shade her eyes. The place was immaculate but for a couple of piles of books.

'Nothing for it,' Jane said, returning to the front door to post a note to him to call them as soon as he returned. 'Now what?'

'Gently back to Sutton. And I mean gently.' Kate pointed to drops the size of two-pence pieces on the windscreen. 'The roads will be like skid-pans after all that lovely weather, and Joe Public won't be able to wait to try his skills. Or not.' But she didn't start the engine.

'You all right?' Jane asked.

'Someone walking over my grave,' she shuddered. Should she take one more look? There was something – no, she was getting silly. 'Look, if we're going to be on really late tonight, we're entitled to a break. Do you want to be dropped off anywhere?'

'Not round here, nor nowhere round Sutton, to be honest. No, I'd rather get back to work, if it's all right by you.'

'No problem.' But there was. For no reason, Kate wanted to go home, to shut her door against the world. It must be the weather.

'You sure you're all right?'

'Tell you what, let's call the hospital: see if Mrs Hamilton's up to visitors. She knows me, after all. They might just let us have five minutes. It'd give us something else to talk to Cornfield about.'

'Suits me. Tell you what, have you noticed you're calling

him Cornfield, not *Mr* Cornfield? You think he's done more than forge a will, don't you?'

'Two minutes,' the nurse said, with all the authority, if not the title or uniform, of the old ward sister. 'And that's the absolute maximum.'

'Thanks. Just before we go in, tell me: has she had any other visitors, family apart?'

'Her nice neighbour called last night with some Polaroid photos of her dog. Just to show he was still all right.'

'And how was she after that?'

'Fine. As fine as she'll ever be. She's a very old lady. Her heart's very tired.'

Jane stayed by the door as Kate slipped into the side ward where Mrs Hamilton lay dozing. Her hair straggled drably across her face. Dentureless, make-up-less, she looked ten years older than when Kate had met her. Her nightie ruthlessly revealed crepey neck, withered breasts, pendulous upper arms. Even in sleep, her fingers fretted the sheet, convulsing every time the old woman in the other bed gasped stertorously. She was in an even worse state, her face butter-yellow, her mouth sagging. Kate felt a sudden spurt of anger in all the pity. Why hadn't Mrs Hamilton's family moved her to the comfort of a private room? Or the nursing home section of the place where Aunt Cassie lived? Surely she had enough capital? Kate'd raise it with the nurse afterwards.

Meanwhile, she walked lightly but not silently to the bed. The last thing she wanted was to make Mrs Hamilton jump.

'I'm not asleep.' The old lady's voice was surprisingly strong. 'I'm resting my eyes. Who is it?'

'Kate Power. The police officer.'

Mrs Hamilton's eyes shot open. 'I have a bone to pick with you, young lady. What nicer way to slip into the next world reading a good book, drinking a cup of fine tea and with your dog at your feet? But you – I understand it was you – brought me back!'

'I thought you might want to finish the book.' Kate put her hand on the old lady's.

'Well, perhaps I should. And how is Edward?'

'Mr Cornfield's still looking after him.' Goodness, what if the dog was afraid of lightning?

'He's a good man. They wouldn't let him see me, you know, but I understand he came every day. Just like him.

'Did you see him the day . . . you were taken ill?'

'I didn't *see* him. I could *hear* him whistling and singing to himself. And – let me see – he called over the fence to ask if he could have another bonfire without disturbing me. It seemed to me, when I began to feel unwell, that I could call him and he would come. But I knew he'd try to do as you did, and – though he does not sing Schubert well – it seemed another lovely factor.' The old lady sighed, then turned her hand to grip Kate's. 'I'd hate to die in here. I'd like to go home first. See Edward. All my precious things . . . Kate, come and see me again. There's something . . .'

The grip slackened. At first Kate panicked. Then she saw the quiet breathing. She straightened to leave, then, moved by an impulse she couldn't explain, she bent and kissed the deep valleys of the old lady's cheek.


'We have to get a vet, and quickly,' Cornfield wept. 'Poor Edward, he always hated thunder and I wasn't here. Oh, Edward.'

'I think it's some sort of stroke,' Jane said. 'Poor old boy. D'you know the vet's emergency number?' She was kneeling beside the old man and the sick dog.

Cornfield gestured at a sheet of paper blu-tacked to the wall by the phone. Kate's job: the others couldn't leave the pathetic panting heap. Edward's head was in Cornfield's lap, a front paw resting, as Mrs Hamilton's had rested in hers, in Jane's hand. She stepped gingerly across the floor – she'd had to disinfect it, couldn't leave it as it was – and dialled, as authoritative to the voice at the other end as if a human life were at stake. And perhaps, when she thought about it, it was.

# Chapter Twenty-Six

This time Kate had a companion in Dave Allen's room for her morning's bollocking: Jane.

'A bloody dog? You don't haul a murderer in because of a bloody dog?'

'Mrs Hamilton's dog,' Kate reminded him. 'And she only wants to live long enough to go home to die with Edward beside her. And we do at least have a statement we both heard that Cornfield didn't try to scare her to death. Whatever else he's guilty of, he's innocent of that. And I reckon he's innocent of Mrs Barr's death too. I read through her GP's notes again this morning, and there's no doubt she was a very sick woman, only kept alive with devoted nursing. Tell me, Gaffer, have you ever dressed anyone's leg-ulcers? Well, Cornfield did, every day.'

'And,' Jane added, 'he's got that alibi for the Duncton death, too.'

Kate nodded. 'Isn't it about time the Forensic Lab came up with the spatter info? I'd bet my pension Duncton did it: there's no sign of the missing sister, no sightings of anyone else. It's got to be him.'

Dave broke and passed round pieces of the Toblerone Kate had bought on the plane. 'The trouble is, you like this bloke, Cornfield, don't you, the pair of you.'

'And you liked him, didn't you?' Kate patted back.

'Ah. But not enough to let him get away with murder. It's just too bloody convenient the husband having done it. Mind you, the medics say he'll probably be in some sort of institution for the rest of his life. Oh, yes – I got that much out of them. Tried again last night, while you were faffing round bloody dogs. Poor bastard. Out of it, isn't he? Quite out of it. I tried the old trick of getting the medic to leave the room leaving the file on the table so I could have a gander.' He grinned. 'Must be losing my grip – it didn't work. Took the bloody thing with him, didn't he? Bugger and blast it all,' he said, slamming his hands on the desk. 'All I want is to take the missus off somewhere special and the bloody case rolls and bloody rolls.'

'I'll get on to Forensics,' Kate said. 'And then . . . oh yes, it's time to talk to Cornfield again. We'd better bring him in here.'

Dave looked up quickly. 'Not if it means him leaving that dog on its own, you don't. You talk to him out there. Better still, wait till tomorrow. If he gets upset, it'll be bad for the dog.'

Neither woman let her face so much as twitch. They were leaving the little office when he called them back. 'What about Barton?'

'"No answer was the stern reply",' Kate said.

'Eh? Oh, I learned that at school, too. Something

about oysters. OK. Keep trying. I think he's important.'

'You're really going for this thirty-year-old death?' Kate asked.

'Any reason why not? Oh, plenty,' he said, subsiding in his chair and breaking off more chunks of chocolate, which, when Kate and Jane waved them aside, he ate himself. 'I've just got this niggle, see? My bunion's twitching.'

Which, as they all knew, was the hallmark of a good cop. The women nodded and left without further argument.


'Christ! Forensics,' Kate declared, putting down the phone, 'had mislaid our bloodstains. But they're working on them now, and so I should bloody think. They'll let us have the results . . .' On the desk in front of her was a note, in an internal mail envelope. The flap was tucked in, but stuck down with sellotape. She turned it back: yes, the block capitals in re-address slot number 9 were Graham's. What the hell was he doing, contacting her like this? It was such a risk. She stuffed it in her bag and headed for the loo. Only after locking herself in a cubicle did she dare look.

> *Dear Kate*, he'd written on lined paper torn from a pad, *If I don't do this now I'm afraid I never will. But I must. I've come to the conclusion that what I'm doing is wrong. I always want to be friends, but it mustn't be more than that. Not any more. I'm sinning. I'm breaking the seventh commandment, and I can't continue to do so.*

She read it again and again. No, not even a signature, let alone a loving valediction. Nothing. Nothing except this. She even looked in the envelope again. Of course there was nothing in the envelope. No more than there was anything about his feelings or hers. No, nothing about her, let alone her feelings. No. No, no, no.

She turned quickly, and retched into the pan. Retched until there was nothing else to come up. When she stood up, she had to squat again. Her legs wouldn't work, and her balance had gone.

Graham had gone. Left her. Graham.

There was a tap on the door.

'Kate? Kate? You all right in there?' Jane asked.

'Sure,' she managed.

'What's up, our kid?'

'Something I ate. It's all right. I shall be out in a second.' She should tear the note into tiny pieces and flush them after her vomit. but she couldn't. Not his handwriting, not his note to her. She crammed it back into the envelope, which she shoved to the bottom of her bag, 'Those baps, I should think,' she said, emerging at last. 'Plus it's period time.'

'You look really bad. Thought you were going to pass out in there. Come along to the first aid room and have a lie down. Then I'll run you back home. OK, chick?'

If Jane was any kinder, Kate knew she'd put her head down on her shoulder and cry, tell her everything. Nearly everything. That her bloke had ditched her, at least. But Jane would have seen the envelope, might even have recognised the writing. Even if she hadn't, the rumours would have reached this far, wouldn't they?

'I'll be fine. Honestly.' She leaned on the washbasin. She'd have to make the effort to bend to splash water on her face, wipe round her mouth. 'There.'

Jane stood, arms akimbo, watching. 'Look, kid, you've been taken bad. You can't work. If you don't want the first aid room, I'll get you straight home. Dave won't mind. In fact, if he sees you looking like that, he'll as likely take you himself.'

And make those observations about married men? Kate shook her head. 'Honestly, I'm all right. Bit of lippie, no one'll tell the difference, will they?' She foraged in her bag, desperate not to touch the letter, and produced her lipstick. 'There. Back in the human race.'

'If you say so. You look more like death warmed up, if you ask me. Actually, what I came to say was there's a fax for you.' Jane stepped back to let Kate go through the door first. 'From Germany.'


'So Edna is dead, after all,' Kate said, passing Dave Allen the fax, which curled irritatingly. 'Poor woman. Killed by her pimp in 1973. Look at this lot. Drug abuse; evidence of at least one termination; chlamydia. And then to be— Jesus, look how she died, poor cow.' The pimp had gone berserk, killing three prostitutes within an hour, told by God, apparently, to change his ways – and, presumably, theirs. God had a lot to answer for, didn't He? Still, being angry with Him was better than throwing up again. If she could just hang on to her anger . . .

Dave looked at the fax again, then up at her. 'So our Dr Barton is a rich man. A very rich man if Cornfield forged that will.'

'Absolutely.'

'I think you should go and break the news. Hey, Kate,' he said, looking at her more closely, 'What's up, my wench?'

'My breakfast,' she said. 'Something I ate yesterday, I should think. Or something I brought home from foreign parts.'

'Ah. Do anything these foreigners will to muck us about. Stomach bugs. *Commissions rogatoires.* One of these days I want us to have a proper chat about that Portuguese business, Kate.' He looked at her under his brows. 'I think you've been like that Steiner bloke: telling the truth but not the whole truth. Understand me?'

She met his gaze but said nothing.

'OK,' he said, smiling ironically. 'Any road, are you fit for this trip to the country?'

'Sure. What line do you want us to take?'

'Why, loads of sympathy, I'd have thought. And then another little poke around the circumstances of the old man's death. Come on, Kate, you must be feeling bad if you need to ask my advice. In fact, maybe I should send you on immediate sick leave.'

She had an idea he was only half-joking.

*

At Kate's suggestion they stopped at a pub for a late sand-wich lunch. An excuse, in Kate's case, for a stiff brandy, which she claimed would settle her stomach and ease her period pains. From time to time, she would shake violently and uncontrollably. When Jane raised concerned eyebrows she made some excuse about having a touch of fever.

'I still think you should go home.'

'I'd rather be working.' And she would. She couldn't face going home to the bedroom where he'd slept with her, the kitchen where they'd sipped coffee, the sitting room where he'd tried once or twice to sit relaxed and insouciant, all the time desperate to go to bed with her. Couldn't face closing the front door forever on their pitifully short time together.

Dr Barton's front door was still firmly shut, as were all his windows. His garden had suffered in the previous day's storm — lupins and other tall plants were prostrate.

Kate peered through the letter-box again. The case was still there. She walked round to the garage. That too was still locked.

She was almost surprised by what she said. 'Time for the old Ways and Means Act, Jane. My bunion started to twitch yesterday and it's going full belt now. I want to know what's going on inside that house. I think I can smell gas: maybe we should break in and make sure every-thing's OK.'

Jane's eyes widened.

'Go and sniff at that letter-box again,' Kate suggested. 'Then if you smell it too, we'll be absolutely forced to break in.'

Shrugging, Jane walked to the front door and did as she was told. But as she straightened real concern furrowed her face. 'You try,' she suggested. 'You see, I reckon I can smell something. But I don't reckon it's gas.'

'Poor bugger,' Jane said, staring down at the late Michael Barton. 'Sitting on a likely twelve million quid and popping his clogs like that.'

Michael Barton lay halfway down his elegant staircase, his neck and at least one arm broken. He had almost certainly been there yesterday when they'd driven away. The news would not go down well with Dave, would it? Another bollocking, this time deserved.

'Looks as if he trod on one of those piles of books and – phut,' Kate said. She pointed to the cascade of paper they'd had to dodge. 'And dropped those as he went flying.'

Jane nodded. 'Silly sod was still wearing his reading glasses by the look of it. Perhaps he couldn't even see where he was putting his feet. My granddad's always doing that. Keeps his glasses on the end of his nose and tries to peer over them. I must have another go at him.' She pressed a tissue hard to her eyes.

Kate put an arm around her shoulders. 'It'd be very quick, I should think. I hope so anyway. OK,' she said, 'thank goodness for good old routine. Coroner's officer.

Undertaker. Post mortem. Inquest. But I've got this sneaking feeling we should preserve the scene, just in case.'

'In case what?'

'In case he didn't die conveniently of natural causes. In case someone pushed him. Though I'm sure they didn't. Thing is, we cocked up yesterday, didn't we? Don't want anyone complaining we didn't get it right this time.'

'Who'd there be to complain? No family, after all.'

'The way this case is going,' Kate said grimly, 'Max Cornfield.'

# Chapter Twenty-Seven

'I must talk to you. I think I'm going mad,' Graham's voice said on her answerphone. But he didn't leave a number she could safely call him on. It was after ten, for goodness' sake, so how could she have called him back in any case? On impulse she dialled his direct office number, and was rewarded by his voice, after one ring.

'Harvey.'

'It's me.'

'Can you come in here? Now?'

'I'm on my way.'

No one seemed to think there was anything unusual about her sprinting up the Steelhouse Lane Police Station stairs as if Old Nick were after her: perhaps the odd officer she passed thought she was still based there. She didn't know what to expect: might have hoped for electric sex, feared — no, surely there was nothing worse to come than this morning's letter?

She tapped on his door and popped her head round. If

he were genuinely working late, if it wasn't just an excuse to his wife, he might have someone with him. But he was alone, grey-faced and drawn. He didn't get up to take her in his arms, but stayed behind the desk, clutching the edge as if to tear the top off. She stayed the far side: she might have been expecting the sort of conversations they'd had in the past about her handling of some case.

'I don't know what to do,' he said at last.

'You seemed to know when you sent me that note.' Any moment now her legs would give way and she'd have to sit. The rest of her would give way too: hunger, tiredness, anxiety — whichever or whichever combination left her ready to weep.

'I meant it. I think I still mean it. But . . .' He released the desk, and then grabbed it again. 'You do understand, don't you? It may be all right for you — fornication's one thing, but adultery . . . I can't, I mustn't . . . But—' He broke off, looking at her as if the answer would appear in her face.

She mustn't let it. Graham had to make his own decisions, as he always had, always did. She might be fifty per cent of the relationship, entitled to half the decision-making, but she'd known from the start that loving him would involve the suspension of those rights. He was the one with the marriage and the religion that made sharing her bed the agony she knew it was, but simply couldn't understand. He always fell on her like a man collapsing in an oasis, but tore himself away more quickly after each encounter.

'I want us to be friends. There's no harm in that. I can't

bear the thought of not seeing you, not talking to you. But I can't – I mustn't – make love to you. Not any more. It's a sin, Kate: you must see that.'

Wasn't there something in the Bible about looking at a woman with lust in your heart being as bad as bedding her? Sooner or later he'd no doubt remember that, but at the moment she couldn't remind him. Yes, just being in a room with him, the opposite side of that insuperable desk, was better than not being with him at all.

'We are friends,' she said. 'We always were. I hope we always will be.'

He pushed away from the desk, to lean on the window sill. 'You – if you find someone else, then you'll be free . . .'

It was the first time he'd mentioned her and her feelings, wasn't it? She was spineless not to point it out, spineless to stutter, 'I don't want anyone else.' But she meant it. She knew the living body beneath the staid office clothes; knew each mole and scar as if she'd studied them. And wanted him now.

He turned. His eyes told her that he wanted her at least as much as she wanted him. Why not claim him? Make him forget his doubts?

Because of her period, that was why. However much he'd desired her in the past, menstruation had always turned him off as if she were unclean. So she stuffed her hands deep in her pockets and waited.

'I'll still visit Cassie,' he said, surprising her. She'd never expected him not to. 'She doesn't know about . . . us, does she?'

'You know I've told no one,' she said, almost as angrily as she felt.

'But has she guessed?'

'For God's sake!'

'That's why I'm doing this,' he said quietly. 'For God's sake.'

She'd no idea how long the words hung between them.

At last, he flicked a glance at his watch. 'It's late. You should be going home.'

'What about you?'

'I'm waiting for a call from America about this case I'm working on. That's why I'm here.'

As if on cue the phone rang. He seized it, managing a brief smile at her. But then his smile faded. 'I told you, I've got to stay till Mellors phones . . . No, of course not. No later than I can help.' He cut the call. As if weighing his decision, he came round the desk, half-opening his arms. Even as she opened her own to embrace him, she dropped them to her sides. It hadn't been a gesture of desire, it was a gesture of utter helplessness. She took his face swiftly between her hands, kissed him on the lips, and left the office before he could speak.

She couldn't fight God. And she no longer wanted to fight his wife. All she had to fight now was herself, and she had a terrible fear that that would be the hardest of all.

# Chapter Twenty-Eight

'You all right, my wench?' Dave Allen asked, peering at Kate's pale face with concern.

'That wretched bug's still hanging round,' she lied. 'But I'm much better, honestly. And those sarnies smell wonderful.'

They did. Smoked bacon done to a crisp, sausages to die for: what a good job there'd never been anything wrong with her stomach except the shock of Graham's letter. If she was looking washed out, who could have blamed her, knowing the circumstances? Meanwhile, she took her place in the team gathered in the incident room, all, by now, looking expectantly at Dave Allen.

'Now, I know that is a bit early, for a Saturday, but I thought the sooner you all knew, the better,' Dave said, a great beam spreading across his face. 'It's good news, bad news time. The good is that we know who killed Mavis Duncton; the bad is that however many guts we've all bust, the best we can get is an "unfit to plead" trial.'

So it was Duncton, poor weird, down-trodden Duncton. The team might have erupted into conversation, but there was none of the jubilation that would have gone with nicking a dyed-in-the-wool villain.

'What next, Gaffer?' Jane asked, when the hubbub was dying down.

'There'll be a little matter of tying up all the loose ends, and although the splatter and all the other forensic tests are conclusive, I still want that paperwork watertight. Just in case. We've still got a loose end in the form of Kate and Jane's dead doctor to worry about. Any news on that?'

'Only that SOCO say we can start looking at the papers he dropped when he fell. He said he was working on some book: maybe it's to do with that.'

'Well, keep the bedtime reading till after the PM. That's scheduled for this afternoon, by the way. Patrick Duncan's doing it. He's sent a message asking if you want to be there, Kate.'

Back at Steelhouse Lane, there'd have been a general snigger. Fortunately no one here seemed to know about her brief fling with him.

'Seems a perfect way to pass a lovely sunny Saturday afternoon,' Kate said as dryly as she could. Even thinking about Steelhouse Lane tightened her throat.

'Right, I'll tell him you're on, then. And the other business – that dodgy will – that'll be going back to Fraud, I should think. Now – ah, come on in, Gaffer,' Dave said, looking over their heads.

Gaffer? Like everyone else, Kate turned. The immaculate figure of Rod Neville appeared, pushing, of all things, a canteen trolley, on top of which stood a couple of red plastic buckets holding bottles with promising necks. On the lower shelf were glasses and cartons of orange juice. Trust Rod to counter their sense of anticlimax with Buck's Fizz.

'Obviously our next move will depend on the results of the post mortem,' Rod said, perching on the edge of Dave's desk. Looking exhausted, Dave leaned back, apparently happy to do no more than host the discussion. 'At least it'll be the job of the local people to notify relatives and so on.'

'I can save them some time there,' Kate said. 'If there were any family, the obvious person to ask would be my fraud suspect, Max Cornfield. He might even know if Barton had any close friends.'

Rod raised his eyes heavenward. 'All roads lead to Rome!'

'Or,' Kate put in, anxious for once to cap him, 'is he the still centre of a turning world? A Level,' she added, turning apologetically to Dave.

What on earth was the matter with him? On her feet in a flash, she asked, 'You all right, Dave?'

'I think I must have that bug of yours,' he said, as if it was an effort to make his mouth work. 'You haven't got some Alka-Seltzer or something, have you?'

She was just going to say she never touched the stuff, not with her cast-iron stomach, when she remembered. 'I ran out. But I can nip and get you some more.' She took another look. 'In fact, I'm on my way.'

'No – I can't...' He clutched his stomach. 'Well, if you wouldn't mind, my wench.'

Kate sped. It was nice to be able to do something for Dave, whose good-heartedness would have seen her through her crisis, she knew, if she'd cared to entrust anyone with it. The chemist's was seething with Saturday shoppers; she thought she'd never get served.

When she got back, however, Dave's office was empty. She left the tablets in the middle of his desk and looked round for Rod. It was unlike him to leave without saying goodbye, now they were back in friendship mode.

Would she and Graham ever get into friendship mode?

She was staring at her desk, wondering what to take back to Lloyd House and the Fraud Squad, when she heard running feet. Jane, hitting a computer keyboard as if intent to punish it for all the world's crashes, looked up briefly but carried on with her work. So did everyone else. Now the job was done, there was a good chance they could leave the paperwork till Monday and scoot off at a reasonable hour. Dave wasn't the sort of man to impose unnecessary overtime, any more than budget-eyed Rod was the sort of man to sanction it. And since the panic bell wasn't ringing, it was none of their business. Kate finished sorting, and strolled over to Jane.

'I'll be in touch the moment I know about Barton. And we've got to decide when's the best time to talk to Cornfield.'

'I phoned him about Edward,' Jane said. 'Apparently he's making a bit of progress. What if we left it till

Monday? Dave's so chuffed about being able to go on his hols now this case is over he won't mind.'

'It's back in Lizzie's in-tray now – and she might well. I'm happy with Monday though. Let him enjoy his loot while he can. Right, everyone,' she added to the room at large, 'let me know when the booze-up is – I've got to go and watch a man cutting up a stiff.' She went from one to another, shaking hands or hugging as the case might be, picked up the files and set off.


'How urgently do you want the tests done?' Pat asked. 'Blood, stomach contents? Not that it isn't all a waste of time.'

'Oh, yesterday, day before.'

'Not urgent at all then.'

'No. But I think our budget might just stretch to fast-tracking them. But you really think it's natural causes?'

'In the absence of anything to tell me the contrary. People do die, Kate: "in the midst of life there is death". Especially if they trot round with their reading glasses on and leave stuff lying on their stairs and . . . Oh, of course it's natural causes. Broken bloody neck. You saw the break. Now, you sit out here while I clean up and then we'll go and have a drink, and you can tell me why you look like the next candidate for my slab.'

If only she could.

If only she could tell him that she might just fancy being just that. That she couldn't deal with the pain pressing on her chest, a real physical pain. That she couldn't bear the weight on her head, the tightness of her throat, the tears burning her eyes. How did the Bach chorale go, the one she'd played at a recent Braysfield Road Baptist funeral? *Ich habe genug*: yes, she'd had enough.

Pat came bustling back, shrugging into a linen jacket. 'There. Though I'm afraid all the showering and scrubbing in the world never convinces me I'm truly free of the smell of— Kate, what is it? In this light you look even worse than you did in there. My dear girl.' He took her by the shoulders and stared at her. 'For a start, when did you last eat?'

She tried to straighten her back. 'This morning. We had a real celebration: we wrapped up our murder.'

'So I heard. I got Dave, remember, when I tried to phone you. A bit of a rough diamond?'

'Oh, don't judge a man by his Black Country accent. He's one of the best, Dave. I wish I could stay with his team. Back to Fraud on Monday, though.' She allowed herself a sigh.

'Fraud and the acerbic Lizzie?'

'Quite.'

'It isn't just that that's getting you down, though.' He held the door for her, and then tucked her arm into his.

'Perhaps I am hungry. And I've not been sleeping well. Too much jauntering round Europe at the public's expense.' Was it the bright sun, the fresh air? She could hardly walk.

'Not a drink just yet, I think. Come on, Kate: I'm

claiming the privilege of an old friend and I'm packing you into your car and taking you home. No, my bike's safe where it is, and anyway you haven't a crash-helmet. I've a chaise longue in the sun that'll just fit you, and while you snooze I'll make you one of my very best Pimms.'

Pimms and thin sandwiches and shortcake. All in his garden, which might have been idyllic had it been more lovingly maintained. As she lazed on the promised sunlounger – trust Pat to describe it in such inflated terms – she amused herself by putting curves into the straight lines, replacing some of the foliage with brightly coloured flowers and generally messing with his obviously low-maintenance plans. It was the sort of garden that Max Cornfield could improve.

He pulled up a chair, passed more shortcake, and was just about to top up her glass when her mobile rang. To take the call or kill it? The latter was tempting. But her thumb found the call button.

'Kate? Rod here. Could you get back to the incident room here in Sutton at once? Thanks.' That was it. No apologies, no explanation, no nothing.

'It's your own fault for having one of the damned things,' Pat said. 'God, I made that Pimms quite strong. Shall I drive you?'

She held up the glass – she'd barely touched it. 'Thanks, but no thanks. I've no idea how long I'll be there.'

'Any idea why he wants you?'

'The only thing I can think of is that the Forensic Lab people have discovered they've sent us the wrong test results or something. Oh, shit and shit and shit.'

'Will you come back for a meal? I don't want you not eating,' he said, wagging a minatory finger. 'Call me when you've finished – that's best.'

'I may have to use this,' she said, managing the first grin for some time as she flourished her mobile at him.


The call from Rod had brought people in wearing a motley collection of gear. Clearly no one had the faintest idea why they were there, and there was a general sulkiness in the air. They'd done their bit, they'd wrapped up a case, they were entitled to a break – and now this. Dave'd have a rebellion on his hands if he wasn't careful.

The door opened and Rod came in. Something about his walk quietened them. That and the pallor of his face and the way his hand shook slightly as he raised it for silence.

'Ladies and gentlemen,' he began. 'There's no easy way to say this. Dave Allen died at three-forty this afternoon.'

# Chapter Twenty-Nine

Near to tears, Rod continued, 'He was taken ill this morning. He was taken to Good Hope Hospital where despite frantic efforts . . .' He swallowed hard. 'His wife and children were with him. A major heart attack followed by a massive one.' He made another obvious effort. 'That's why I asked you to come in here. For no other reason. I didn't want you to hear piecemeal rumours. He was a good, decent man, and I'd ask you to stand and join me in a minute's silence.'

Kate let the tears course down her face. There was no reason to pretend. Several of the men were openly weeping, and any moment Jane would hit hysteria.

At last — he'd let them grieve for far more than a minute — Rod cleared his throat and spoke again. 'I'll let you know all the official arrangements as soon as I know them. I know as many of us as possible will want to pay our last respects. Meanwhile, until everything's finally tied up, I shall be taking day-to-day responsibility for the case, and I'll be with you at eight on Monday. Thank you.'

*

Kate was too stunned to know at what point Rod fell into step with her.

'Leave your car here,' he said. 'I'll run you home. Either your place or mine.' When she hesitated, he added, 'I need some company too, Kate. I was with him. I did my best . . .'

She made an effort she didn't know she was capable of. 'If it was that bad, no one could have saved him. Me and my stupid stomach tablets,' she added, bitterly.

'It was the last thing he said: "She's a good little wench". Then he clutched his chest and I knew it wasn't indigestion and . . . Oh, Kate . . .'

She opened her passenger door. 'Come on.'

He slumped in, had to be reminded about his seat-belt. 'I was supposed to be driving you,' he said as she tackled the Parade. 'You looked ill before. I was worried about your going to the post mortem.'

'Pat the Path gave me afternoon tea. Which is more than you've had, I should imagine. Your place or mine?'

'Mine's marginally nearer and you've never seen it, have you? Into the city centre, and I'll navigate from there.'


Rod lived in an open-plan house in an open-plan estate in Harborne, a suburb to the west of the city. Despite its unpromising seventies exterior, the interior opened Kate's eyes. She'd known Rod was keen on art, but had never expected him to fill his home with the sort of touches Aunt Cassie would have thought a woman's province. *Objets trouvés* in one corner, a dried flower arrangement in a potentially ugly space under the open-treaded stairs, not to mention the sort of pictures on the walls that wouldn't be out of place in a gallery. Some things she registered; most she didn't. She trailed after Rod into his kitchen; he put the kettle on, reached mugs, then dived into a cupboard, for a whisky bottle.

'The glasses are behind you.'

She passed them to him silently, watched his hand shake as he poured several fingers into each. He drank deeply, the sort of macho swig that would have made her choke.

'What a waste of single malt,' he said.

'On an empty stomach too. I'm not much of a cook, Rod, but—' She looked round the kitchen.

He dug in the fridge: a loaf, three sorts of cheese in a plastic box, spreadable butter. He stared at his booty in something like revulsion: 'And none of it low-fat. Christ!'

'Worry about your cholesterol tomorrow,' she said. 'You need something now. Comfort food.'

He shoved the cheese back in the fridge, reaching into a cupboard beside it. He slammed a tin of organic baked beans on to the surface beside the bread. 'There. Comfort food. And not this' – he poured the whisky down the sink – 'but some red wine. How about that?'

Kate nodded, but clung to the whisky as if it would warm her outside as well as in.

She ought to leave. She ought to frame sensible sentences about cabs and leaving the car on his drive till tomorrow.

She ought to make sensible arrangements about retrieving it. But the oughts collapsed as soon as she erected them. All she wanted to do was curl up and sleep.

It wasn't just the drink. Very soon her whisky had joined Rod's down the drain. Perhaps it was the relief of tears. Tears which had started as mourning for Dave but had very soon become tears for her and Graham. Not that Rod had asked any questions. He'd simply taken her in his arms and held her.

And now he was very nearly asleep. Any moment he'd keel over on to his sofa. She looked around for something to cover him with: after the bright day, the evening was chilly. But to get up and close his patio door would almost certainly wake him. She'd got goose-pimples on her bare arms. She'd better shut that door.

'You won't go, will you?' he asked suddenly.

'But I—'

'I don't want you to go.' He struggled upright. 'You know what I want. I want you to come to bed with me. Shit, Kate, I'm too pissed to fuck with you, but what I want more than anything else is a warm breathing body beside me.'

She ought to worry about the consequences. They'd agreed to be friends. She didn't want another lover . . . She loved Graham. She didn't want the complications of having a senior officer as a lover. She didn't know what she wanted.

'Oh, Kate,' he said, 'I just want someone to hold on to.'

She turned back to him. That was what she wanted too.

*

She'd known, dimly, as she fell asleep, that things wouldn't be quite as simple in the sober light of morning. Nor were they. Some time during the night – perhaps when she came back from the bathroom – he'd pulled her close to him, her back against his chest, his hands covering her breasts. She woke to find her nipples as hard and erect as the cock pressed between her buttocks.

'Don't go,' he groaned, reaching for her as she tried to inch away.

She hitched on to an elbow to face him. 'I'm slap in the middle of my period.'

He kissed her. 'I'm sure we can find other ways of giving each other pleasure.'

Her hair was still damp from the shower when she faced him over the breakfast table, but from the expression on his face there was nothing wrong with her appearance at all. If only Graham had ever once looked at her with such open affection.

'Rod,' she said, wishing she didn't have to, 'this morning was great. Wonderful.' It had been. Rod was the most considerate lover she'd ever known. 'But – and I know it doesn't look like it – I'm not ready, not yet . . .'

'Am I up against someone living or dead?' he asked, paying unnatural attention to the marmalade.

He deserved the truth.

'Living. But it's over. Don't ask me who.'

He pushed away the jar and scraped his chair clear of

the table. 'For God's sake, Kate, the whole of Lloyd House knows about you and Graham Harvey.' He stood, but restlessly.

'It's over,' she repeated.

'So you expect me to hang round while you get over your broken heart?'

'I don't expect anything. We were going to be friends, remember. That's what we agreed.'

'Easy enough to say while Harvey was poking you.'

'We seemed to be friends yesterday,' she said, her voice cracking despite herself. 'Rod: you're the sort of man I could love . . . the sort I want to love. But until – until Dave died – I was . . . do you know . . . I thought – well, it had crossed my mind that I might . . . top myself. That's how I felt.'

'Until Dave—?' Curiosity replaced anger in his eyes. And then fear and love, as if he'd registered the last part of her sentence.

'Until I realised that if forty-nine wasn't enough for Dave, thirty wasn't enough for me. I wanted a bit longer.' She managed a grim smile.

'Anyone else know how you felt?'

'It's the sort of thing I'd only tell . . . a friend.' And preferably a friend who could say something, not turn to fill the kettle.

'Did you say thirty years weren't enough for you? I thought you were twenty-nine.'

'Even in the Fraud Squad Lizzie allows us the occasional birthday.'

'So long as you don't make it more than one a year!' He set the kettle on its stand and turned back to her. 'What can I buy you?'

'Friends give each other presents. Anything friendly.'

She watched emotions cross and re-cross his face. At last the words seemed to force their way out of his mouth. 'What's Harvey bought you?'

She forced the words out of her mouth. He'd exposed his feelings; it was only fair that she should expose hers. 'Do you want the honest truth? He's never bought me anything. Ever.' It was her turn to turn from him.

'You poor girl,' he said, taking her at last in his arms as if she'd announced another bereavement.


'You're very quiet,' Aunt Cassie observed. 'And you're looking peaky. Too many parties, I suppose.' Although she no doubt meant it as a joke, it came out as sour criticism.

Kate had always avoided mentioning death to Cassie. After the insouciance with which Cassie had announced the death of her fellow card-player, however, she wouldn't hold back the brutal truth. 'Someone died yesterday. Someone I cared for very much. The man who was the boss in the Sutton Coldfield case.'

'I thought that was a woman? Oh, I can't keep up with all these different bosses of yours,' she grumbled.

'No. A man.'

'Not that young man that comes to see me! Oh, I shall mis him.'

'No. It's no one you know.' Kate found she couldn't say Graham's name. 'A man called Dave. He was only in his forties, desperate to go on holiday to celebrate his silver wedding. And he'd wrapped up the case we were working on and dropped dead.' Her voice wouldn't work any more.

'That's what comes of not looking after yourself,' Cassie observed complacently. 'You want to watch your diet. That's the secret of a good long life.'

No one had said that, of course. Everyone had known he was overweight and stuffed down too many chips. But no one had suggested that it was Dave's own fault. Trust Cassie at her smuggest.

The trouble was, Kate wasn't sure if she could trust herself. She'd never before felt so close to comprehensively losing her temper with the old woman. She poured her a gin – no, she couldn't face one for herself – and waited.

'They're taking us out tomorrow,' Cassie said. 'Some of us. In a minibus. They thought we'd like to see a bit of the country. Hartlebury, round there. Have you been yet?'

'No, not yet.'

'It'd do you good to get out a bit. You want to remember: all work and no play makes Jill a dull girl. It's not much fun for me, my girl, when you come and sit here moping.'

'I'd best push off then. When a friend dies, you can't be the life and soul of the party.' She bent to kiss Cassie. 'Goodnight.'

She was just opening the door to leave when it opened to admit Graham. He pressed an envelope into her hand,

and walked briskly over to Cassie. Well, that was one promise he'd kept. While they talked, she opened the envelope; one from Woolworth's.

*I have to talk to you. Now. My office. 9.00.*

As before, Kate tapped lightly on Graham's door before opening it. This time he was on the phone, hardly acknowledging her as he talked and made notes. She did the things she'd done before they became lovers: checked the plants on his window-sill, boiled his kettle to make his preferred herbal tea.

At last he cut the call, but kept writing for several moments, though probably not as long as she thought he did.

When she put the mug on his desk, he managed a smile. Then he came round the desk and took her hands, gripping them so hard it hurt.

'I can't do it,' he said. 'I can't give you up. I can't. I need you. I need you.' She could see the effort he was making. 'I love you.'

He'd never said that before. Not in those simple words.

'And I love you.' She took a deep breath. 'But I don't think we can go on as we are.'

He shook his head blindly. 'What do you mean?'

'Just that every meeting seems to give you more pain than pleasure. I don't think you're a man for furtive affairs.' She couldn't tell him, could she, of the emptiness of her life, of the silent phone.

'I've been thinking,' he said. 'Divorce.'

Her heart leapt, but plummeted again at the sight of his face. 'Your church permits divorce?'

'It doesn't encourage it. Prefers couples to accept counselling . . . But my wife doesn't want counselling.'

Her head jerked up. 'Your wife knows?'

'No. No. Not about us as such. But even she admits we're not happy, you see, and I did my best to persuade her. But her health's so poor . . .'

What did that have to do with anything? 'Have you mentioned divorce to her? In as many words?'

'Of course not. That'd sound like blackmail!'

She fiddled with her mug and then asked, 'What are the consequences of divorce in your church?'

'Hardly good. They'd ask me to stop preaching, might ask me to leave the council.'

'They'd ostracise you?'

He turned back to the desk. 'Not as such. But I can't imagine . . . you see, I'd be the guilty party . . .'

'I always thought it took two to wreck a marriage,' she said more tartly than she meant.

He snorted. 'Well, you would say that. Wasn't your Robin a married man when you lived with him?'

How dare he? 'He'd left his wife well before we became lovers. In any case, Graham, the law doesn't apportion guilt these days; why should the church? Why don't you leave it to God? "Let him who is without guilt cast the first stone".' This was getting nowhere: who wanted to discuss theology when they should be talking about their future?

'You're right. I don't even know how to set about things, you know,' he added. 'Putting things in motion. I don't know how to break it to her. Not in her state of health.'

As clearly as if he'd been in the room beside her, she heard Dave Allen's verdict: *Married men don't leave their wives.*

'Where would I live?'

Graham, not pathos! 'That's not a problem,' she said briskly. 'You know my house would welcome you with open arms.'

'I couldn't. Not until we were married. I can't. Don't you understand?'

'I'm trying to.' And trying equally hard not to cry. He wouldn't make it, would he? He'd never do it. 'So what will you do?'

He shook his head. 'I don't know where to start.'

'You start by moving into your spare room—'

'Don't you think that's where I've been for the last eight years?'

'Well, you pack a case and go and see a solicitor tomorrow.' Most people might sort out their own divorces these days, but a solicitor might put some steel into Graham's spine, simply in the interests of his subsequent fees.

'In the middle of this case?'

'Or on Tuesday or Wednesday or whenever.' She held back, as if not wanting to get too impatient with a slow child. 'Graham, everything depends on you. I can't tell you what to do. You'd never forgive me if I gave the wrong advice: never forgive me for setting your feet on what promises to be a long lonely path.' He wouldn't. Even if he got his divorce, even if they got married, there'd be a large part of Graham's heart that would blame her for his straying from the paths of righteousness. She took a painful breath and took his hands. They lay limp, not responding to her grip. 'Whatever you want, whatever you need – I'll try to give it to you. If you really want me. If.' She stood tall to kiss him, and, turning on her heel, left his room without a backward glance. She waited two minutes in the corridor lest he call her back. All she heard was the ringing of his phone and his voice murmuring into it.

She passed a young constable. 'God, Harvey's burning the midnight oil,' he said.

'That's what you have to do if you're a copper,' she said lightly. 'You have to marry the job.' And for the first time, she felt a rush of compassion for Graham's wife.

# Chapter Thirty

Kate didn't find it hard to ignore the answerphone's flashing light. Whoever, whatever, would simply have to wait till the following morning. All she wanted now was a hot bath, the stiffest of whiskies and the chance of a night's sleep. But at two-thirty she was still wondering if by chance it could have been Graham trying to contact her, announcing a change of heart, a real decision.

'Sergeant Kate, I'm sorry to phone you on your home number,' came Cornfield's voice. 'But it really is important that I see you. Would Monday afternoon be convenient? Perhaps you would be kind enough to tell me where I should present myself.'

*Present myself?* What did he mean by such an official term? Come on, Kate. You know what it means. He's going to make some sort of statement and wants to do it in the appropriate place. You've got him. You've got him!

'Wheel him in here,' Lizzie said. 'Then we can whip him over to Steelhouse Lane and charge him. D'you want me to sit in on the interview?'

'That nice kid from Dave's MIU — shit, Lizzie. Has anyone told you yet? About Dave?'

'What about which Dave?'

'Dave Allen. The DCI in charge of the Duncton investigation.' As if the stupid woman couldn't work it out.

'What about him?' Her voice was so off-hand it was clear she hadn't picked up the pain in Kate's.

'I'm sorry. He collapsed and died on Saturday. Heart.' She waited for some reaction. Getting nothing, she added, 'He was a week away from his silver wedding anniversary.'

'Trust you to play the sentiment card, Kate. You're just as dead whatever the date.'

'I was thinking about his wife, Lizzie.'

'She should have thought about his diet, if you ask me.'

It dawned on Kate that one day Lizzie would be just like Cassie — was halfway there already, come to think of it. She asked, 'Any news of your hospital appointment yet?'

Lizzie looked furtive. 'I'll get on to it today.'

Kate looked hard at her. 'I think you'd find a slow death from cancer worse than a quick heart attack,' she said, and left.

Derek was just making tea when she walked into their office, and he cocked a warning eyebrow at her desk. And at Rod, apparently absorbed in the *Guardian*.

'Bad news about Dave Allen,' Derek said. 'The Gaffer just told me,' he added awkwardly.

'Very bad,' she agreed.

Derek peered at her. 'Looks like you've taken it real hard.'

'He was a decent man, Derek, and a first-class cop. I liked him very much. But,' she continued, turning to Rod, 'I thought you'd be in Sutton, Gaffer.'

'I was. It took about three minutes to ensure everything continued on its well-oiled wheels. Dave had a good team, there. I thought I'd pop in to see how you were. Kate was there when Dave started his attack,' he told Derek.

'He said it was indigestion.'

'Poor bugger.' Derek passed her and Rod mugs of overmilked coffee, which Rod took without turning an immaculate hair.

'Actually, I've got news for you, Gaffer,' Kate said, trying for an efficiency she didn't feel. 'Max Cornfield wants to talk to us. Lizzie thought here. OK if I get Jane along?'

'Absolutely. It'll take her mind off things. Poor kid looked terrible this morning – well, they all did.'

'You're a bit washed out yourself,' she observed, as much for Derek's benefit as anything.

Rod nodded. 'It wasn't the best of weekends. Look, all this stuff you've told me about Cornfield and his millions – any chance I could sit in with you and Jane while you talk to him? I'd like to see a master-fraudster at work.'

'Master-fraudsters get away with it,' she said. 'Actually, if you've got time, it'd be a great idea. Add a bit of gravitas.'

'And it'll re-skill me a bit. Thanks.' He gathered his newspaper, checked, apparently, that he'd not disarranged her desk, and took himself off. 'See you later.'

'If you ask me, he's got his eye on you,' Derek observed.

'Look, Derek, we've been through all this. I've had a crap weekend, the highlight of which was a visit to my great-aunt in the Hotel Geriatrica and I do not want any more crap now. And if Lizzie comes sniffing round for gossip, you can tell her what I said.'

'OK, Sergeant,' he said.

'For fuck's sake, you can drop that, too. If you don't,' she added, managing a grin, 'I shall have to use the ultimate weapon in my armoury and start calling you Ben again. Get it?'

'Not that! Anything but that!'

'Well, you've been warned,' she said, still smiling, but applying herself to her desk, and finding, inevitably, a note from Rod tucked in with the rest of her mail.

*Dear Kate*

*I thought a friend might give another friend a book for her birthday. Unfortunately the one I found is rather too large to leave on a desk. Would you let me hand it over at dinner tonight? I thought that new place in Brindley Place? If you've no other plans, of course. Could I collect you at seven-thirty?*

*Rod*

She rather thought he could. Perhaps he might even run to a card. It was weird having a birthday with no cards. No nothing.

In fact, that was what she felt this morning. Nothing. She explored her mind as if it were a tooth minus a filling.

There were rough edges, from Graham and from Dave, but in the centre, a great gaping hollow. Work might be the best thing to fill it. She stared resentfully at the piles of paper on her desk.

After her mini-spat with Derek she didn't feel like suggesting a lunch-time drink. But she wanted to be fresh for her encounter with Max Cornfield so she just might take herself for a walk. What if she met Graham? There was always a chance. Not if she took herself in the opposite direction from his usual haunts. So she set off down Livery Street, fairly briskly, because an idea was creeping into her head. Thirty seemed an important birthday, something of a milestone. It might not be the end of her third decade till this time next year, in real terms, but in emotional ones — yes, it had to be. She looked at her hands, still steady, still full of life despite the weekend. She needed to promise herself that whatever happened to rock her off course again, it wouldn't defeat her; that she'd no longer even contemplate suicide. Had she meant it? Or had she simply been over-whelmed by a dreadful combination? Whichever it was, she mustn't give in. Dave's death had taught her that. She would do what she'd promised those nice people in the Jewellery Quarter what seemed like months ago. She'd go and treat herself. No need to wait for Graham to give her anything. No point, more like. As for Rod, only time would tell. And somehow, she wasn't sure the auguries were good. No. She must do this for herself. Do what she'd never done before:

march into a shop and spend a very great deal of money on something for herself. Not a car, not furniture. Nothing useful. Just an affirmation, a very visible affirmation, that her life could go on. Oh yes, there'd be some bad times ahead, some viciously lonely days and nights. This – whatever it was, she didn't know yet – would keep her company.

To her surprise they recognised her.

'Any more fraud, Sergeant?' asked the woman with the rings to die for.

'Plenty, but none that need worry us today,' she smiled. 'Not on my birthday.' There, it was out.

'Congratulations!' came a little chorus from the men working behind the shop.

'And you're going to buy yourself a present? Good for you. Now,' the assistant spread her hands in an expansive gesture, 'what do you fancy? A nice chain?'

'I've had enough of chains,' Kate said positively.


She was just opening a hasty baguette when the phone rang. It was Lizzie, with the news that a punter was waiting for her in Reception. Hell, it must be Max Cornfield, a good half-hour early.

But it wasn't Cornfield, nor was the punter alone in Reception. Well, for all the strange things career police officers dealt with in their years in the service, jungle explorers complete with pith helmets were rare sights. Particularly when they stripped off their safari suits to nothing but a well-filled elephant trunk.

God, she'd been had, hadn't she. She should have twigged: why should Lizzie have called her? Scarlet from the navel up, her hands were being gripped by the explorer, intent on making her oil his body. Not just the pecs. to die for. All parts.

And she had to get out of the situation with neither a disciplinary nor the derision of her mates.

'Come on,' she whispered urgently. 'A Hollywood embrace, please – tip me right back.'

As she went over, she might have been in the arms of Clarke Gable. But she didn't kiss him. She whispered tenderly in his ear, 'You make me massage your bloody trunk and I do you for indecent assault.'

He swung her with more panache than she'd have credited over his other side. 'You wouldn't.'

'Before you could say prick,' she confirmed. 'Just give me the message and scarper.'

He slobbered a huge wet kiss on to her – well, he was entitled to a little professional revenge – and returned her to the vertical. 'It's in the right ear,' he whispered. 'You have to grope for it.'

'I don't think I do,' she said, holding out a hand like a schoolteacher demanding an illicit note. 'Do I?'

*A happy birthday from Lizzie and all in the Fraud Squad.* Well, that was nice. She supposed. And when she'd had time to reflect on it, when she was no longer debating whether to snarl or laugh or both, she might think it was.

# Chapter Thirty-One

Kate was just leaving her office to meet Cornfield in reception when Rod put his head round the door.

'I've brought you this lot,' he said, producing a polythene bag wearing an evidence label. 'The papers Barton dropped when he fell.'

'Have you had time to look at any of them yet?'

'Time? What's time? Anyway, I know you love paperwork and wouldn't dare deny you — especially on your birthday.'

She stuck her tongue out. 'Gee, thanks, Gaffer.' There might be no one in the room to see, but that didn't mean no one could hear. 'Cornfield's down in reception—'

'No, he isn't. Jane found him hanging around and took him straight to an interview room. OK? Into battle.'

Max stood up as they entered, the smile that Jane had somehow brought to his face fading abruptly.

'This is Detective Superintendent Neville,' Kate said. 'Superintendent Neville, this is Mr Max Cornfield, who last spoke to us in connection the the Duncton case.'

'I am so very sorry to hear about Mr Allen,' Cornfield

said, 'I hope you will accept my condolences.'

There were embarrassed smiles as they all sat down. Jane switched on the tape recorder and introduced the protagonists.

Kate leaned forward, 'Mr Cornfield, you left a message saying that you wished to talk to us. How can we help?'

He shook his head. 'I don't know why you ask, Kate. Three police officers – you're clearly not expecting a chat about the weather. I should imagine you have a very good idea of what I want to say. I want to tell you how I came to forge the signature of my very dear friend Leon Horowitz.'

Rod raised his hand. 'Mr Cornfield, might I recommend that you ask your solicitor to be present?'

'Thank you. But I know what I want to say and am prepared to take the consequences. Oh, no, I'm not! Don't you see? But I must.'

'Why don't you get us all some tea, Jane?' Rod asked, looking at Cornfield with concern on his face. 'You do realise that forgery may well carry a prison sentence, and that you will forfeit whatever you gained by your forgery?'

'I am not unaware of that,' Cornfield said, swallowing hard.

'What's the latest news of Mrs Hamilton?' Kate asked, to settle him again.

She was rewarded with a smile. 'She will be allowed home on Wednesday. She tells me she needs to talk to you urgently, Kate. About something in her past.'

Kate stared. '*Her* past?'

'When you speak to her, remember that she is a very sick woman.' He smiled enigmatically. 'No one is pretending, least of all Mrs Hamilton, that she will live long. But we all have to die, and she wants to die at home, with her dog beside her. The hope is that Edward will play his part.'

'Won't she need round-the-clock care?'

Bother Rod for interrupting her. 'What did the old lady want to talk about?'

Was Cornfield's smile sad or cynical? He ignored Rod's question. 'Mr Neville, if I am to lose my home, I will be glad of the shelter. Until my trial, that is.'

'You're going to batten on another old woman's affections and hope to get her to change her will in your favour?' Rod jumped in again. Well, he was entitled to. And perhaps he was right to. But he didn't follow it up.

'Mrs Hamilton has a family to whom to leave her property. Mrs Barr had a family, but if ever one was dysfunctional, hers was. I became her family. I became everything to her, in the end. That was why I did what I did.' He was upright in the chair, jabbing the table in emphasis.

'Max: for quite a long time, I've wanted to know exactly what you did,' Kate said. 'And I've met with evasion upon evasion, from you and from your friends. Wouldn't you like to get it all off your chest?'

'You've been harassing my friends,' he countered.

Kate raised her eyebrows coldly. 'I've been *questioning* your friends about a potentially very serious crime. Forgery

– to gain a fortune the size of the one you're likely to get – is serious.'

Jane brought in a tray with four plastic cups. Even in this situation Rod couldn't resist a disparaging look at the cups and their contents. Kate told the tape recorder what was happening, and passed Cornfield his.

'Thank you. I didn't want to do it. I didn't want to have anything to do with any of it. I told you, I begged her to call a solicitor. But she decided, that last Saturday morning, that she had to do it there and then. She knew my friends were coming to see me – they were at a convention at the NEC,' he said to Rod, who nodded impartially. 'She asked me to summon them earlier, so that they could be witnesses. As you know, Joseph made it in time. But Leon insisted that he finish his game, and promised to come on later. His train was derailed, so he was late. Mrs Barr gave up on him. Wouldn't wait. Insisted I sign it in his name. Joseph will verify this, as will Leon himself. But now Joseph tells me that you're accusing him of conspiracy, as if we planned this all along. Kate, Jane: can you convince your colleague that I'm telling the truth? I never planned it. I warned her, pleaded with her, implored her. But she was so ill – was dead within the week.'

'Did you kill her?' Rod asked.

'As God is my witness, no! I was afraid that she was in so much pain that she would ask me to help her. But ultimately she clung to life. She was afraid to go. And much as I wished to end her suffering, I couldn't.'

'If we are in any doubt, we can ask for an exhumation order,' Rod told him.

'Dear God, what sort of man do you think I am? I loved that woman, body and soul. How could I harm her?'

'You never thought her ill enough to call the doctor?'

'Superintendent, I cannot believe that you haven't checked her medical records. Oh, not you, some underling. She had severely ulcerated legs and feet, and developed a form of septicaemia. The GP called from time to time, but could give her only palliative care, as long as she declined to go into hospital. In the end, she refused to let him see her.'

'Or did you refuse to let him see her?' Rod pursued.

Cornfield spread his hands. 'If he had seen her and been able to prescribe strong painkillers, wouldn't it have made my life easier? Of course I wanted him to see her. Officer, why don't you simply charge me and be done with it?' His voice broke, but he regained control immediately. 'Here is my passport. I understand from Kate that you wouldn't want me to leave the country. Or will you oppose bail?'

Rod smiled. 'Not if you're going to be nursing Mrs Hamilton, not to mention her dog.' He turned to Kate. 'Might we have a word outside?'

Kate nodded, telling the tape recorder they were taking a break.

Cornfield coughed apologetically. 'I'm sure there are rules about allowing people in my position to wander round in search of a lavatory.'

'Let me accompany you myself,' Rod said.

Jane and Kate followed them out of the room, stopping in the corridor.

'God, I could really use a fag,' Jane said. 'Kate, does he know about Dr Barton being dead?'

'Not as far as I know. I was thinking of dropping it on him later. Maybe you should take up the questioning for a bit and you could tell him. Might provoke something.'

'You're sure the boss wouldn't want to do it?'

Kate leaned towards her conspiratorially. 'I don't know about you, but I reckon his interviewing skills are a bit rusty. I'd rather trust you.'

'Fair enough. Look, I wouldn't mind a pee myself. Where's the ladies'?'

'Like the man said, "Let me accompany you myself."'

Rod was waiting for the women by the interview room door. Jane went in ahead.

'What did you want to talk about, Gaffer?'

'Whether, to be honest, you wanted to continue with this. Even if we get the DPP to take it on, if he pleads guilty, he'll get a year's suspended sentence, that's all.'

'And lose everything. You know he never had any salary all that time he was working for her? That he lived all that time in a badly converted garage? That he nursed her all that time for nothing? What's the justice in it?'

He shook his head sadly. 'It's not justice we're talking about, Kate. It's the law.' Without consulting the others,

Rod started the questioning. But his enquiry sounded genuinely curious. 'Tell me, Max, how have you been surviving financially?'

'The same way I survived while Mrs Barr was bedridden. She gave me power of attorney – the one time I managed to get her to see a solicitor – so I could deal with all her financial affairs. You will find all the cheque stubs in her bureau.'

'I never doubted I would.' Rod could have instilled a threatening note into his voice, but didn't. 'But since her death?'

A shadow of distaste crossed his face. 'I was forced to borrow.'

'From?' Kate didn't want to hear a compromising answer. She didn't want to hear he was in debt to Steiner or Horowitz, lest it add weight to the conspiracy idea. Or would failure to ask them look like a guilty conscience?

'From Mrs Hamilton. I had known her for years, if not with any intimacy. I asked the day after Mrs Barr's death. You will find the receipt in these papers of hers. She particularly asked me to give them to you in person.'

'Thank you,' Kate said, meaning it. But on edge, now. Why on earth should Mrs Hamilton want her to have anything? She stowed the box folder under her chair.

There was a short pause.

'What I'd really like to ask you,' Jane began, 'is about Mr Barr's death all those years ago. You see, I don't like it. Mr Barr sounds as if he was a really nasty piece of knitting, sir; into child abuse and I don't know what. Now, young Michael was away at medical school, wasn't he, Max?'

'That's right, at Nottingham University.'

'And Edna had a big row with the family about her sex life and you escorted her to Berlin?'

'That's right. My friend Joseph tried to care for her but she left him, and became, I suspect, a prostitute. He told you this the other day, I understand,' he said, bowing gently to Kate.

'Yes.'

'And Mr Barr very conveniently died shovelling snow at about this time?'

'Yes. And I know one should never speak ill of the dead, but the world was a better, cleaner place without him.'

'Who killed him?' Kate asked.

Cornfield started. 'I beg your pardon?'

'We have a medical student with access to drugs, we have a girl raped by her father, we have you, a young man in love with Barr's wife. Are you seriously telling me that no one spiked his tea?'

'Kate! That's a terrible thing to suggest.' He said it with so little emphasis she was disconcerted.

'Terrible things happen in terrible families,' Rod prompted.

'Terrible things did happen in that terrible family. Barr raped his daughter and impregnated her. I took her to Berlin, Kate, to find an abortionist. We are talking about the days before the nineteen sixty-seven Act,' he added, as if Rod wouldn't understand. 'As for Barr's death. I always regarded it as an act of God. If only He existed.'

So you're denying any part in Barr's murder?'

'Absolutely. My dear sir, I'm sure you're mistaken. I'm sure no one would have touched him. They were all far too afraid of him for one thing. Me too,' he added ruefully.

'I'm not talking about touching him,' Rod said. 'I'm talking about popping something in his morning tea to cause heart failure. You were the gardener – you had access to foxgloves. Michael had access to digitalis. Didn't one of you—?'

'I give you my word,' Cornfield said. 'My word of honour. And I'm sure Michael would never . . . What does he say? Ask him!'

Rod leaned forward and coughed, gently. 'Mr Cornfield: perhaps we should have broken this news to you earlier. Dr Barton passed away last week.'

'Dear God. Dear God. What a tragic family. Did he – I'm sorry, I have to ask – did he die . . . naturally?'

'Do you doubt that he would?' Rod asked.

'Officer, if you and your colleagues have been poking around in his sad past, he might easily have wanted to end it all. He might equally, of course, have died of a broken heart. Can you tell me how he died?'

'A depressingly mundane death. He fell downstairs and broke his neck. Kate and Jane found him.'

Cornfield lowered his eyes to the table, as if in prayer. But he turned suddenly to Kate. 'When we were talking about Edna's flight to Berlin, I sensed that you – no, sensed

is too strong a word. Did something, some flicker, come
into your eyes? Is poor Edna dead, too?'

Kate nodded. 'Many years ago. A sadly predictable
death.'

'Drugs? Prostitution?'

'Killed by her pimp.'

Cornfield closed his eyes. 'Oh,' he said, opening them
again, 'how I wish I could believe in God and offer a prayer
for their sad souls.'


'You're letting me go, officer?' Cornfield asked Rod a few
minutes later. 'I expected you to charge me. I've even
brought my overnight things.'

Poor naïve bugger.

Rod ushered him gently out of the room. 'Stay in
Birmingham. Don't attempt to go anywhere without notifying us. We may have to talk again, and I can't guarantee
that you won't be charged at a later date.'

'Tell me,' Cornfield began, 'what I should do about the
house. Presumably everything goes to the government if
there are no relatives.'

'Yes, the Crown. Who will, of course, make strenuous
efforts to find next of kin.'

'I'm afraid they will search in vain. Call me petty,
Superintendent, but while I would happily have helped
Michael, and possibly less happily helped Maeve, sort
out the house and garden, I can't feel I could do the same
for the government.'

'You must feel very bitter,' Rod observed.

Cornfield shrugged massively. 'I came with next to nothing; I leave with next to nothing. I've managed, as Kate will no doubt tell you, on next to nothing. So long as I have my health, my friends and my chess, what's the problem?' He dropped his voice, averting his eyes. Did he add something? Something about losing the love of his life? Kate couldn't be sure.

Whatever he might have said, he braced his shoulders. 'This evening I will pack my things and move – pro tem – to Mrs Hamilton's. And I do assure you that I will be drawing a small salary, and that her will is lodged with her bank. I witnessed it. I am not a beneficiary,' he added dryly. 'Good day to you. Kate. Jane.' He nodded and began a dignified progress down the long corridor, Rod at his elbow.

'Poor old bugger,' Jane said. 'All that in the palm of his hand and then – phut. How'll he manage? Hey, what's up, our kid?'

Kate was clutching her head, and beginning to laugh. 'Jane – where's your notebook? The one we had when we talked to Barton. There's a statement there, signed and witnessed by two police officers. Remember?'

# Chapter Thirty-Two

At first Kate feared Max would faint. She should have announced it more tactfully. But the words had burst out, and not in the order she'd intended.

'Here you are,' she'd gasped, stumbling to a halt ahead of him. 'All signed and witnessed by two police officers. Max, the Law may be about to punish you, but at least you're going to get justice.'

Rod stared. 'Kate?' he asked coldly.

She tried to gather her wits. 'The other day Jane and I were talking to Michael Barton. And he made us write this down and witness his signature.' She flourished the notebook. 'Goodness knows how the law stands, but it looks to me as if you're a genuine beneficiary in a genuine will. Unless,' she added more soberly, 'he's made a later one.'

Max leaned against the wall, speechless.

Rod asked with commendable presence of mind, 'Has a search been made for one?'

'That'd be the local force's job. But I'll get on to it. Rod – can someone inherit in these circumstances?'

'Don't rely on me – I'm only a policeman.' He turned

to Max, who was now regaining his colour. 'But for God
sake get your solicitor on to this now.'


'Time for home, I'd say,' Rod observed, draining his cup
they were in his room having a self-congratulatory coffe
courtesy of Rod's wonderful machine.

'What about Mrs Hamilton's papers?' Kate asked. Sh
was intrigued, almost intrigued enough to push back he
meal with Rod. But she didn't want to say that in front c
Jane.

Probably Rod didn't want the meal postponed. But
seemed he didn't want to say that in front of Jane either.

'Leave them till the morning,' he said. 'Probably no mor
use than Michael Barton's papers. Interesting observation
on the mores of the period, but nothing else,' he explaine
to Jane. He got to his feet, looking at his watch.


The rush hour had already begun. Kate contemplated th
queues to Kings Heath with less than enthusiasm:
would be so much easier to nip out and buy a dress fc
tonight. That way she could come back to look at thos
papers. They couldn't wait till the morning, could they? I
would save Rod a long circular trip, too, as she pointe
out over the internal phone; though he insisted he'd hav
been perfectly happy to make it, she could tell he wa
relieved. If she'd got a box-file of papers, he'd got a who
in-tray.

A very swift sortie to Rackhams – even quicker because the saleswomen left her in very little doubt that it was extremely close to closing time – for a beautifully cut short layered dress and some strappy sandals and it was back to the papers. And not all that long before she was knocking on Rod's door and shoving a sheet under his nose.

'We've got ourselves our murderer,' she said quietly. 'It's all here. She's had a bad heart for years, apparently. I wonder how she's survived so long.'

'Remember the creaking gate proverb,' he said. 'So how and why?'

'Why: because she could hear, and often see, the damage he was doing his kids. How: by grinding up some tablets and giving them to Edna to put on his breakfast porridge! He was the only one allowed to have sugar on his cereal, apparently – a hangover from rationing, Mrs Hamilton says. Rod, now what?'

'She wanted you to know. You.'

'A sort of deathbed confession?'

He shook his head. 'You'll have to ask her. When the medics say she's ready for that sort of questioning. God, Kate, she won't live long enough to go on trial. If she did, she wouldn't get a sentence. Can you imagine any jury convicting? A judge sending her down? Jesus!' He closed his eyes, ageing his face five years.

Kate put a hand out to touch his arm. The last few days had been as bad for him as for anyone, hadn't they?

'The great thing is that this absolves Max,' she said. 'Oh, God, you don't think that that's why she's done it?'

'Are you going to give her the third degree to find out?'

'Not unless you authorise me to.'

'Not in a million years! Hell, I'm going to have to take advice about this, Kate. In the meantime, come on. Time to celebrate.'


The champagne was making Kate giggly. Not that she hadn't been before. Giggly and tearful and over the moon about the Barton business and outraged by the strippogram and puzzled by Lizzie and weeping inside for Graham and grateful to Rod for his amused forbearance.

'The next stage is where I fall asleep with my face in the soup,' she announced, as he held her chair for her.

'How very fortunate that we've chosen the hot d'oeuvre,' he said.

'And ordered mineral water, I hope.'

'Indeed.' He leaned forward, elbows on the table. 'I've never seen you so relaxed before.'

'For relaxed read pissed,' she grinned. 'What a day, Rod. Oh, I do hope that old man gets his loot.' She clasped her hands in mock prayer.

'I'm sure . . .' he began, before his face clouded. 'I gather . . .' His eyes dropped to her ring. 'I've wanted to ask all day . . . Do I gather that Graham . . . ?'

She shook her head emphatically. 'I bought it for myself. There's a very serious explanation I'll favour you with on a less festive occasion, but this was from me with love to me.' She spread her hand. The big ruby flared in the candlelight. 'I hope – you don't think it's vulgar, do you?'

'Are friends allowed to say that deep rich reds suit you? With hair as dark as yours and skin so fine . . . Sorry, that doesn't sound like a friend at all.'

'My Irish ancestry, I suppose,' she reflected, realising that she was hardly rebuffing him. 'But I've descended further than most. I've never even been to Ireland to check out my roots.'

'It's very fashionable. One day I'd like . . . Ah, I'd forgotten this.' He burrowed under the table and passed her a large, heavy parcel.

She stared at the professional wrapping. 'It's a shame to undo it.' Why had he left it till now? Why not simply handed it over in the car? Perhaps Rod had less of the policeman, more of the showman, in his veins than she'd realised. Anyway, she took the knife he proffered and slit her way gingerly in. An encyclopaedia of antiques. 'Rod, it's wonderful. It's just what I need. God, what clichés. But I mean them. Thank you.'

Of course, he'd handed it across the table so she wouldn't have to kiss him – and perhaps so that he wouldn't have to risk the rejection of not being kissed. But the look in his eyes told her that he hoped a book concerned with the past might bring them together in the future.

Only time could tell. They were both adult enough to understand words like rebound and second-best, which would float unbidden between them until she'd evaluated her feelings for Graham. Evaluated? Conquered!

Her ring flashed again. Only when she'd learned to love herself, it said, could she start returning someone else's love. Rod's or whoever's.

'Hors d'oeuvres, madam?' the waiter enquired.